OUR STOLEN PIECES

JAMES HUNT

❀ Created with Vellum

---

*D*awn pierced the cracks of the bedroom blinds. Patricia Montgomery lay in bed on her side, facing the window, her body marked with thin lines of sunlight. Stirred by the morning, Patricia rolled away from the light and next to her husband, slipping her arm around his waist. She pressed her body against the warmth of his back and nestled her nose against the nape of his neck.

Dan woke and rolled from his side and onto his back, allowing Patricia to rest her head on his chest.

"Good morning," Patricia said, her eyes closed and her voice a whisper.

"Good morning," Dan replied, kissing the top of his wife's head.

"Did you get any sleep?" Patricia asked.

Dan cleared his throat. "I think the giggling stopped somewhere around two o'clock in the morning, so I got a few hours."

Their daughter Sarah had hosted a slumber party.

"We should probably get breakfast started," Patricia said. "Hell hath no fury like a hungry tween."

"I doubt they're awake," Dan said, his eyes still closed.

"Well, I'm getting hungry," Patricia said.

Dan chuckled. "And the truth comes out." He flipped the sheets off of him and rolled out of bed, letting Patricia's head rest on his pillow. He guided his feet into his slippers and shuffled toward the door, stretching his back and arms, yawning. He always looked more like a lumbering beast than a grown man in the mornings. He stopped at the door and turned around. "French toast?"

Patricia smiled. "You know me too well."

"I'll warm up the griddle, but it's your job to wake up the girls," Dan said.

"Are you scared?" Patricia asked.

"Yes," Dan said then opened the door and walked down the hallway.

"Chicken!" Patricia called out after him but then laughed at Dan's clucking response.

Patricia rose from the bed, donned her robe and her slippers, and then opened the blinds of their bedroom window, flooding the room with sunlight. She pressed her hand against the glass. It was cool but not cold. The last bits of winter had finally thawed, and Seattle's spring was in full bloom.

Pots and pans clanged from the kitchen as Patricia exited the bedroom hallway and neared the stairwell by the front door. She walked up the carpeted stairs, the last three steps leading up to the second floor trumpeting their ceremonial groan.

Dan always joked those stairs would be their alarm for when their daughter was older and tried to sneak in and out of the house, and he vowed not to fix them until she moved out.

The second floor was quiet when Patricia neared her daughter's bedroom. The girls were most likely still sleeping, but she knew they'd sleep all day if no one woke them.

Sarah's bedroom door was closed and was decorated with a "please knock before entering" sign. Gone were the days of rainbows, princesses, and stuffed animals. She was in middle school now and had transitioned from fairy tales to boy bands. Patricia knew her daughter was growing up, but the acknowledgment didn't make the facts any easier to process. Both she and Dan were dreading the day when Sarah finally brought home her first boyfriend.

Patricia knocked on the door, one hand on the knob. Sarah had strict instructions to never keep the door locked, and in turn, Patricia and Dan promised to knock before they entered. "Sarah? Girls?"

Patricia had expected to hear nothing, but instead, she heard the hurried whispers. The kind of whispers meant for secrets.

"Girls?" Patricia opened the door, and the whispers stopped. The girls were awake, everyone sitting on their sleeping bags scattered around Sarah's bed, looking up at Patricia like a deer caught in headlights. Empty bags of chips and crumpled cans of soda lay among the haphazard sleeping arrangements.

But aside from the mess, Patricia saw nothing wrong. No drugs. No booze. No boys, though she would have to check under the bed and in the closet to be certain.

Patricia looked at her daughter. "Sarah, what's going on?"

Sarah sat cross-legged on the bed with her lips shut tight while the rest of her friends looked up to her as if she were their wise tribal leader.

"Sarah," Patricia said, her voice stern. "Out with it, young lady."

Sarah twisted her mouth, hesitant, but finally acquiesced. "Emily and Amelia left."

Patricia frowned. "What?" But as she glanced around the room, she saw that the seven girls had shrunk to five. "Where did they go?"

"We don't know," Sarah answered. "They were here until we all fell asleep, but when Chrissy woke up to go to the bathroom, they were gone."

Patricia looked to Chrissy. She was the smallest of the girls, braces on her teeth, and wearing a T-shirt that fit her like a ballroom gown. "What time did you wake up, Chrissy?"

"I'm not sure really," Chrissy said. "It was before the sun came up, though."

Small drips of panic started to creep into Patricia's

4

voice, her mind struggling to find a reasonable explanation. "Did they take their things?"

"They took their backpacks, but left their sleeping bags," Sarah said. "Oh, and Amelia left her cell phone. Chrissy, give it to my mom."

Chrissy handed the bejeweled smartphone to Patricia, who took it as if the device might hurt her. Kids used phones like a third appendage. For Amelia to take everything else but leave the phone was strange.

"Did something happen last night?" Patricia looked at her daughter. "Did Amelia and Emily get in a fight with anyone?"

"No," Sarah answered. "Everything was fine."

The rest of the girls nodded along.

Patricia stared down at the phone, and those drips of panic opened up into a steady stream. But she knew there had to be something the girls weren't telling her, afraid they might get in trouble.

"Girls," Patricia said, crossing the room and sitting on the bed next to Sarah. "This is important, and I want you to be honest with me. I promise you I will not get upset, but I need the truth. Was anyone doing anything they weren't supposed to last night?"

Patricia waited, examining the girls' reactions, particularly her daughter's. Sarah had always been a bad liar, and if something did happen, Patricia was hoping Sarah would be the one who came clean.

"Honest, Mom," Sarah said. "We didn't do anything wrong."

Patricia studied her daughter and saw no hint of deception. And that scared her to death.

Patricia stood and then quickly left her daughter's room. She clutched Amelia's phone in her hand as she descended the stairs. She glanced down at the black screen and then pressed the home button. She didn't know Amelia's password, so she was locked out.

"Dan!" Patricia reached for the door, flinging it open. "I need you to call the police!" She was out the door before she heard her husband's response and hurried down the walkway to the sidewalk.

The neighborhood was quiet, as it typically was this early on a Saturday morning. They lived in a nice neighborhood, most of the residents younger couples with children. It was a safe place. Or so she had thought.

"Honey?" Dan stepped out of the house and jogged to his wife's side. "Hey, what's going on?"

"Amelia and Emily are gone," Patricia said. "And Amelia left her phone behind."

Dan blinked, unsure if he'd heard his wife correctly. "What? Where did they go?"

"I don't know." Patricia's chest tightened, and her stomach grew uneasy. She bit her lower lip, praying she would see the girls walking down the street, coming back from the store.

"Maybe they just went home?" Dan asked.

It was possible, but then why would Amelia leave her phone?

"Hey," Dan said, gently taking his wife by the shoulders. "Everything is going to be fine. I'm sure they went home. So let's just call their parents before we go off the deep end, okay?"

Patricia nodded. "Okay. Yeah."

Dan escorted his wife back into the house, and Patricia continued to clutch Amelia's phone close to her chest, dreading the conversations that came next.

erry Martin stood in front of the bathroom mirror, gripping the sides of their pedestal sink, staring at her reflection. Dressed in her green blouse and black slacks, Kerry knew she looked the part, but the million worrying thoughts racing through her mind chipped away at her confidence.

Kerry shut her eyes and drew a deep breath. "It's just another day." She exhaled slowly and repeated the breathing exercise a few more rounds and then convinced herself that it had helped.

When Kerry opened her eyes again, she lowered her gaze from her reflection to the detective's shield clipped to her belt. She touched it, making sure it wasn't a figment of her imagination, and a smile broke through the worry on her face.

Kerry had joined Seattle's police department shortly after she turned nineteen. No one wanted her to succeed, and she had failed her first two attempts training at the academy. She had been failed through no fault of her own. It had been an uphill battle, the odds stacked against her, but Kerry had refused to quit.

Fourteen years of working the streets, building her experience and learning the job from the ground up had finally paid off. She had proved her ability, and she was now ready to break free of her father's treacherous legacy.

Kerry lifted her gaze back to her reflection. A pale, freckled complexion stared back, two steel-blue eyes focused and ready. She had trimmed her auburn hair shorter, the ends reaching past her neck and touching her shoulders. At thirty-four, she had officially begun her career as a Seattle detective.

But even after the long, hard-fought battle for this accomplishment, there was still a tickling of doubt in the back of her mind. She couldn't completely quiet the voice of her father, who continued to whisper their similarities. But she was nothing like him.

In all her years on the force, Kerry had never broken procedure, because she knew even the smallest infraction would give her commanding officers the excuse they'd been looking for, a reason to discharge her and take her badge. People had no lost love for the daughter of Roy Solomon.

Despite the rumors, Kerry wasn't her father—no matter how loud his voice became in her head.

Kerry let go of the sink and straightened with confidence. "You earned this."

She walked from the bathroom to her bedside, and unlocked the gun safe beneath her nightstand. Inside were two weapons, her .45 ACP Smith and Wesson service pistol and her personal Glock 19. She grabbed the .45 along with the magazines and holster, loaded her weapon, and then clipped the holster with additional ammunition to her belt. She reached for the Glock, which was a 9mm, and concealed it in her ankle holster. She had registered the weapon with the department and had been approved to carry it on duty.

Voices drifted from the kitchen as Kerry walked out of the master bedroom of their single-story, split-floor-plan house, reminding her of why she had wanted the badge in the first place: to help keep her family safe.

In the kitchen, Kerry found her family still dressed in their pajamas.

"Good morning, Detective!" Brian smiled at his wife from the skillet, flipping pancakes barefoot in his boxers and a Mariners shirt. At thirty-seven, he was prematurely bald, but the way he filled out his attire more than made up for his lack of hair. "Are you excited for your first day?"

Kerry joined him by the stove, kissing his lips. "Excited. Nervous. Terrified. The usual."

Brian wrapped his arms around his wife, making her feel safe in his embrace. "You're going to do great."

"Thanks," Kerry said. "And I appreciate you taking the lead on weekends until I can get a different shift.

Once I get some seniority, I'll be able to make my own schedule."

"It's fine," Brian said. "I mean, the kids and I will miss you, sure, but don't feel guilty." He turned to their children, both of whom were watching Saturday-morning cartoons from the kitchen table as they shoveled pancakes into their mouths. "Mom doesn't have to feel guilty, right kids?"

A unanimous moan, which sounded liked a no, escaped their mouths, and Brian turned back to his wife.

"See? I'll be with them all weekend, and they won't even notice me, so we're in the same boat," Brian said. "Do you know who you're being partnered with yet?"

"No," Kerry said. "But I assume I'll spend some time shadowing the sergeant for a few weeks before I'm assigned a regular partner."

"And what about the new LT?" Brian asked.

Kerry shrugged. "I mean, she was one of the best detectives in the city when she was on the beat. I've never met her, but I've heard she's smart. And it'll be nice to have a female boss for a change."

"New boss, new partner, new position," Brian said. "Sounds like a fresh start."

Kerry nodded, but she couldn't stop thinking about all of the attention she would be getting now that she was a detective. She knew she was still in the hot seat, and any mistake she made moving forward could result in her losing the one thing she had worked so hard to obtain.

"Hey," Brian said, noticing her trepidation. "Today is a good day."

Kerry forced a smile. "I know."

Brian flipped the pancakes onto a plate and then set the spatula down, focusing all of his attention on his wife. "I know you're nervous. And I know how difficult this road has been for you, but this is your time. You're going to do great."

Kerry smiled more naturally this time. Her husband always had a way of making the stress melt away. "Thanks."

"You're welcome." Brian then turned to the pancakes and handed her the plate. "Now, eat."

Kerry kissed him and then joined her kids at the table. She turned the television off, which triggered groans until Kerry looked at her son, Jake, who was her youngest at six, and Daisy, her oldest, who was nine. "Hey. I want to spend some time with you before I go. Okay?"

Both kids glanced at each other then sighed as they spun around from the television.

"Moms can be so needy sometimes," Jake said.

Kerry kissed the top of his head. "Yes. We can."

* * *

DETECTIVE JIM NORTH had parked his rusted Mazda Protegé in the back of the precinct parking lot. He had arrived ten minutes earlier but hadn't moved since he parked. He had just gotten his suit back from the cleaners, the navy color blending well with his tan, and the trim cut clinging to his physique. He did his best to tame his thick brown hair which he kept short and neat, and his energetic chocolate-brown eyes were focused and alert.

He was a young man, too young to be a detective if you believed his superiors, but his short six-year career with the department had been storied. When he'd first started out, everyone had seen him as the young buck with a chip on his broad shoulders. And while most officers grew out of that phase, Jim had wallowed in it even after earning his detective's shield.

Now, he stared through his dirtied windshield at the unassuming one-story brick building ahead of him. It was his third new precinct in as many years.

The reassignment hadn't come as a surprise. Jim had been told by multiple superiors that he had an issue with keeping people in the loop, an opinion he didn't agree with because at the end of the day, all that mattered was solving the case. And while others judged him on certain superficial standards, Jim judged himself on the standard of locating abducted children. And his record was immaculate.

At twenty-five years of age, Jim had recovered more missing persons in his three years as a detective than any other officer in the country.

But while Jim had a stellar record for closing cases, his dust-ups with his superiors and the revolving door of partners who had been assigned to him had given him a lone-wolf perception amongst his peers.

Still, people tolerated him because of his success in the field, but all of that changed eight weeks ago when Jim's latest partnership ended with an IA investigation.

Jim had caught his partner not only catching bribes from local drug dealers, but orchestrating shipment drop-offs in areas where he knew officers wouldn't be stationed. But the moment Jim had alerted IA, his partner didn't skip a beat when he leveraged the same accusations against him.

It wasn't unusual for a dirty cop to drag down the person who outed them, and under normal circumstances IA would have taken it as nothing more than speculation. But his former lieutenant had been itching to get rid of him, and he jumped at the opportunity to give Jim an LOA while the investigation played out.

Jim managed to go over the lieutenant's head and found a loophole which stated he could stay on the job so long as he transferred to another precinct. He had tried every precinct in the city, but by the time he managed to apply for transfers, word has spread about him ratting out his former partner. He had broken an unspoken rule, and his brothers and sisters in blue had shunned him for it.

Seattle's police department, like most police departments, was like family. They protected one another fiercely, and any person who broke the family's sacred trust was branded a traitor.

Jim glanced over to the passenger seat, where he had placed his shield and his gun. The thought of quitting and leaving to start over somewhere else had crossed his mind more than once. But each time he considered running, he remembered the last time he had decided to run away.

It had been a long time ago, back when he was still an orphan in the foster system, but he still remembered it like it was yesterday. Every time he picked at that old scab, it still bled. And it was that fresh blood that pushed Jim forward.

Jim stared down at his open palms, which had been scarred when he was a boy. The wounds had healed long ago, but the calluses of that night remained. Jim ran a finger down one of the larger marks, the raised scar tissue white and pink.

Running away wasn't an option.

Jim grabbed his badge and gun. He placed the pistol in the shoulder holster beneath his jacket and clipped the badge to his belt. He drew in a breath, steeling himself for the fury he knew was waiting for him on the inside, and then stepped out of his vehicle.

Jim moved across the parking lot quickly, his stride long and purposeful. The suit was slightly stiff, as he hadn't worn it in years. But since the Five was the only precinct who took him in, Jim thought it best to make a good impression. He stepped inside the building and headed for the desk sergeant on duty, who had his head down, filling out some paperwork. When the sergeant didn't look up, Jim tapped the desk.

"Yeah?" the sergeant asked.

"I'm the new reassign from Twelve," Jim said. "I have a meeting with Lieutenant Mullocks."

Jim had heard stories about the Five's lieutenant. She had a bit of a reputation herself, having made the papers on multiple cases during her days as a detective. But she was more known in connection with the man she used to work with, an old partner that Jim had learned had died in a shootout somewhere in the Washington wilderness a few years back.

"Name?" The sergeant still didn't look up, and Jim noticed the man had a crossword puzzle on top of his paperwork.

"Jim North."

The sergeant paused then lifted his gaze from the crossword puzzle. Jim recognized the look in the man's eye. It was the same look he'd been on the receiving end of for the past eight weeks. Confidential information spread through the department like wildfire.

The slightest hint of disgust fell over the sergeant's face before he managed to hide it. "Lieutenant's office is down the hall, past the bullpen, and on the left. You'll see her name marked on the door." He buzzed Jim inside and watched him until he was out of sight.

The precinct was busy for a Saturday morning, the influx of officers indicating the morning shift change. Uniforms and plainclothes officers were huddled together, talking, laughing, joking around in the camaraderie in which Jim had never joined.

Most of them were too distracted with their work or conversation to notice Jim. But he knew it was only a matter of time before the desk sergeant spread the word that Jim North was the new detective at the Five.

Listening to everyone on his way through the precinct, Jim had flashbacks to his youth, listening to the children in the large halls, avoiding the groups that whispered about him.

But Jim kept his eyes ahead, focused on his goal, never forgetting the promise he made to himself all of those years ago.

LIEUTENANT SUSAN MULLOCKS sat behind her new desk, patiently listening to her new captain. She studied her superior with a pair of striking green eyes that blended nicely with her pale complexion, freckles, and dark-brown hair. She was a petite woman, the chair swallowing her up, but despite her size, she carried a large presence of authority.

"I understand you wanting to shake things up, Lieutenant," Kierney said. "But this pairing of yours isn't going to work."

Captain Kierney was a younger man for his position who tended to trust statistics more than insight. It was a method that had catapulted him into the captain's post before he was forty.

Mullocks had expected his visit this morning because she knew that her new appointments would be landing on his desk. And while she expected some pushback, she hadn't expected Captain Kierney's vehement objections.

But Mullocks had her own history with the department, and she had the sinking suspicion that while the captain strongly objected to her new choices for partners, this meeting was more about measuring how resistant she was going to be to his opinion.

"Captain," Mullocks said, reaching for the box of strawberry Pop-Tarts next to her monitor. "I left my position at the Eighteen to come here and build something new. And while you've made great progress on the homicide cases in this precinct, you ranked dead last on Missing Persons."

"And it's one of the reasons why I wanted to steal you away from the Twelve," Kierney said. "And I understand the need to retool, but this?" He pointed to the pair of files on her desk. "I think you might be biting off more than you can chew."

Mullocks leaned forward, picking the first file off the desk. "Kerry Martin has been a cop for fourteen years. She passed the detective's exam six years ago, and every application she made for an open detective's position was denied."

Kierney tilted his head to the side. "Lieutenant, you know why her application was rejected. And you know why she's worked the same street beat since she graduated from the academy. Her father was the most notorious crooked cop in Seattle's history. Roy Solomon murdered one of our own. He was a cop killer."

"And if you look at Kerry's file, you'll find nothing but a clean, sterling record," Mullocks replied. "She's the only officer in the city with her level of experience with zero citations."

Kierney motioned to the second file. "And him?"

"Detective Jim North has resolved more missing-person cases and returned more kids to their parents in the past three years than any other detective in the nation," Mullocks said. "The kid is young, but he's a bloodhound."

Kierney leaned forward in his chair. "And he's worked through more partners and been transferred more times than any other cop in the city. His file is full of complaints from other cops, civilians, reporters —he even hung up on a phone call with the mayor. The *mayor*. Not to mention what his last partner accused him of doing."

"Detective North turned over a dirty cop to IA, and in return and out of spite, the guy spouted off some lies about him to save face." Mullocks crossed her arms over her chest. "But that's not why you don't want him here."

Kierney bit the inside of his cheek and then leaned back into his chair. "No. That's not why I want him here. Not that it matters. But do you really want to bring a rat into this precinct? Someone who goes to IA without consulting their superior officers first? Because you know that's what he did, right? He went outside the chain of command."

Mullocks rocked in her chair for a few beats and then stood, walked around the desk, and leaned her backside against it as she crossed her arms, staring down at Kierney. "These two are unorthodox officers. I'm aware of that, and I am no stranger to the optics of the job. But sometimes two broken pieces fit together. And if there is anyone in this city who understands what this job entails, what it takes to bring kids home, it's me."

Kierney remained stoic, the pair in a standoff. Mullocks had laid all her chips on the table, and all she could hope for was a chance.

"You were a good detective," Kierney said. "And yes, you've made a reputation for yourself as a lieutenant that'll put you in my chair one day." He took a breath and glanced back to the files, shaking his head. "But this is mixing fire and gasoline, Lieutenant." He turned his attention back to her. "Is this really the hill you want to die on?"

"I don't plan on failing, sir."

Kierney cracked a smile, shaking his head as he stood. "All right, Lieutenant. Consider your new team approved." He shook her hand, his grip firm. "But if this blows back on us, it will not end well for you."

Throughout her career, Mullocks had been part of more conversations like this than she could remember. And while she was confident in her choices and her ability to lead, she was growing tired of her superiors refusing to trust her instincts.

"I understand, Captain."

"Good."

The door to the office opened suddenly and a man stepped inside. He was dressed in a suit and tie with a shirt, which he wore uncomfortably. And he looked younger than his age suggested. But people had said the same about her when she first started out.

"I'm Jim North," he said. "I had a meeting scheduled this morning."

"And you're right on time," Mullocks said. "Jim, this is Captain Kierney."

"Morning." Kierney's tone was dismissive as he kept his communication mainly toward Mullocks. "I'll leave you to it, Lieutenant. Keep me updated on the progress."

"Yes, sir."

Kierney walked toward the door, and while Jim nodded to his superior, Kierney avoided eye contact with the detective as he stepped out of the office and shut the door.

"Why don't you have a seat, Detective," Mullocks said and then returned to her own chair.

Once the pair were settled, Mullocks caught Jim's eye glancing at the two files on her desk.

"I'm assuming mine is the thicker file," Jim said.

"I like to do my homework on the people I bring on my team," Mullocks said.

"I understand," Jim said.

Mullocks studied him, trying to get a read on the man behind all of the paperwork that had been filed about him, but in the end, she decided to stick with what she knew best: getting to the point.

"The last time I saw a jacket file your size, I was looking at my own," Mullocks said, picking up Jim's file. "One of the youngest officers to earn his shield, but you've sifted through partners like pairs of shoes. Do you have a problem working with people, Detective?"

Jim didn't flinch. This wasn't the first conversation he'd had with a new lieutenant.

"No," Jim said. "But I don't tolerate incompetence."

Mullocks laughed and tossed his file back on the table. She bit into her Pop-Tart. "You're a good detective. The best I've seen in a long time. But if you keep on running as a lone wolf, you're not going to last much longer, Jim."

It was no secret Mullocks's unit had been the only precinct to agree to Jim's transfer. With the IA investigation opened against him, the threats had gotten so bad within his old unit that the captain had had no choice but to move him out while Internal Affairs continued their investigation.

Jim opened his left palm and ran his finger over it for a moment and then quickly closed it again as he returned both hands to his lap. "Lieutenant, I understand the circumstances around my transfer here aren't ideal, but I can assure you that my main priority is the recovery of any missing-person case that comes across my desk."

"I figured as much." Mullocks chewed her Pop-Tart and aimed the remaining pastry at Jim. "But you painted a target on your back, and I need to know you're going to be able to handle the shitstorm you're about to wade through now you're back on the job. I'm sure you know that your new captain happened to be good friends with your old partner?"

Judging by the surprise that flashed over his face, Mullocks saw this was new information for him.

"I can play nice, Lieutenant," Jim said. "And everyone is entitled to their own opinion of me."

Mullocks leaned back in her chair, finishing her Pop-Tart. "Just like an asshole, everybody's got one. You know, I do have some experience when it comes to rubbing folks the wrong way. And it might feel like you're buried under a mountain of dogshit right now, but the truth will have its day."

"We'll see," Jim said.

Mullocks dusted her hands of the remaining Pop-Tart. "I was hoping your new partner would be here by now, but—"

"I'm here."

A woman entered the office, panting to catch her breath. She was tall but hid her height by wearing flats.

"Sorry, Lieutenant. Traffic was a nightmare."

"That's all right," Mullocks said. "We were just about to get started. Detective Kerry Martin, I'd like to introduce you to your new partner, Detective Jim North."

Jim stuck out his hand, but it lingered in the open air between the chairs, before Kerry broke through her own paralysis.

"Sorry. Hi." Kerry shook his hand, her grip strong, her palm a little sweaty.

"Detective Martin earned her shield last week," Mullocks said. "I'd been looking for someone to partner her up with and thought you two would be a good match." She looked at both of them. "Kerry, I'll let you show Jim around, give him the lay of the land."

"Yes, ma'am," Kerry said.

"Lieutenant?" An officer leaned into the open door. "I have two sets of parents here who say their daughters disappeared from a slumber party."

"Looks like the tour will have to wait," Mullocks said, standing up. "Jim, you take the lead on this. You know the drill." She shook both of their hands, hoping that her instincts hadn't dulled. "Don't let me down."

3

---

*K*erry studied the monitors displaying the video feed from the two interrogation rooms where the parents waited for news. She saw their nervous glances, their fidgeting arms and bouncing legs. As a mother, she knew those parents were experiencing the unthinkable. A missing child was the nightmare scenario for every parent.

In both rooms, the coffee they'd been given had remained untouched, all of them waiting for an update, but Kerry knew that instead of answers, they would only be given more questions.

Kerry glanced from the monitors to her new partner, the only other cop in the department she knew who was hated more than her own father, or herself. She had heard the stories about him like everyone else, but she was surprised at how young he looked. He might have to shave maybe once a week by the look of his face. She had to be at least a decade older than him, and he had already been a detective for three years.

But Kerry tried to remember that she didn't have the whole story. After all, people judged her for the actions of her father. Until he proved otherwise, Kerry decided to give Jim the benefit of the doubt. And besides, it wasn't as if anyone else was chomping at the bit to be partnered with her.

Jim was speaking to the officer who had taken the parents' statements when they arrived. He hadn't said much to her since they'd left the lieutenant's office. Kerry wasn't sure if he was naturally reserved or if he was just getting acquainted with his new surroundings. She left the monitors and joined Jim's side.

"What about the parents who hosted the slumber party?" Jim asked.

The officer who had taken the statements was Larry Bennigan. He and Kerry had been partnered for a few months during his rookie year. He had come a long way since being a doe-eyed officer fresh from the academy.

"Dan and Patricia Montgomery," Larry said, reading from the report. "They called Emily and Amelia's parents early this morning when they discovered the children were gone."

"Find their address and have a uniform officer sit on their house," Jim said. "And get me a background check on those parents as well."

Once Larry was gone, Jim returned to the interrogation room monitors, continuing to flip through the pages Larry had given him. Kerry waited for him to give her an update, but when he remained silent, she spoke up.

"What are we looking at?" Kerry asked.

"Two missing girls: Emily Wilks, aged twelve, and Amelia Johnson, aged eleven," Jim answered, his eyes still glued to the paperwork. "I had one of the officers pull background checks on both sets of parents. The Johnsons are clean, a few speeding tickets, but nothing major." He stopped on one particular page and handed it to Kerry. "Emily's parents are a different story. Both arrested on drug charges. The mother has done time, but the father has managed to stay out of the system. But three years ago, there was a domestic-disturbance dispute at the house. Cops showed up, and both individuals had physical injuries, but because the mother was under the influence, she took the ride downtown." He pocketed his hands and stared at the screens. "Ralph, Emily's father, divorced her a few months after that incident."

Kerry scanned the rest of the pages, catching up on what Jim already knew. "Vanessa Wilks is currently on three years' probation after serving a two-year sentence for possession and intent to distribute." She handed the pages back to Jim, who took them while never taking his eyes off the screen. "If both of Emily's parents were druggies, then an unstable home might be a good reason to flee."

"According to the paperwork, Ralph Wilks has sole custody," Jim said. "No charges, drug or otherwise, filed against him for the past seven years. The paper trail shows a man who cleaned up his act."

Kerry studied Ralph on the monitor. He sat alone in the room, arms on the table, head down. He bounced his leg nervously. "If he was abusive when he was on drugs, then he still might have been abusive off of them. You don't need to be high to be violent."

"No," Jim said. "You don't."

"So, what's the play?" Kerry asked.

"We'll start with Amelia's parents," Jim answered. "See what they know. Then we'll talk to Emily's father."

"Nine times out of ten, it's usually a friend or family member who takes the kids, right?" Kerry asked. "Shouldn't we go and find Emily's mom?"

"I have a uniform tracking her down," Jim answered. "We'll focus on the parents here until we know where Vanessa Wilks is or isn't."

Kerry followed Jim toward room two and kept the notepad and pen she'd brought with her to take notes tight to her chest.

Jim paused with his hand on the door handle and then turned back to Kerry. "Don't be afraid to jump in with questions. If you think it's pertinent to ask, ask it. Just remember we don't want to accuse anyone too early and close them off. We need the parents to cooperate with us, and it's easier for them to do that when they trust us."

"Right," Kerry said.

The interrogation room was small, crowded, and bland. The Johnsons were still seated at the table, both of them fidgeting, when Kerry and Jim entered the room. Jim handled the introductions, which were quick and efficient.

Natalie Johnson, Amelia's mother, was ghostly pale and plagued with tremors. Tom Johnson, the father, sat off to the side. His arms were crossed over his chest, and he leaned back. There was distance between the two of them, both physically and emotionally.

"We're going to ask you some questions," Jim said, laying the groundwork. "Some questions might not sound pertinent to the case, but we need to build a strong image of your daughter in our heads to help in our recovery efforts. Okay?"

Natalie Johnson nodded, her movement quick, while Tom barely moved his head.

"When was the last time you saw your daughter?" Jim asked.

"Friday night," Natalie answered, her voice trembling. "I dropped her off at the Montgomerys' at seven."

"How well do you know the Montgomerys?" Jim asked.

"Well enough for me to trust them with my daughter's well-being," Natalie said.

Tom scoffed. "Unbelievable. I mean, where are they now?" Tom pressed a meaty finger onto the table. "They should be down here answering your questions too. How could they have let this happen?"

"Tom, please." Natalie cast a dagger-like stare at her husband. "Now is not the time."

Jim dismissed the outburst. "We have an officer

over at the Montgomery household as we speak. We'll be heading over to question them when we're finished here." Jim glanced down at the notes, quickly changing subjects. "I see here you already gave a good physical description of your daughter along with the clothes she'd packed for the sleepover, which is helpful. What can you tell me about her behavior over the past few weeks?"

Natalie quickly glanced at her husband and then cast her eyes down to the table. "Home life has been a little hectic."

Kerry looked up from her notes, pausing for a moment as Jim leaned closer.

"Hectic how?" Jim asked.

Natalie kept her gaze to the table. "Tom and I are getting divorced."

"When did that start?" Jim asked.

"A few months ago," Natalie answered.

"How does our divorce have anything to do with this?" Tom asked. "You think she ran off because of what's happening at home? That's bullshit."

"Tom." Natalie spoke between clenched teeth. "They're just trying to help."

"We understand your frustration, Mr. Johnson," Kerry said.

"Frustration?" Tom bolted out of his chair and leaned halfway across the table. "I'm not frustrated, I'm fucking livid!" He slapped his palm over the desk. "My daughter goes over to a slumber party and then disappears! How the hell does that happen?"

Jim raised his hand, his voice stern. "Mr. Johnson, sit down." His voice boomed in the room, and it pushed Tom back into his chair. "Right now, we're gathering information. That's all. We ask questions because we want answers. And the more answers we have, the better."

"Of course," Natalie said then glared at her future ex-husband.

"How has Amelia been handling your divorce?" Jim asked.

Natalie cleared her throat, nodding. "Good. We explained it to her as clearly as we could and told her that it had nothing to do with her. And therapy has helped."

"Who is her therapist?" Jim asked.

"Dr. Gary Weathers," Natalie answered.

"How long has she been in therapy?" Jim asked.

"Since we talked to her about the divorce," Natalie answered. "Ralph said—"

"Emily's father?" Kerry asked.

"Yes," Natalie answered, her voice catching in her throat. "Um, he gave us the number for the therapist that Emily sees."

Jim leaned back, nodding along. "Do both girls know they see the same therapist?"

"Yes," Natalie answered.

"So the girls must be close," Jim said.

Natalie smiled. "They've been best friends since the third grade. Attached at the hip. We used to call them M&M because of their names."

"How had Emily and Amelia been getting along lately?" Jim asked.

"Good, as far as I knew," Natalie answered. "Amelia was very excited about the slumber party."

"What is Amelia's online presence like?" Jim asked.

Natalie frowned. "What do you mean?"

"Does she have a Facebook page or Instagram, any social media accounts?"

"No, her father and I both agreed she wouldn't have any of that until she was older," Natalie answered. "We know how toxic social media accounts can be on children her age. And with cyberbullying and everything that's happening—no. It's just too much."

"What about a phone?" Jim asked.

"She does have a phone for emergencies," Natalie asked. "But we monitor her activity on the internet, and she can only access websites we've preapproved. The Montgomerys told me she left the phone at the house and—"

Natalie Johnson covered her mouth, the tears finally breaking loose as she shut her eyes and bowed her head. She sobbed quietly to herself, her shoulders shaking, but Tom Johnson never moved a muscle to comfort her.

Kerry leaned across the table, grabbing hold of Natalie's hand and squeezing. She spoke no words but didn't let go of Natalie's hand until the mother regained her composure.

"Thank you," Natalie said. "I'm sorry about that."

"There's nothing to apologize for, Mrs. Johnson,"

Jim said, glancing back at Kerry and offering an approving nod. "Does your daughter play any sports, musical instruments, or is she part of any organization that would put her in contact with other adults?"

"No," Natalie answered. "But she does well in school."

Jim worked his way back along the timeline, asking about Amelia's twenty-four hours before the disappearance. According to the parents, everything had seemed normal.

Kerry chimed in whenever something piqued her interest, but for the most part, she resigned herself to listen. Despite Jim's age, he carried himself like a veteran. But he was clinical in his questioning. He offered no empathy for the situation.

When they finished, Jim and Kerry thanked the Johnsons for their time and headed toward the door. But just before Kerry stepped outside, Natalie Johnson called out to her.

"Do you have children, Detective?" Natalie asked.

"Yes, ma'am," Kerry answered.

"Then you know," Natalie said, her voice trembling. "You know the fear of losing them."

"I do," Kerry replied.

"Find her," Natalie said, desperate hope clinging to her voice. "Bring my little girl home."

This might have been her first day as a detective, but Kerry knew better than to make promises she couldn't keep. But even before she spoke, she felt the conflict bubbling up inside. It was the same conflict she had struggled with her entire life: the intersection of life and work.

"We'll do everything we can, Mrs. Johnson," Kerry said.

A sad smile broke over Natalie's face. It wasn't the answer she wanted, but it was the only comfort Kerry could provide.

Kerry excused herself and closed the door. She joined Jim in the hallway and found him looking at her, the files tucked under his arm. "What?"

"You said the right thing," Jim answered.

Kerry sighed, walking past him toward the next room. "It didn't feel right."

"It usually doesn't," Jim said and then stopped her before they entered the next room. "We're dealing with parents who have lost the one thing more precious to them than anything else in the world. They're caught up in their personal hell. We're not here to make them promises to alleviate their fears. But if we do our job right, we can find their children and bring them home."

It was the sincerity in Jim's voice that surprised her. After listening to him drone in the conference room with zero emotion, she hadn't expected to see any now.

"It's easy to get personally involved in these cases," Jim said. "But, we stay the course."

"Yeah," Kerry answered. "Thanks."

Jim nodded. "You ready for the next one, or do you need a break?"

"I'm fine," Kerry said.

"Okay. Here we go." Jim opened the door. "Mr.

Wilks, we appreciate your patience."

Ralph Wilks was middle-aged with thinning hair, but he was still handsome. He had a square jaw and a muscular physique. The few wrinkles and gray stubble that framed his face spoke more to a life lived than a man worn down. He perked up when Jim and Kerry entered the room, eagerly leaning forward. "Have you heard anything yet?"

"Right now, we're in the collection phase of the investigation, Mr. Wilks," Jim said.

"Please, call me Ralph."

Jim nodded as he sat down and opened the file in his lap. "What can you tell me about Emily?"

Ralph smiled at his daughter's name. "She's smart. A good kid who doesn't get into trouble much."

"I understand that you and your wife are divorced," Jim said.

"Yes," Ralph answered. "I have sole custody of Emily. Have you found Vanessa? Does she have Emily?"

"We're examining all facets of the case right now," Jim said. "According to our records, she's had drug issues in the past?"

Ralph crossed his arms, leaning back into his chair. "My ex-wife is an addict. And she refuses to get help. I tried everything in the book, sent her to programs, rehab, but nothing worked. It just got to a point where I didn't know what else I could do. All I knew was that I didn't want Emily exposed to that lifestyle. So I ended it."

"How often does Emily see her mother?" Jim asked.

"Vanessa gets one supervised visit per week," Ralph answered. "But she's missed her last two appointments. Emily was pretty upset about it."

"What's Emily's relationship like with her mother?" Kerry asked.

"Complicated," Ralph answered. "When she was younger, her world revolved around those visits with Vanessa. And despite everything the woman has done, I know Emily still loves her, but... the older she gets, the harder it is for her to hold onto that relationship."

"Does your wife have any contact with your daughter outside of those weekly supervised visits?" Jim asked. "Phone calls, emails, texts?"

"No," Ralph answered. "Vanessa gets one hour on Wednesday afternoons, and that's it. If I had any say in the matter, she wouldn't even get that." Ralph fidgeted in his seat. "She has disappointed and failed our daughter repeatedly. And while Emily keeps forgiving her, I stopped doing that a long time ago." He leaned forward, scowling. "When Emily was a toddler, Vanessa used to pawn her toys for cash so she could buy dope. What kind of person does that?"

"You've had your own history with drug abuse, yes?" Jim asked.

Ralph flinched, uncrossing his arms and staring into his palm, picking a callus. "I had demons. Bad ones. But I put all of that behind me. I've been sober for seven years now." He knocked on the table for luck and then smiled.

The room was quiet for a moment, and Kerry

glanced at Jim, who only stared down at the file in his lap. She was about to say something when he finally spoke.

"In addition to some of the drug charges your wife had, she was also arrested for a domestic dispute three years ago," Jim said, lifting his gaze from the report. "Tell us about that incident."

It was like watching a deer caught in headlights. Ralph opened his mouth, struggling to speak, and then shut it, cleared his throat, and fidgeted in his seat. "I don't, um—" He rubbed his eyes and then finally crossed his arms. "She was the one arrested for that confrontation."

"Was it violent?" Jim asked.

Ralph struggled to find his footing in the conversation. "Yes—I mean, we had a fight. A neighbor called the police. Vanessa was high, and she was arrested."

"The officers who responded to the disturbance said that both of you were physically injured." Jim removed a photograph from the file and placed it on the table for Ralph to see.

Vanessa Wilks had wild, untamed hair and a bloodied lip and a black eye. She wore a vacant expression, her pupils dilated, her eyes red and glazed.

Ralph didn't look at the picture and instead stared directly into Jim's eyes. "I was defending myself."

"So you hit her," Jim said.

"She had a knife in her hand, she came after me, and I had to disarm her," Ralph said, struggling to keep his anger in check.

"Was this the first time you had to defend yourself?" Jim asked. "Or were there other instances?"

"I'm not a woman beater," Ralph said.

Jim nodded and then returned the picture of Vanessa to the file. "Did Emily see that altercation?"

Ralph lowered his gaze, shifting his posture in his chair. "Yes. Unfortunately, she was home." He cleared his throat. "My daughter has been through a lot. I'm ashamed to admit that for a long time, I was part of the problem. But after the divorce, I checked Emily into therapy, so she had the opportunity to work through some of the horrible things she saw at such a young age."

Jim checked his notes again. "That would be Dr. Weathers. You referred the Johnsons' daughter to him, correct?"

"Yes," Jim answered.

"Why did you do that?" Jim asked.

Ralph frowned. "Because they're getting a divorce."

"Who told you that?"

Ralph hesitated. "Natalie told me."

"And do you and Mrs. Johnson speak regularly?" Jim asked.

Kerry stopped taking notes, picking up on what Jim was trying to nail down. If there was a love triangle happening, then the pool of suspects had just widened to include more people than Vanessa Wilks.

"Our daughters are best friends," Ralph answered. "We talk."

Kerry knew Jim could press the man further, but

this was where Jim exercised restraint and used the opportunity to transition the conversation back to Emily.

"Does Emily have any social media accounts?" Jim asked.

"No," Ralph said. "I keep a close eye on that stuff."

"Cell phone?" Jim asked.

Again, Ralph shook his head. "I don't want her to have one yet. But she's kept asking me for one."

Jim took a moment to open the case file one more time and flipped through the pages. "Looks like we have a picture and description of Emily." He closed the file and stood. "We're going to keep an officer stationed at your house, and we'll be over soon to examine Emily's room. In the meantime, if you remember anything else that's useful, please don't hesitate to reach out."

Ralph stood as Jim and Kerry stood. "How long do you think it will be until we hear something?"

"We'll reach out when we have new information," Jim said. "Thank you for your time, Mr. Wilks. We'll be in touch."

With statements taken and all of the information they required for the Amber Alert collected, Kerry and Jim watched the parents leave.

The Johnsons had come in different vehicles, and Tom left without saying a word to his wife. But Ralph Wilks, Emily's single father, lingered and embraced Natalie Johnson as she broke down crying.

The pair were too far away for Kerry or Jim to

overhear their conversation, but Kerry didn't need to hear them talk to understand what was happening.

"What are the odds that Ralph Wilks might have something to do with the Johnsons' divorce?" Kerry asked, watching as Ralph and Natalie walked arm in arm out of the precinct together.

"I'd say they're high," Jim answered. "What are you thinking?"

"Well," Kerry answered, glancing down to her notepad and flipping through the pages until she landed on the notes that she had written about Ralph. "The obvious choice is Emily's mother, but that doesn't explain why Amelia would go unless Amelia hasn't been handling the divorce as well as her parents thought."

"I agree," Jim said. "I'll finish the Amber Alert reports for both girls and submit them to the lieutenant."

Kerry studied Jim's face and noticed the tiny lines between his eyes as he thought. "What?"

"Our missing kids were at a house in a room filled with other girls," Jim said, speaking the words aloud. "And they just decided to get up and leave."

"Maybe home life is worse off than the parents are saying?" Kerry asked.

"I think the girls planned to run away, but I don't know if they were running away from something, or running to something." Jim looked to the clock on the wall and saw that it was almost eleven. "Let's finish up our legwork here and then hit the road."

4

*J*im's and Kerry's desks were pressed up against one another. It was the same setup as all the other detectives in the precinct.

Kerry had the phone wedged between her left ear and shoulder while she quickly jotted down notes. "Uh-huh. Yeah. Okay, thank you." She hung up and caught Jim's attention. "That was Vanessa Wilks's parole officer. She's been MIA for the past seventeen days. No contact with her PO or the halfway house where she's been living."

"Put out the APB," Jim said, typing on his computer. "I'm almost done with these reports, and then I want us to head over to the Montgomerys' house. I want to speak with their daughter, see if we can learn anything she might have been hiding from her parents."

"On it," Kerry said, and she stood, taking a step away from her desk before she spun back around. "You need any coffee?"

41

"Black," Jim answered.

Just before Kerry left, a trio of officers blocked her path then surrounded their desks like a pack of wolves.

"Well, look what we have here." The officer who spoke was in his blues, and around Jim's age. He was stocky, his head shaved, and the muscle along his left jaw wouldn't stop twitching. "The daughter of a cop killer, and a rat. The new LT must be missing a few screws to bring you two on board."

"Back off, Wyatt," Kerry said, standing her ground.

Jim broke from his typing, glancing at Wyatt's other cronies who stood nearby, scowling. He had hoped to avoid any conflict in the new precinct for as long as he could, but he knew confrontation was unavoidable.

Wyatt turned his gaze to Jim, and the twitch along his jaw intensified. "Only a coward goes behind their partner's back and rats them out to IA. You're a disgrace to the badge." Wyatt stepped around Kerry, and the man's partners moved in closer, taking their cues from their leader.

Jim remained seated. He had seen the tough-guy act before.

Wyatt bent forward and got into Jim's face. "I wouldn't make yourself too comfortable, Rat. Because vermin tend to find their ways into traps."

Jim never flinched, staring straight into Wyatt's eyes. "I'd be careful with threats, Wyatt. Because you might have to back up those big words one day."

Wyatt's cheeks flushed red, and for a moment Jim thought they were going to have it out on the precinct floor. But the officer backed off, and his cronies followed suit, the trio walking away.

Even after the cops were gone, the precinct's attention was still focused on Jim. But he didn't pay them any mind and returned to work, and eventually, everyone else did too.

Kerry rejoined Jim's side once the commotion was over. "You all right?"

"It'll take more than that boy band to rattle me," Jim answered and then glanced up at Kerry. "Are you all right?"

"Yeah," Kerry answered and then sat on the edge of his desk, crossing her arms. "I don't think you have anything to worry about with them. Wyatt's always been a dick."

"I'm not worried," Jim said, focused on his work.

"Right," Kerry said, and then stood. "You said black for the coffee right?"

"Yes," Jim answered.

Once Kerry was gone again, Jim paused his work, wondering what Wyatt had meant when he called Kerry the daughter of a traitor. He opened up a new browser window and typed Kerry Martin in the search box, and the title of the first article on the search page explained everything.

Daughter of former Seattle Detective Roy Solomon joins the force.

The news pushed Jim back into his chair. Everyone in the city knew Roy Solomon. The man was the dirtiest cop in Seattle history. And of all the people Jim could have been paired with, he couldn't help but laugh at the fact it was Roy Solomon's daughter.

Having Jim here was probably a godsend for her, because there was finally someone else for everyone to hate more than her. And it explained why it had taken her so long to earn her detective's shield. People had already made up their minds about her without giving her a chance.

Just like him.

Jim exited out of the browser window and returned to his work. He typed quickly, and with a few more keystrokes, the Amber Alerts were finished. He forwarded the reports to the lieutenant and appropriate departments and turned his attention to the timeline.

Aside from establishing the Amber Alert quickly, putting together a timeline was key to ensure success. If Jim and Kerry couldn't get a solid lead in the first twelve hours of the case, then the odds of recovering the children dropped in half. And after only forty-eight hours, chances of recovery dropped to practically zero.

But they did have a lead in the form of Emily's mother. All they had to do was track her down, and with every cop in the city searching for her, Jim hoped it wouldn't take long.

Every case Jim worked was nothing more than a map. Most of the time, the map was blank save for two simple things: Jim was on one side of the map, and the person he needed to help was on the other.

No two cases were ever exactly the same, and at

times, it was maddening. New information could change the course of the investigation at the drop of a hat, which could be good or bad. And between eyewitnesses, testimony, evidence, and the million other little things that came about during an investigation, it was easy to get lost. Just like now.

But whenever Jim was faced with those moments, he made sure to remember that no matter how complex the road to the solution, the endgame was always the same: shortening the time and distance between himself and the person who was missing.

Jim started the timeline for the case with the girls being dropped off at the Montgomery home for the slumber party. Amelia had arrived at seven o'clock, and Emily had ridden home with the Montgomerys' daughter, Sarah, after school at three o'clock.

The parents had arrived at the precinct this morning at nine fifteen, and assuming the girls had remained at the Montgomery house until at least midnight, that would put them missing for almost ten hours already.

Jim needed to get a better understanding of when the children had disappeared in the middle of the night and what had been happening at the slumber party.

Jim returned to his notes and then tapped on the name Dr. Gary Weathers who had been both girl's therapist. He typed the therapist's name into Google and found his office number and dialed it on his cell phone. While the phone rang, Jim ran Gary's name through their criminal database, searching for any past warrants or arrests. The guy was clean save for one instance ten years ago.

Weathers had filed a police report against a couple who had attempted to blackmail him. According to the notes in the file, a couple was using their child to make up lies about inappropriate contact between themselves and whatever therapist was their mark.

The parents were arrested and convicted, and Weathers was cleared of any wrongdoing.

The phone continued to ring with no answer, and Jim hung up. He jotted down the doctor's office address and made a mental note to stop by for a chat.

Jim checked the time again and glanced around to find the coffee maker. He stood and headed toward the back of the building, and along the way, Jim noticed the stares.

People had always whispered about him behind his back, but this was the first time he'd noticed genuine malice.

The handful of threatening letters, the dust-ups in the locker room, and the vandalism to his property had been enough to prompt his old lieutenant to put him on a LOA, but Jim knew his old lieutenant didn't do it for Jim's safety. The man just wanted him gone.

Jim had broken the unspoken rule of damaging the silent blue wall. For those who had gone to extremes to protect that wall, for Jim to breach trust within the ranks was sacrilege. So he had been branded a rat.

It was a complicated political field Jim had to navigate, because while he understood the importance of trust, he wasn't going to turn a blind eye when he saw something wrong.

No matter the situation or the personal cost, when Jim saw someone breaking the law, using their power and privilege to hurt other people for their personal gain, he refused to keep silent, blue wall be damned.

Jim finally spied an officer stepping out of a room with a cup of coffee in hand, and Jim zeroed in on the breakroom. But when he neared the entrance, he paused, listening to the voices inside.

"Kerry, listen," the man said. "I know how hard you worked to earn your shield. It wasn't easy for you. But I promise you that we're going to take care of the problem."

"Ken, I barely know the guy," Kerry said. "And if things get bad, then I'll just request someone else. Hell, Jim does it all the time. I mean, you've heard the rumors."

"I have," Ken said. "He can't be trusted, Kerry. Be careful what you say around him."

"Yeah," Kerry said. "I will."

"And listen," Ken said. "North is a marked man. No one betrays one of their own and sticks around for very long. Once he's gone, I'll make sure you get a real cop on your side. One that doesn't squeal to IA at the first sign of trouble."

Jim flinched and turned away from the breakroom, returning to his desk. It had been a long time since office gossip had irked him in such a way. And while Jim thought Kerry was pleasant and a sharp investigator, he knew that deep down, all people were the same. He had known that since he was a child.

Jim could break all kinds of records as a detective. He could have a perfect case rate, and all people would talk about would be how no one liked to work with him and how he obsessed over a case at the cost of everything else. But wasn't that what they were supposed to do? Wasn't that why they wore the badge in the first place?

Kerry returned and set his coffee on the desk. "Sorry for the wait. The pot was empty. But nothing beats a fresh batch." She smiled, sipping the coffee, but then lowered the cup. "What's wrong?"

Jim stared at the coffee, steam rising from the cup. He picked it up, shaking his head. "Nothing. I called the therapist's office and didn't get an answer." He sipped the caffeine, careful not to burn his tongue, and then stood. "We'll swing by the office after we visit the families' houses."

"Oh, we're going now?" Kerry asked.

"Yeah," Jim answered, picking up the case file they had already started putting together. "We should head over to the Montgomerys' house first. It's as close to a crime scene as we're going to get." He looked to Kerry, gesturing to the coffee. "Any lids?"

"Huh? Oh, I didn't see any."

Jim shrugged. "I guess we'll just have to dodge the potholes. Do you have a cruiser?"

"Yeah," Kerry answered.

"Good," Jim said. "Let's go."

Jim rode shotgun while Kerry drove. She kept the car clean, which he appreciated. He hated when cops didn't take care of their rides. He understood the nature of their job made it difficult to keep order in the vehicles, but there was nothing worse than hopping into a ride that had been roasting under the hot sun with old fast-food wrappers and half-filled cups of coffee or soda.

Jim did his best not to let what he'd heard affect the case. Deep down, Jim understood Kerry's hesitation. He imagined she might be getting some brushback from the other detectives in their unit because of their pairing. No one wanted to be the leper, but a close second was being partnered with the leper. Because like the disease itself, Jim knew he was contagious.

Jim reached for the radio dial and turned the volume up one notch. All of those visits at the gun range, even with the proper ear protection, were starting to take its toll on him. Hearing aids were in his future.

"So how long have you been on the force?" Kerry asked, keeping both hands on the wheel and her eyes on the road.

Jim knew it was an olive branch, but he had always struggled with small talk. "Six years."

"You must have been pretty young when you made detective, huh?"

"Yeah." Jim glanced out the window, looking away from his partner and catching a shadow of his own reflection in the glass.

Kerry shifted in her seat and flexed her grip on the wheel. The silence had grown awkward, and Jim knew it. No amount of radio chatter was going to save him now. But Jim couldn't stop thinking about the conversation he'd overheard in the breakroom.

"I've been trying to get my shield for the past six years," Kerry said.

"Mmm." Jim nodded, staring at the buildings they passed.

"So why'd you join—"

"Kerry, listen," Jim said, cutting her off. "We're partners. Not friends. We work the case together, so let's concentrate on our job."

"Yeah," Kerry said. "Sure."

Jim's tone was harsher than he'd intended, but he knew how this would end: the same way it always ended for him. He would get paired with someone, it wouldn't work, and then he would be left to fend for himself. He'd been on his own for as long as he could remember. There was no reason for that to change now.

5

*T*he rest of the drive to the Montgomerys' house was made in silence. Kerry had been taken aback by Jim's tone, but it matched the rumors about how he was difficult to work with.

Still, Kerry couldn't help but feel there was something else going on with the man. Sure, he had built a wall around himself, but she had seen plenty of cops do the same. But Jim's wall had been constructed a long time ago.

The Montgomerys lived in a well-to-do neighborhood, which made sense given the father's profession. According to the background check, Dan Montgomery was a software designer and worked in a local Microsoft branch office.

Kerry parked on the street outside the Montgomery home and followed Jim to the door.

Jim rang the doorbell, and Patricia and Dan Montgomery answered, both welcoming the detectives into their home.

Kerry examined the house on their walk to the living room. It was a typical family home. Pictures were on display, the house was tidy. It reminded Kerry of her own home.

Patricia led Kerry and Jim into the living room, where there were two sofas. Jim and Kerry sat down on the larger couch, while Patricia and Dan took the love seat.

"Can we get you anything?" Patricia asked, her tone nervous. "Water? Coffee?"

"No, thank you," Jim said. "Is Sarah here?"

"She's upstairs," Dan answered. "We weren't sure if you needed to talk to her or not. She's a bit shaken up right now."

"That's fine," Jim said. "We'd like to talk to both of you first."

"Of course," Patricia said. "Whatever we can do to help."

Jim opened the case file and went to work. "Why don't you tell me what happened?"

Patricia kept her left hand closed in a fist close to her throat, little pieces of white tissue poking between her fingers. "I woke up around seven o'clock this morning, and I walked upstairs to check on the girls. Sarah had friends over last night. When I entered the room to wake them up, I discovered Emily and Amelia were gone."

Kerry jotted down her notes but noticed Jim continued to study the parents.

"What did the girls tell you?" Jim asked.

"The girls said everyone fell asleep around two o'clock, and then one of the girls woke up before sunrise to pee, and she noticed Emily and Amelia were gone."

"Who was the first girl to wake up?"

"Chrissy Thompson," Patricia answered.

"Did you hear anything in the middle of the night? Was there any kind of arguing?"

"No arguing," Patricia said. "Dan said they were giggling late into the night. And the girls said everyone was getting along just fine."

Kerry had gone to her fair share of slumber parties growing up, and there was always some kind of spat when a big group of girls around that age got together in a confined space.

"Do you have a security system at home?" Jim asked.

"No," Dan answered. "It's such a safe neighborhood, we never thought we'd need one."

"We'll need a list of names of all the girls that were at the party," Jim said. "Is it all right if we speak to Sarah now?"

"Of course." Dan stood and walked out of the living room. His footsteps echoed up the stairs and onto the second floor.

Kerry watched Patricia fidget nervously on the couch. She could understand the worry. Kerry's daughter had sleepovers, and she couldn't imagine losing any of the girls on her watch.

"How are the others holding up?" Patricia asked.

"We can't comment on the investigation at this time," Jim answered.

"Oh, yes, of course." Patricia apologized quickly and then bowed her head.

With the silence lingering and the mother looking as though she were on the verge of a mental breakdown, Kerry interjected.

"Sarah is your only child?" Kerry asked.

"Yes." Patricia smiled.

"So are you home base then?" Kerry asked, smiling.

"I'm sorry?" Patricia asked, confused.

"For sleepovers," Kerry said. "My daughter is nine, and our home has become the forward operating base for most of her friends." She laughed. "It's hard when they're still in elementary school, but I can't imagine dealing with girls on the cusp of becoming teenagers."

Patricia nodded. "It's an adjustment. Sarah has sleepovers all the time. Sometimes the girls can get a little rambunctious, but never—" She bowed her head, hands clasped together very tightly as she took a moment to collect herself. "Never anything like this."

Dan returned with their daughter, and Sarah sat on the couch next to her mother, while Dan stood off to the side. The cushions swallowed her up, and the young girl kept her head down and her hands clasped between her knees. She was nervous.

"Sarah?" Patricia placed her arm over her daughter's

shoulders. "These detectives have some questions about Emily and Amelia. Okay?"

Sarah nodded, but she didn't look up.

"Sarah, what do you remember from the slumber party last night?" Jim asked.

Sarah was quiet for a moment and then looked to her mother, who nodded patiently. "Well. We were having a lot of fun. Samantha kept burping because of all the soda she was drinking, and that made us laugh." A smirk crossed her face. "I had some good ones."

"What about Emily and Amelia?" Jim asked. "Were they joining in on the fun?"

Sarah nodded. "Yeah. Both of them were having a lot of fun. I don't know why they left."

Kerry watched Sarah closely. She'd had enough conversations with her own daughter to know something was wrong. Whenever kids wanted to hide the truth, they provided you with small pieces of things that had actually happened. But they made sure to keep the bulk of the truth to themselves.

"Sarah," Kerry said. "Did Emily and Amelia talk to one another a lot last night? Maybe just to themselves?"

Sarah scrunched her face in thought. "I guess so. But they're always like that."

"And who stayed up the latest last night?" Kerry asked.

Sarah struggled to hide her smile. "Me."

"I was always the night owl too," Kerry said, gaining the girl's confidence. "Sometimes, I used to pretend to be asleep just so I could see what the other girls would do. Did you ever do that?"

Sarah giggled but covered her mouth quickly. "Sometimes."

"Did you do that last night?" Kerry asked. "Did you see something after everyone thought you were asleep?"

Sarah hesitated but eventually nodded. "I saw a light."

Jim leaned forward. "What kind of light?"

"It was dull at first, like a glow," Sarah answered, again scrunching her face as she concentrated. "It was coming from under Emily's sleeping bag. She had pulled her cover all the way over her head." Sarah mimicked the motion with her hands. "She was whispering to someone. I think she had a phone."

Kerry looked to Jim, remembering how Emily's father, Ralph, had been adamant about his daughter not having a phone.

"Are you sure it was Emily?" Jim asked.

"Yes," Sarah answered, nodding with confidence. "She was the only one with a pink sleeping bag. It was her."

"Sarah," Kerry said. "Were you able to see what kind of phone she was using?"

"No," Sarah said.

Jim looked from Sarah to her parents. "I'd like to look in her room."

Mrs. Montgomery nodded. "Of course."

Kerry and Jim followed the mother upstairs.

"Her room's a bit of a mess still," Patricia said. "We didn't want to pick anything up in case there was evidence or something you needed."

Jim said nothing as he passed through the door, stepping around the landmines of sleeping bags that riddled the floor.

"Thank you," Kerry said, making up for Jim's lack of manners.

Jim studied the area and found the pink sleeping bag that belonged to Emily, which was next to a green one. "Is the green bag Amelia's?"

"Yes," Patricia answered.

Jim donned a pair of gloves. Kerry turned back to Sarah and her mother, reaching for her own pair of gloves. "We'll be up here for a while if you two want to stay downstairs."

"Okay, sure." Patricia guided her daughter away from the room. "Let's go, Sarah."

Kerry joined Jim, who was crouched by the green sleeping bag, looking through the contents. "They slept close to one another. Maybe Amelia and Emily were just talking to each other, and Amelia had her phone out?"

"Maybe," Jim answered.

Kerry turned toward the window. She unlocked it and tried to open it, but the window jammed after only opening a few inches, and she gave up. "No way they could have gone out through the window." She turned around, pointing toward the door. "They walked out the front door when they left." She shook her head. "They must have been quiet as church mice."

"I've got something," Jim said, his arm stretched into the bottom of the pink sleeping bag.

Kerry crouched by his side as Jim removed a small envelope. It was addressed to no one, but it hadn't been opened yet. "Emily's bag?"

"Yeah," Jim answered, turning the envelope over in his hands a few times before holding it up to the light. "There's a letter inside."

Kerry watched as Jim carefully opened the envelope. "We can pull DNA off of it for whoever licked it, even though it was probably the girls."

Jim said nothing as he removed a folded piece of paper. When he opened it to read, Kerry couldn't see what was written. She was about to ask for it when Jim handed it over to her.

Kerry frowned as she read the letter aloud. "'Don't worry about us. We're going someplace where we can be together. We'll be safe. Someplace where we can be free. But we want you to know, we know.'" She reread the letter a few more times and then looked up at Jim. "What is it you think they know?"

Jim studied the sleeping bags, checking both again to make sure they hadn't missed anything else. "Remember how friendly Mr. Wilks and Mrs. Johnson looked?"

Kerry tucked the letter back into the envelope. "So you think the girls took off because they found out their parents were sleeping with one another?"

"That combined with a difficult time at home." Jim shrugged. "The pieces fit."

Kerry bagged the letter and envelope in an evidence bag and then removed her gloves. "We might have a better idea of where they might have gone after we look at their rooms. Leaving the letter behind hints at signs of premeditation. I think they had been planning this for a long time."

"'Someplace where we can be free,'" Jim said, repeating the words. "Don't you think that's odd for a pair of girls to talk like that?" He stood and then removed his own gloves.

Kerry tilted her head from side to side. "It's a little strange. But kids that age are always different."

"Right," Jim said.

After another quick sweep of the room to make sure they hadn't missed anything, Jim and Kerry returned downstairs. They provided their thanks to the Montgomery family and then returned to the squad car. The moment the doors shut, Jim shared his thoughts.

"We've got a secret phone, a secret letter, a possible secret affair, and a mother with a drug and criminal history," Jim said, ticking off each statement with his fingers. He glanced back at the house and was quiet for a moment before he turned back to Kerry. "Did Mr. Montgomery trigger any red flags with you?"

"No," Kerry answered. "I think those parents are more nervous about being sued by other parents than being considered suspects."

"Yeah," Jim said, his expression still set in deep concentration.

Kerry buckled her seat belt. "If Emily was on the phone last night, she might have been talking to her mother. Maybe that's where the girls went? Maybe they were meeting Vanessa Wilks?"

"It's possible." Jim tapped his finger on his knee and then glanced out the window to the surrounding neighborhood. "We need uniforms to canvass the streets. Talk to the neighbors and see if they heard or saw anything."

Kerry nodded but then thought back to the letter. "You mentioned before you weren't sure if the girls were running away from something or running to something."

Jim looked at her. "Yeah?"

"In the letter they left behind they mentioned they were going someplace safe," Kerry said. "If they didn't think the adults in their life could create a safe space, maybe they found someone who could? Maybe they were running to someone they trusted."

"Are you talking about Vanessa Wilks?" Jim asked. "Her profile doesn't suggest stability and safety."

"Maybe it's someone else," Kerry said, starting the car. "We can stop and speak with the girls' therapist on our way to Amelia's house. See if Dr. Weathers can offer any insight into our missing children or who they might have been speaking with."

Jim buckled his seat belt. "I wouldn't be so sure.

Kids are good at hiding things. I know I was when I was that age."

"Anything about Dr. Weathers we should know?" Kerry asked.

"I ran a background check on him," Jim answered. "Guy came back clean except for some blackmail ten years ago."

"Blackmail?" Kerry asked.

"Apparently two adults were running a scam on therapists," Jim answered. "They would bring in their kid for therapy, convince their kid to say the therapist was inappropriate with them, and then demand cash for their silence. Dr. Weathers called their bluff."

"Sounds like he lucked out," Kerry said.

"Maybe," Jim replied.

Kerry dismissed the comment as she drove away from the Montgomery household, hoping their next visit would provide more answers as to where the girls might have gone. And who, if anyone, they might have met.

---

6

*D*octor Gary Weathers's office was on the outskirts of Seattle's southeast corridor in an old but well-maintained commercial district. The office was a small suite part of a larger building. The small waiting area smelled musty, and even though the room had no windows, it was drafty.

The waiting room reminded Jim of the offices he used to visit as a child. And even after all of these years his stomach still churned with unease. He had hated therapy during his time in foster care.

The carpet was plush but old, and it crunched beneath Jim's feet as he walked from the door to the elderly woman sitting behind a desk, squinting at her computer behind a pair of thick glasses.

"Hello, ma'am," Jim said, removing his badge from his belt to catch the old woman's attention. "I'm Detective Jim North, and this is my partner, Detective Martin." Jim motioned to Kerry as he clipped his badge back to his belt. "We need to speak to Dr. Weathers about two of his clients."

The secretary must have been in her late sixties. Wrinkles lined her face, and her skin was loose and aged with dark spots. Her hair was a cloud of delicate white curls set in a perm, and she had decorated herself with gaudy necklaces and bangles. "Did you have an appointment?"

"No," Jim answered. "But we need to speak to him soon or—"

The door behind the old woman opened, and a young woman stepped out, accompanied by a tall, handsome gentleman with short gray hair.

The woman wiped her nose with a tissue and then shook the man's hand. "Thank you so much, Dr. Weathers. Really. Thank you."

"Today was a good session, Katy," Dr. Weathers said, smiling warmly. "I'll see you next week."

"Yes, and thank you again." Katy turned toward the door, waving goodbye to the secretary along the way before she flashed a smile in Jim's direction.

Once his patient was gone, Dr. Weathers stepped from his office, pocketing his hands as he stared at Jim and Kerry. "Can I help you two?"

Jim opened his jacket, revealing his badge once again, and repeated his introductions. "We need a few moments of your time."

Dr. Weathers, dressed in navy slacks, expensive dress shoes, and a light-brown cardigan, checked his watch, which Jim noticed was a Rolex. Business must have been good.

"I've got a few minutes before my next appointment." Dr. Weathers cleared his doorway and then waved the detectives into his office.

Once Jim and Kerry were inside, they took a seat at the pair of chairs by his desk. Jim noticed the plaques on the walls showcasing his multiple degrees and license to practice, along with a few awards and certificates. The office was furnished with another couch, another large armchair, and plants that filled each corner of the room. Like the waiting room, the office was windowless, and aside from the furniture and plants, there was no other décor.

Dr. Weathers finished speaking with his secretary then returned to the room, shutting the door for privacy. "Sorry about that. I just hired a new assistant, and she's a little long in the tooth. I'm afraid she's not as efficient as my previous secretary, Lindsey." He sat down and made himself comfortable. "Detectives, how can I be of assistance?"

"We had some questions on a pair of children you were working with," Jim said. "Emily Wilks and Amelia Johnson."

Dr. Weathers's warm smile slackened. He was quiet for a moment and then lowered his gaze. "What happened to them?"

"What makes you think something happened?" Jim asked.

"Police detectives don't come to visit me about children I've counseled to deliver good news," Dr. Weathers said. "Tell me."

"Emily Wilks and Amelia Johnson disappeared from a slumber party last night," Jim said. "We hoped that you could provide us with some insight into why they might have run away."

Dr. Weathers's face remained grave and concerned. "Two very different girls. Two very different homes."

"Different how?" Kerry asked.

Dr. Weathers crossed his legs, transitioning himself to a more comfortable position. "Amelia grew up in a fairly stable home. It wasn't until recently that her home life had become troublesome, and even then her parents made sure to keep her in the loop about what was happening. She was someone who needed a hand to hold during the transition and to learn healthy ways of coping in her new environment. I also encouraged her to keep a journal to provide her an opportunity to examine her emotions externally."

"And Emily?" Jim asked.

Dr. Weathers sighed. "Emily had a more traumatic past. The majority of our sessions were finding a way to sift through all of those memories, working on ways to confront and accept what happened in the past and ways of approaching any similar situations she might encounter in the future."

"Situations involving her mother," Kerry said.

"Yes," Dr. Weathers replied. "I know Emily's mother continues to struggle with addiction."

Jim did his best to sit still, to remain professional,

but it was the cadence of the doctor's voice that irked him. Time suddenly rolled backward, and he was no longer a detective with Seattle PD and instead was nine years old, sitting on the couch and listening to a man tell him it was okay to speak up. But when you were little and powerless and the only life you had known depended on the cruel actions of adults, silence was your only weapon.

"Did the girls confide anything to you?" Jim asked. "Anything they discovered at home or about each other?"

Dr. Weathers shrugged, pressing the tips of his fingers together, each of them lined up perfectly with its counterpart. "We spoke about many things, Detective. But rest assured, if I saw any signs of abuse or trouble, I would have reported it."

"So neither girl had been physically or emotionally abused?" Jim asked.

"No," Dr. Weathers answered. "Not as far as I could tell." He smiled, then wagged a finger at Jim. "You're not a fan of people like me, are you, Detective?"

Jim smiled politely. "Did the girls mention any places that might have been special to them? Anywhere they might have gone if they wanted to leave their homes and parents behind?"

"I never had the impression that either girl wanted to run away from home," Dr. Weathers answered. "But no, the girls never mentioned any specific location special to them."

"And they didn't speak about any other adults in

their life?" Jim asked. "Anyone who they looked up to or admired?"

"No."

Jim nodded, jotting his notes down. "And just one last question. Can you tell me where you were between the hours of two o'clock and six o'clock this morning?"

Dr. Weathers remained stoic. "I was at home, sleeping."

"Can anyone corroborate that?" Jim asked.

Dr. Weathers rocked forward in his chair and rested his elbows on his desk. "Detective, I have been a therapist for thirty-two years. I understand the job, and I know what even the smallest indiscretion can do to a man in my position. I can assure you I have done nothing wrong."

"I'm not asking you about your work history, Dr. Weathers, I'm asking if anyone can confirm your whereabouts last night." Jim retained a neutral tone, but inside he was glad he'd managed to irk the therapist. It felt like payback for all of the sessions Jim had had to sit through as a kid. It might have been petty, but he didn't care.

"No," Dr. Weathers answered. "As I said, I was alone."

Jim flipped his notebook closed and pocketed it in his jacket. "We appreciate your time. If you think of anything else, please give us a call." Jim placed his card on the desk. "I'm sure we'll be in touch soon."

Dr. Weathers picked up the card and handed it back to Jim. "You can give that to my secretary."

Jim plucked the card from between the doctor's fingers and quickly left the room. He dropped off the card with the old woman, repeating to her the same message he'd given the doctor.

The secretary nodded, her tone serious. "I'll be sure to keep this handy. It's my first week with Dr. Weathers, and I'm still getting the hang of the system. I'm afraid I'm not as quick as Lindsey was." She smiled and chuckled.

"I appreciate that, ma'am," Jim said and then leaned closer, lowering his voice. "How has it been working for Dr. Weathers?"

"Oh, it's been fine," she answered and then frowned. "But I'm afraid I've gotten under his skin a little bit, being new and all."

"How long have you worked here?" Jim asked.

"About a week," she answered.

"The previous assistant, Lindsey—do you have her contact information?" Jim asked.

"Let me see, I think so." The old lady rummaged through a few drawers, and after her search, she wrote the number down on a slip of paper. "Here you go."

Jim smiled, folding the paper into his palm. "Have a good day."

Kerry followed Jim outside, and both remained silent until they returned to the car parked across the street. Jim stared at the building through the windshield, beads of sweat already starting to form on his forehead from the heat.

"You want to talk to the old assistant?" Kerry asked.

Jim unfolded the paper. "Anyone who worked closely with him might be able to provide us better insight about him." He tucked the paper back into his pocket. "We'll give Lindsey a call after we visit the other houses."

Jim buckled his seat belt, but when Kerry didn't start the car, he looked at her. "What?"

"Was he right in there?" Kerry asked. "About you not liking therapists?"

Jim faced forward. "I've been around enough of those head shrinks to know the ones who are so full of themselves they think the air they breathe is holy."

"And is this from recent experience, or something from your past?" Kerry asked.

Jim blushed. The last thing he wanted to do was share anything with Kerry about his childhood, so he deflected the conversation to the investigation. "We'll head to Amelia's house first and check out her room next. See if we can't find that journal or diary—"

"Unit Seventeen, come in," dispatch crackled over the radio.

Kerry reached for the receiver. "Go for Seventeen."

"We have a hit on your APB for Vanessa Wilks. She's being brought back to the Five."

Kerry and Jim exchanged a glance, and Kerry pressed the talk button down on the receiver. "Did she have the girls?"

"Negative," dispatch answered. "She was alone."

"She still might know something about Emily's phone," Jim said. "Let's go and have a chat."

7

*D*rugs had taken their toll on Vanessa Wilks.
She twitched like a strung-out junkie, and
the bags under her eyes marked more than a few nights
without sleep. Her clothes were dirty and stained, her
hair nothing but a tangled rat's nest, and a few sores
had grown at the corners of her mouth.

Years of substance abuse had made her skin sallow,
and she was deathly underweight, nothing but bones.
Kerry was surprised the woman was even alive. And
because Kerry knew this woman was a mother with a
missing child, the fact she was more concerned with
scoring dope than locating Emily put a bad taste in
Kerry's mouth before the woman even spoke.

"You guys don't normally give me so much pomp
and circumstance," Vanessa said, scratching her forearms, which were covered with dirty long sleeves.
"Usually, it's just quick processing, and I go into the
tank for a night."

"You're not here on drug charges, Mrs. Wilks," Jim said.

Vanessa snorted. "Mrs. Wilks. I'm no more a misses than you are, buddy. Been divorced for years now. I don't have that bastard's name anymore. Not that I ever really wanted it." She drummed her fingers on the table. The nails were yellowed and cracked. They varied in length, but Kerry saw that the pinky fingernails on both hands were the longest. "So, what do you want?"

"You're in violation of your parole," Jim answered. "You haven't checked in for the past three weeks, and we want to know where you've been and what you've been doing and who you've been talking to."

"That's easy." Vanessa leaned forward. "Um, fuck you. Fuck you. And fuck you." She leaned back into the chair and crossed her arms. She smirked, amused with herself.

Kerry had her notepad in her lap, but she hadn't written anything down yet. She couldn't take her eyes off of the steaming pile of garbage across the table.

"When was the last time you spoke with Emily?" Jim asked.

"Emily?" Vanessa scrunched up her face as if she didn't even recognize the name, but then she corrected herself. "God, I don't know. A couple weeks, maybe?"

"Mrs. Wilks, did you—"

"I told you, I'm not a fucking missus anymore!" Vanessa slammed both fists on the table with a surprising degree of strength. "Stop calling me that!"

"If you don't like the name, then why did you keep it?" Kerry asked.

Vanessa pivoted her anger toward Kerry. "What?"

"You used the name Wilks on all of your parole papers," Kerry answered. "You never changed your name after the divorce. Why?"

Vanessa opened her mouth as if she was going to say something smart, but then shut it and unclenched her fists as she leaned back in her chair. She narrowed her eyes at Kerry. "You're a cheeky bitch, aren't you?"

"Vanessa, did you give your daughter a phone?" Jim asked, redirecting the line of questioning to the matter at hand.

Vanessa shrugged, but she was still looking at Kerry. "Maybe."

"I need a yes or a no," Jim said.

Vanessa crossed her arms and finally looked to Jim. "What's in it for me?"

Kerry shook her head, muttering under her breath, "Unbelievable."

"Oh, you better believe it, sweetheart," Vanessa said. "I'm not going to give up anything until I know what's in it for me."

"What's in it for you is that we might be able to find your daughter!" Kerry snapped at the woman.

Vanessa dropped her guard. "What do you mean to find my daughter?" She glanced between Jim and Kerry. "What the hell are you talking about?"

Jim took a breath. "Your daughter disappeared from a slumber party last night, and one of the girls saw her speaking on a phone. According to her father, she doesn't have a cell phone." He studied the mother's reaction. "Did you give Emily a phone to contact you with?"

Kerry waited to see what the woman would say, and she was surprised to see the genuine disbelief spread across her face. "That doesn't..." She shook her head. "No, that can't be right. She's gone?"

"Vanessa," Jim said, raising his voice. "Did you give your daughter a phone?"

And just like that, the fight ran out of Vanessa, like flicking off a switch. She hunched forward. Her eyes reddened, and her lips trembled.

"Yes," Vanessa said. "I gave her a phone."

"When was that?" Jim asked.

"A few months ago," Vanessa said, a single tear falling from the corner of her left eye. "I just got fed up with only being able to talk to her once a week."

"That's in violation of the custody arrangement," Kerry said.

"Yeah, and you think I give two shits about that agreement?" A flash of Vanessa's anger returned. "No one gets to tell me when I see my daughter. No piece of paper is going to stop me from talking to her. No matter what Ralph says."

"And you're sure the last time you spoke to her was a couple of weeks ago?" Jim asked. "It's important for us to know when you spoke with her last, Vanessa."

Vanessa shut her eyes, sending a cascade of tears down her dirty cheeks. "I don't know." She wiped at her eyes, smudging the dirt and tears along her face. "I could have gotten a call from her when I was high, and I just don't remember."

Kerry scribbled down the phrase *Vanessa's phone is in evidence* on her notepad and then showed it to Jim, who nodded.

"Emmy just left some party in the middle of the night?" Vanessa asked. "Was she with anyone?"

"We're not at liberty to discuss the details—"

"She's my fucking daughter!" Vanessa slammed her fists on the table again. "I have every fucking right to know exactly what the fuck is happening!" She quickly stood, knocking the chair into the wall behind her.

Jim raised his hand. "Vanessa, sit down."

"No! I want answers! Did he do something? Did he?"

Jim leaned forward. "Did who do something?"

"Ralph! That fucking asshole!"

Jim pointed toward the chair. "Vanessa, if you can just—"

"Sit your ass down!" Kerry roared, her voice booming in the small room, and both Jim and Vanessa looked to her with surprise.

Vanessa hesitated for a moment, but then she finally leaned off of the table, picked up her chair, and sat down. "I don't know what paint-by-numbers bullshit Ralph told you, but he is no saint."

"We know about his drug history," Jim said.

"I'm not talking about his addict days," Vanessa said. "I'm talking about him fooling around with little girls."

The air was suddenly sucked out of the room, and Kerry leaned forward onto the table while Jim returned to his seat.

"Your ex-husband wasn't flagged in the sexual offender registry," Jim said.

"Just because it wasn't reported didn't mean it didn't happen," Vanessa replied.

Jim had been around more than his fair share of perverts throughout his childhood and his career in law enforcement, and if what Vanessa was telling them was true, then he was losing his instincts. "You're telling me Ralph Wilks sexually assaulted a minor?"

"Yeah," Vanessa answered. "That's what I'm telling you."

"Who?" Kerry asked.

"I didn't catch her name, but she couldn't have been older than sixteen," Vanessa said. "It was back when we were still married. I came home and caught him in bed with her. I chased the girl off and then whipped Ralph's ass for cheating on me."

"So you're not sure if she was a minor," Jim said.

"She left her jacket behind," Vanessa said. "And I found a high school ID. But Ralph snatched it out of my hands before I had a chance to go to the cops. I don't know what he did with it. Burned it. Shredded it. Maybe he gave it back to the girl."

"Did you ever see him do anything inappropriate with Emily?" Kerry asked.

Vanessa's face slackened, and she stared down at the table. She wiped beneath her nose and shrugged. "I never saw him do anything. I don't know how young he liked them. I don't think it was that young. Hell, I don't know; I was high most of the time."

"Was he ever violent with Emily?" Jim asked.

"Once," Vanessa answered. "And I told that to the judge, the lawyer, the cops, but none of them fucking believed me."

"Why?" Jim asked.

"Because I'm a junkie, sweetheart," Vanessa said then looked to Kerry. "No one ever believes a bitch with needle marks in her arms. Plus, he was always smarter than me." She picked at her dirty fingernails. "Clever too. He was better at hiding who he really was than me. But I don't make any apologies. I might be a shit mom, but I never laid a hand on my little girl."

"No," Kerry said. "You just abandoned her for your next drug fix."

Vanessa chuckled. "Yeah, you go ahead and judge me, little Miss Priss. I know how much you hate me. I can tell you got kids. But you press Ralph hard. You talk to him about the person he used to be. Hell, he probably still is. It's not like people don't relapse."

Jim followed up with a few more questions, but Vanessa remained tight-lipped, and he ended the interview, leaving her to be processed with her parole officer, who was on his way to pick her up.

Outside of the interrogation room, Kerry vented her frustration. "I can't believe that woman. I'll never understand parents like that. Never. I couldn't imagine abandoning my kids. Not on the worst day of my life."

"We need to talk to Ralph again," Jim said. "See how much of what Vanessa told us was fact and how much of it was out of petty anger."

Kerry stopped pacing. "What do you think? Did we misread the father? Do you think Ralph Wilks is a pedophile?"

"My gut tells me no," Jim said. "If he was sleeping with other women when he was using, then it's not impossible an underage girl could have been in the mix. Girls can get fake IDs, drink in bars, go home with men they don't know."

Kerry took a breath and tried to calm down. "It's sick."

"It is. But it's part of the job." Jim rubbed his eyes, and his voice cracked from fatigue. "We need to pull Emily's number off Vanessa's phone and see if we can get a trace. If we're lucky, she still has it on her."

"And if we're not lucky?" Kerry asked.

Jim checked the time, noting they were already past the twelve-hour mark, which meant their chances of a successful recovery had already dropped in half. "Then we need to work faster."

Kerry and Jim returned to their desks. Her mind was still spinning from her conversation with Vanessa Wilks, her mind unable to grasp the concept of abandoning her children for anything. But she wasn't an addict.

"We can take my car again," Kerry said, quickly checking her emails before they left. "Hey, did you hear me—" She looked up from her computer screen and saw Jim staring at something. She followed his line of sight to his desk where she saw the fake rubber rat.

Kerry straightened up and then glanced around the room, noticing how the precinct had gone quiet, and every pair of eyes was watching Jim. She saw the contempt on their faces, their sneers, their hatred for a man they didn't even know.

It was the same hatred that had been directed at Kerry when she was first hired. And she'd be damned if she was going to let someone else go through that too.

Kerry reached for the rubber rat and held it high above her head for everyone to see. Once she had everyone's attention she picked up the waste basket and slammed the rubber rat into it. She returned the trash bin to the floor and then dusted her hands.

"You ready?" Kerry asked, turning to her partner.

Jim wore a deer-caught-in-headlights expression, but he quickly recovered. "Yeah."

The pair walked out together, and Kerry caught Jim's smile on their way to the car.

8

_____

*K*erry drove to Emily Wilks's house, Jim riding shotgun with his phone glued to his ear. He grunted in frustration and then ended the call.

"What's wrong?" Kerry asked.

"Tech is saying Emily's phone is turned off," Jim answered. "We'll have to wait until we hear back from the carrier and get the last cell tower coordinates. But that won't necessarily give us Emily's current location."

"How long will it take for a tech to get a ping on the phone?" Kerry asked.

"It depends on the carrier." Jim pinched the bridge of his nose then rubbed his eyes, and when he opened them again, his vision was momentarily blotched with black spots and white stars. "If Amelia was smart enough to leave her phone behind, then Emily might have been smart enough to ditch hers too. Wherever these girls went, they didn't want to be found."

"What about the former secretary?" Kerry asked. "Lindsey, right?"

"Nothing yet," Jim answered. "I emailed her and I'm still waiting for a reply."

The pair fell into silence, and Jim struggled to find a connection between Dr. Weathers and the girls. Aside from the blackmail scandal he had been caught up in a while back, the man was squeaky-clean. But the fact he was the therapist for both girls, along with his intimate knowledge about their lives, added up to a potential for trouble.

Kerry had been right about his prejudice against therapists. He hated how they could manipulate someone into changing their minds. And while therapy had worked for some kids, it had never worked for Jim.

"How are you holding up?" Kerry asked.

Jim frowned. "What do you mean?"

"I mean with the IA investigation, the incidents at work, being in a new precinct, new partner," Kerry answered. "You've got a lot going on."

Jim shifted uncomfortably in his seat and glanced out the window. "I'm fine."

Kerry arched her eyebrows and exhaled a long sigh. "Yeah. Okay."

Jim knew Kerry was trying to connect with him. It was what partners were supposed to do. But he had always put the case first.

A lifetime of solitude had hardened him and made it difficult to connect with anyone. But Jim thought if there were only one detective in the city he could connect with, it might be someone who had just as hard a time as him growing up.

"Thanks for the backup at the station," Jim said. "With the rat."

"You're welcome," Kerry said. "I know what it's like to be hated amongst your peers."

Jim remembered the article he found on Kerry about her father.

"Roy Solomon must cast a long shadow."

"Too long," Kerry said.

"Do you ever go to see him?" Jim asked.

Kerry adjusted her grip on the wheel. "No. As far as I'm concerned, Roy Solomon is already dead."

Jim had heard the brutal stories about her father, but judging by the disgust in Kerry's voice, Jim thought that for once, maybe the rumor mill had gotten it right.

Jim also understood the desire and psychological need to bury the past. But he had never worked with another cop who had a similar experience to his own about being shunned based solely on who he was as a person instead of his casework.

"Why'd you do it?" Jim asked.

"Do what?"

"Join the force." Jim flipped the end of his tie. "After what you saw your dad do, why would you think becoming a cop was a good idea?"

Kerry nodded, drumming her fingers on the steering wheel. "People always ask me that, and I usually tell them I did it because I wanted to clear the family name. But I did it because I wanted to understand. I wanted to know how my father, a man who I had loved and respected as a kid, could become two different people. I wanted to prove to my father that I could resist the temptation. I wanted to prove to him that I was better."

The answer surprised Jim, but hearing it made him respect her more. "What was it like after your dad was caught?"

"I was brought in for questioning," Kerry answered.

"But you were just a kid," Jim said.

Kerry scoffed. "Well, it's not every day the city's biggest crime lord ends up being a detective for Seattle PD." She rolled her shoulders. "They wanted to see if they could get any dirt on him through me, but I honestly didn't know anything about what he was doing or why he was doing it. I was just a babe in the woods, lost and afraid."

"I didn't really know how bad he was until I got older. But growing up, I didn't know him as the crooked cop. I only knew him as Dad." She took a deep breath. "He was a good father. Always home when we needed him. We never wanted for anything. He wasn't violent at home. He loved me and my mom." She shrugged. "And then the story broke about all of the drugs that he'd been running and how he was leading an entire platoon of cops to help keep drugs on the streets. The kickbacks, the bribes." She remained very still, and then her voice became quiet. "And then we heard about the bodies. The people he'd killed. That broke my mom." She shook her head. "None of us saw it coming."

Jim had been around his fair share of scumbags, but he knew Roy Solomon was a different breed. They talked about him a lot at the academy. He had become a study case for corruption.

Kerry frowned and then shook her head. "I do remember my mother though." She grew still and quiet. "I remember the way she looked and how much she cried when she found out what happened." She pinched her eyebrows together, several wrinkles creasing the skin. "After the police had come and collected my father, and after we were allowed to go home, I remember the officer that escorted us inside the house, and I remember him apologizing to my mother for everything that had happened. And then I remember my mother just screaming at the cop. It was like she had all of this pent-up rage and all of this hate, and she needed to let it out, and she aimed all of it on this poor kid fresh out of the academy." Kerry swallowed, her grip on the steering wheel tightening once more. "I don't remember what she said, but I remember how it made me feel."

When Kerry grew silent, Jim spoke up. "What did you feel?"

Kerry's voice grew small and quiet as she reflected on those moments in her past. "I had never seen her blow up like that, and I knew I was witnessing something. It was a transformation. Something shifted in my mother, and she was never the same again." She took a breath and fought the tears that were starting to form. "She became a different person. She became angry and bitter, and she shut herself off from the rest of the world."

"I did visit him once, you know," Kerry said. "It was right after I graduated from the academy. I was so nervous about seeing him. It had been years since the last time we were face-to-face." The muscles along her forearms rippled from the flexed grip over the steering wheel. "I almost didn't go through with it." She shook her head. "You wouldn't believe the things I learned about him during my time in the academy. Everyone had stories about him, and the moment people realized he was my father, I was immediately shunned. People think that genetics are contagious when you come from a bad family. No one trusted me, and it's taken me this long to make people believe that I'm not my father."

Her mouth suddenly went dry, creating a ball of sandpaper-like air that traveled down her throat when she tried to swallow.

"I was shaking so much when I finally made it to the waiting room where other people had come to visit prisoners. It was cold and drafty, and there was a lingering scent of disinfectant on the tables, chairs, and floor. And it was so bland, no colors, just gray and white. And then the buzzer sounded, and the inmates flooded the room. A few people stood up, searching for the ones they came to visit, but I remained seated and kept my head down. I was sweating so much, and I was having a hard time breathing, and my blood was rushing so fast to my head that my brain was pulsating. I felt everything. And just when I was about to leave, I heard my father's voice, and I looked up."

Jim was locked into the story.

"He had aged a lot," Kerry said. "His jet-black hair had grayed, and he had gotten thin, rail thin. Dark circles rested beneath his eyes. Overall, his time in prison hadn't done him any favors, but when we made eye contact with one another, he smiled, and for a moment, I saw the man who ate breakfast with me on Sunday mornings and would make smiley faces on my pancakes. But it was all a lie, an illusion to hide who he really was, and that was a man who no longer cared for upholding the law and protecting the public, and I told him everything that I had kept bottled up inside of me since the day my mother and I discovered what he really did when he was on the job.

"And I still remember the look of pain and shame on his face as I laid into him. Every word that came out of my mouth was like a stab to his gut, and every wince and grimace I saw only fueled my rage. It was like I had all of this poison built up in my system, and the only way that I could get it out was by throwing it back up in his face."

Kerry remembered how he had looked, remembered how much she had hated him and how glad she was at the pain she was now causing him. Because as bad as prison might have been for him, his actions had created a prison for Kerry and her mother too, a prison built of doubt and suspicion from everyone who knew who they were. They had become outcasts in their own city, shunned by the very people who had once been friends and even other family members.

"But when I was done—and it took a long time before I was finished—I was still angry," Kerry said. "It was like, even though I had dumped all of this hate and rage into this man who was supposed to take care of me and protect me, and ultimately betrayed and humiliated me, I thought the hate in me would be gone. But it stayed. It wasn't until I met my husband that I realized that all of the trauma and heartbreak and betrayal I experienced helped shape me into the person I am today. But hate only begets hate. Anger only begets anger."

Jim was silent, the noises of the road filling the space in the interior of the vehicle. "How did you do it? How did you stop being angry?"

Kerry paused, reflecting on the question. "I'm not sure I ever really got rid of all of it." And then a slight smile graced her lips. "My kids have helped. The moment I became a mother, I realized how those kids would affect the rest of my life. I realized just how different my future and my world had become when I finally held my firstborn in my arms. There was no other feeling in the world like it, and I just couldn't wait to give them everything that they needed, and I vowed to never make them feel the way I felt. I wouldn't set a trap for them to fall into by pretending to be someone that I wasn't.

"And that's when I realized that was what my father had done. He thought he could keep everything separate and divided, but the split put too much pressure on him, and he eventually lost track of who he was. The lies and the truth blended together, and all of the false stories and fake narratives finally caught up with him." She took a breath and nodded. "I told myself that I wouldn't fall into the same traps. And I intend to keep that promise."

Jim took a moment to absorb and process everything Kerry had shared, and he realized how similar they truly were. Both of them had experienced trauma. Both of them had gone through something terrible, and survived.

"That was a lot," Kerry said. "Sorry."

"No," Jim said. "It's fine, really."

Kerry took a moment to wipe her eyes, recomposing herself before she turned the conversation back to Jim. "So what about you? What's your deal?"

Jim struggled to remain tight-lipped. This had been the longest conversation he'd had with another detective about anything other than a case in the past two years. But what was more, he found it hard not to like Kerry. She was different. Older than his usual pairing, but she was calm. And what might have been equally hopeful and frightening to him was the fact that he was beginning to trust her.

"My foster father was the one who got me interested in wanting to become a cop," Jim said.

"Foster father," Kerry replied. "So you're adopted.

Jim nodded and then looked out the window. His foster parents were good people and did the best they could with him. But even with them around, deep down, he always felt alone.

"Do you know what happened to your real parents?" Kerry asked.

Jim shook his head. "No."

"Did you ever go and look for them?" Kerry asked.

"When I was really little, I sometimes wondered what my parents were like," Jim answered. "I would lie awake at night and try and figure out who they were as people based on things that I did and liked." He smirked at the thought. "It was stupid things like how I always used to keep my feet poked out from under the covers because I would get hot when I slept. Or how, when I was a kid, I would take my green beans and stuff them in my pocket because I didn't want to eat them."

"Must be hard not knowing where you came from," Kerry said.

"Yeah." Jim took a breath. "I came close one time. I mean, I am a cop, and it's not like I couldn't search through some records if I wanted to, but I stopped myself."

"Why?" Kerry asked.

Jim was quiet for a moment, the answer on the tip of his tongue, but he kept it locked behind tight lips for a long time before he finally answered. "Because she left me."

Kerry frowned.

"My mother had me, didn't want me, or couldn't take care of me, or both," Jim said. "And then she dropped me in the system. She knew who I was, and she didn't want me." He shrugged. "So why would I want her?"

"Jim, it's more complicated than that," Kerry said. "And I think you know that too."

"You're probably right," Jim said. "Hell, I know you're right. But it's the answer that I learned to live with, and it's the only thing that helped get me through all of the shit that happened before all of this." He shrugged. "It's how I cope."

"But you liked your foster parents?" Kerry asked. "The ones who adopted you?"

Jim smiled fondly. "Yes."

"Do you get to see them a lot?" Kerry asked. "Or did you even grow up in Seattle?"

"No, I grew up here," Jim answered. "They still foster kids, but I don't get to see them as often as I should."

"How long did you live with them?" Kerry asked.

Jim bowed his head and picked at his fingernails. "After I turned sixteen."

"And where were you before?" Kerry asked.

Jim's cheeks grew red-hot, and sweat broke out on his forehead. "I bounced around a lot. Typical foster kid story. The one no one wanted."

Kerry was quiet for a moment. "I replied to a few calls with foster kids over the years." She shook her head. "Some of those places were bad."

"Most of them are," Jim said.

Kerry glanced at Jim. "Did you ever go through anything like that?"

Jim was sweltering now, his undershirt soaked. "Yeah." His voice grew quiet, his mind drifting back to the horrors of his childhood.

"Jim?" Kerry asked. "Are you all right?"

Jim rolled down the window, the whipping wind cooling his face. He stayed that way until the sweats subsided and then leaned back into his seat and rolled up the window. "It got hot in here, didn't it?" Jim hoped she'd drop the subject. He didn't want to talk about it anymore.

"I'll turn up the A/C," Kerry said.

Jim stuck his face against the air vent. It had been a long time since he'd put himself back in the shoes of his childhood. But he knew he'd keep dwelling on it until he let it out. So he did.

"Before you asked me why I joined the force," Jim said.

"Yeah?" Kerry asked.

Jim steeled himself for the conversation he was about to have. It had been a long time since he'd spoken about it aloud.

"When I was in middle school I was with these other foster parents," Jim said. "The home was run by this alcoholic couple. Kind of like Emily's parents, but more violent. So I took off one night. I must have run away from home dozens of times. Usually, I'd get picked up by some cop, and they would run my name in the system and take me back to where I was trying to escape from. But that night, someone else picked me up. Someone even worse than my foster parents." Jim glanced out the window, making sure Kerry couldn't see his cheeks burning hot red. "I had bummed rides before, so I didn't think this one was any different. Because I grew up in the system, I had a pretty good radar detector for creeps. You just start to instinctively know who they are. Like a smell." He shifted in his seat, still keeping his eyes forward. "Anyway, I get in the car, and before I can even buckle my seat belt, he chloroforms me."

"Jesus," Kerry said.

"I don't know how long I was out, but when I woke up, I was in a cage," Jim said. "I'm pretty sure it was a dog cage. The guy even put a bowl of water inside for me. It was dark, but after my eyes adjusted, I saw there was another kid in a cage next to me. Another boy. We were in some kind of warehouse. When I woke up, I started screaming for help, but that only brought the man back."

Jim shut his eyes, and suddenly he was thrust back in time. He could still remember the smell, the cold, and the hard floor of the metal cage.

"I kept asking him what he wanted, but he just kept staring at me," Jim said. "Eventually, he opened the cage with the kid next to me and then dragged him out. The kid was so limp I thought he was dead, but then I saw his eyes open, and they looked at me. Right in my eyes." Jim turned two of his fingers and pointed them at himself. "I stared at that boy as the man pulled down his pants and then raped the boy. I don't remember how long the guy took, but the way the kid just remained motionless like a doll... I knew it wasn't the first time it had happened."

Jim lowered his gaze and opened his palms, exposing the scars along with his hands.

"After the guy finished, he dragged the boy and put him back in the cage," Jim said. "Then he walked over to me and said, 'that's what I want.' And then he walked away. Once he was gone, I pissed myself."

Kerry struggled to find the words. "Jim, I... I'm so sorry that happened to you."

Jim drew in a slow, rattling breath. "It didn't happen to me."

Kerry frowned, not following what he was saying. "What?"

"The guy who kidnapped us left, and he was gone for a long time," Jim answered. "After I saw what happened to the other boy, I told myself I wouldn't let him do that to me. So I started pressing on the cage, looking for any weak spots. The thing was old, rusted. I don't like to think about how many kids he locked inside—probably dozens. I found a few bars that were loose and started pulling. I pulled so hard that I ripped my palms to shreds." He opened and closed his hands, remembering the pain. "I was bleeding everywhere, but I told myself that if I didn't escape, then bleeding to death was better than getting raped.

"I just kept pulling and pulling and pulling," Jim

continued. "Eventually, I managed to open up the bars wide enough for me to squeeze out. I scraped up my back from the rusted edges. After I freed myself, I walked over to the kid's cage. He had fallen asleep, and I rattled it to wake him up. He finally looked at me, and when he saw me, I could tell he thought he was dreaming. He knew there was no way for me to be out of my cage, so he just went back to sleep. But I rattled it again, and he looked at me, and I saw his eye flicker and come alive with hope. He scrambled to all fours and then poked his fingers through the cage, touching my bloodied fingertips. He begged me to let him out, but his cage was locked like mine. I tried finding any weak spots, but the cage was new, the steel ridged and unforgiving.

"And then he started to cry and scream and beg for me to let him out. But I didn't know where the guy put the key, and that's when I heard someone coming." Jim swallowed and shut his eyes, his voice growing smaller as he shrank into the seat. "I knew it was the guy coming back, and I knew I wasn't strong enough to face him on my own. So I looked back at the kid in his cage, the boy who had been raped so many times he had grown numb to the action, the boy who was crying and begging me to let him out, and I left." A single tear rolled down the side of Jim's face. "I just ran as fast as I could, found a window, and jumped out. And then I just kept on running until I stumbled out onto a road, and someone finally stopped to pick me up."

Jim opened his eyes and wiped away the tear that

had fallen. He took a deep breath and then finally looked Kerry in the eyes.

"I see that little boy's face every day," Jim said. "I couldn't save him. So I saved myself. And I vowed to never do that again."

Kerry was quiet for a long time. She tried opening her mouth, but every time she attempted to speak, the words escaped her. Eventually she placed her hand on Jim's arm and squeezed tight. "I'm sorry. I'm so sorry you saw all of that. But Jim... It wasn't your fault."

Jim nodded, the motion solemn and somber. "I tell myself that. And sometimes it works. It's gotten easier as I've grown older. I mean, I was just a kid, right? Just a scared-shitless little kid who didn't want to get raped. So I ran. I ran because I wanted to stay alive." He looked at Kerry. "But I still feel the same. I still feel the pain. And I work so hard to find other kids because in my head, I think the more I save, the more I'm able to bring back, the less pain that one will cause me. The one I couldn't bring back. The one I couldn't save."

Kerry kept hold of Jim's arm, and in that brief moment, she saw what was on the other side of that brick wall, and she understood why the walls were built so high and so thick.

"They never caught the guy," Jim said. "He's still out there somewhere. And I keep looking for him too. He might be dead now. I'm not sure. They never found that little boy either. I've checked the missing-person files and looked for his picture, but I've never been able to find that either. Hell, he might have been some runaway too. Some foster kid who was in the wrong place at the wrong time."

Jim bowed his head and cried for a moment. It was over quickly, and when he finished, all that was left were the red blotches on his cheeks and the red veins in his eyes.

"So that's why I do what I do, Kerry," Jim said, regaining control of his emotions once more, rebuilding his wall. "That's why I don't quit on a case."

Kerry nodded and then released Jim's arm. "I'm sorry."

"I'm not," Jim said. "It gives me purpose. It drives me to bring kids home."

"Then that's what we'll do," Kerry said. "We'll bring these girls home."

It was quiet for a moment, and then Jim finally spoke again. "We're quite the pair, aren't we?"

Kerry laughed. "I'd heard Lieutenant Mullocks liked to rock the boat, but I'm pretty sure we might capsize it."

"Maybe we will," Jim said, but deep down he didn't think that was the case. For the first time in his career, Jim thought he might be paired with the right person. Someone who understood what it meant to be broken.

The neighborhoods they passed on the way to Mr. Wilks's house were significantly poorer neighborhoods than where the Montgomerys lived. Jim suspected that Mr. Wilks might still be paying for his past sins.

"What the hell?" Kerry asked.

Jim reached for the radio. "I need a unit over to 297

Shire Street." He clicked off and braced himself against the dashboard as Kerry floored the cruiser, flipping the lights and siren.

Two men were brawling on Wilks's front lawn, and as Kerry mounted the curb and drove onto the grass, Jim saw the men involved were Tom Johnson and Ralph Wilks.

erry was out of the car first, followed closely by Jim. Tom Johnson was on top of Ralph Wilks, punching the man repeatedly.

"You son of a bitch!" Mr. Johnson screamed, his face beet red from anger and exertion. "You goddamn bastard!"

"That's enough!" Kerry was the first one to draw her weapon. She aimed it at Johnson, but even the gun wouldn't get him to stop, and Jim tackled the man to the ground, pinned his arms behind his back, and cuffed him.

Wilks lay on his back, exhausted, and Kerry flipped him to his stomach and cuffed him. Once both men were secure, Kerry and Jim took a step back.

"You're a dead man!" Johnson screamed. "You hear me? You're a dead man!"

"Quiet!" Jim barked then glanced at the crowd of neighbors who had gathered around them and saw several different phones recording their movements. "I need everyone back! Back now!"

Kerry helped with crowd control, while Jim picked Johnson up from the lawn. He glanced over to Wilks, whose nose and lip were busted from the altercation. He still lay on the grass, unable to stand.

"Kerry," Jim said, catching her attention as she pushed the neighbors back, and gestured to Wilks. "Take him inside."

Kerry nodded and then helped Wilks up off the grass and held his arm to keep him upright, but before they made it inside, another car pulled into the driveway, and Natalie Johnson stepped out of the vehicle, making a beeline to Tom. "What did you do?"

Jim did his best to keep himself between Natalie and her soon-to-be ex-husband.

"What the hell did you do!" Natalie screamed. She swung her hand at Tom's head, missing only by an inch and nearly hitting Jim.

"Hey, that's enough!" Jim yelled and created some distance between himself and the enraged woman. "Mrs. Johnson, you need to step back, now!"

The fight ran out of Natalie Johnson very quickly, and she covered her mouth and began to cry.

Wanting to avoid another outburst, Jim quickly escorted Tom Johnson to the cruiser and shoved him in the back seat while Kerry took Wilks into the house.

"Mind telling me what you're doing here, Mr. Johnson?" Jim asked.

Johnson remained silent.

"If you talk to me now, you'll make it easier on yourself," Jim said.

"Talk to him," Johnson said, keeping his head down. "Talk to my wife."

Jim glanced at Ralph's house, remembering how cozy he had been with Natalie Johnson at the precinct. He shut the door, locking Johnson in the back of the squad car, and then reached for the radio, calling for an ambulance, and then he joined Natalie in the yard. "Mrs. Johnson, I think we need to talk."

Natalie nodded, and then Jim walked her inside the house, but made sure to keep Ralph and her separated until they sorted everything out.

Once backup arrived, Jim had the uniformed officers handle crowd control and gave strict instructions for the officers not to engage with any reporters that might show up.

When the paramedics arrived, Jim escorted them into the house, where they treated Wilks at the kitchen table, a wad of bloodied tissues crumpled on the table as he kept the pressure on his nose.

Kerry stood nearby, and Jim joined her while the paramedics worked on Wilks.

"Did he say anything?" Jim asked.

"Nope," Kerry answered.

"Where's Mrs. Johnson?"

"Bathroom." Kerry leaned closer so the pair could discuss their plan of attack. "Who do you want to work first? I vote for Mr. Wilks. He's probably still hurting from that beating he took. He'll probably be easier to crack."

"Agreed," Jim answered. "We need to figure out if they know anything about the girls, but we also need to see if they have any motivation for being involved with the girls' disappearance."

"We should press Wilks on the accusations Vanessa told us about when he slept with a high school student," Kerry said. "See how he reacts."

"Either father might have gotten involved with the other's daughter," Jim said.

Kerry grimaced. "It's hard to imagine it."

"I've seen worse," Jim said.

When the paramedics finished, they walked over to Jim and Kerry. "We need to take him to the hospital for an X-ray."

"No." Wilks lowered the tissue from his nose. It had finally stopped bleeding. "I'll go later if I need it, but I don't want to go to the hospital."

"Mr. Wilks," the paramedic said, "I highly recommend—"

"I said I'm fine!" Wilks raised his voice.

The paramedics didn't press the issue any further. They collected their gear and departed.

Wilks remained at the kitchen table, picking at the pile of bloodied tissues.

Jim walked over to the table and sat down opposite Wilks.

"What happened?" Jim asked.

"What do you think happened?" Wilks answered.

"I have a shitty imagination," Jim replied. "Tell me."

"He came over," Wilks said. "And he started saying all of this shit…" He bowed and shook his head. "I told him to leave, and the next thing I know, he started swinging at me."

"He just knocked on your door and started shouting and screaming for no reason," Kerry said, repeating Wilks's statement back to him without any sympathy.

Wilks gently touched his nose again. "Yeah."

Jim and Kerry exchanged a glance, and then Jim turned to Wilks and continued his questioning.

"Does this have anything to do with the Johnsons' divorce?" Jim let his words linger in the air, making sure Wilks understood his tone.

Wilks shook his head. "I don't know why they're getting a divorce, all right? What, you think I slept with Natalie? Is that it?"

"It crossed our minds," Kerry answered.

"No," Wilks said. "I did not have an affair with Natalie. I don't know why that lunatic decided to come after me in the middle of the day like that. We're all stressed. We want to find our daughters, so why don't you focus your investigative prowess on that instead of asking me stupid fucking questions!" Wilks slammed his fist on the table to hammer home his point, but what was meant to be his exclamation point to the end of the discussion only looked like a child who had been caught in his own lies.

The man had taken a fine beating. The welts along Wilks's face had swollen even larger than before. With one eye swollen shut and a busted lip Wilks looked like the losing boxer at a press conference.

"Mr. Wilks," Jim said. "The less time we spend talking about why Mr. Johnson beat you up, the more time we have to be out looking for your daughter. So why don't you save us both a lot of trouble and just tell me why Mr. Johnson attacked you."

Wilks was quiet for a moment and then drummed his fingers on the table. He remained sheepish, refusing to speak about the cause of the altercation. Jim needed the man to clear the air so they could move forward, but for whatever reason, Wilks was holding back.

"Do you consider yourself a ladies' man, Ralph?" Jim asked.

Wilks frowned. "What?"

"You cheated on your ex-wife a few times," Jim said.

Wilks was quiet for a moment, unsure where the conversation was going. "I don't see what that has to do with—"

"Did you ever bring any young girls home, Ralph?" Jim asked.

Wilks blinked a few times, his mouth hanging open before he found his voice. "No. No, of course not."

"How do you know?" Jim asked.

"What do you mean, how do I know?" Wilks answered. "I'm not some creep, all right? Yeah, I cheated on my wife with other women, but the key word is *women*. Not children."

"Your ex-wife had something different to say about that," Kerry said.

"She's a fucking junkie!" Wilks exploded from his chair. "You can't be fucking serious about this."

"He said–she said moments rarely go over well in court," Jim said.

Wilks was shaken, his body trembling. His cheeks turned bright red, and when he spoke, he did so slowly and softly. "The youngest girl I ever brought home was eighteen. I know that because I saw her high school ID card."

"So you had sex with a high school student?" Kerry asked, her voice disgusted. "You have a daughter, for Christ's sake."

"She had already graduated," Wilks answered. "I know that because she was the daughter of a guy I used to buy dope from. It was a one-time thing. Vanessa had come home and caught us and then freaked out when she saw how young the girl was. That's why she made up that shit about me sleeping with a minor. Okay? That's it."

Jim bided his time, letting Mr. Wilks marinate in his own fear. "That's not enough, Mr. Wilks. Because right now, we're dealing with two missing girls who have run away from their homes, which, by your own admission, have been less than accommodating for a child."

Wilks shook his head, stuttering as he struggled to comprehend what Jim was telling him. "Are you saying you think I had something to do with the girls disappearing?"

Jim never broke his collected composure, making

sure Wilks understood the gravity of the allegations. "You have a past of drug abuse, violence, and a taste for infidelity and young women. It doesn't paint a very flattering picture, especially when I have the sense that you're holding back information."

Wilks shut his eyes and clenched his fists tight. "I swear to God I didn't do anything to those girls!" He opened his eyes, his gaze pleading.

"Tell us," Jim said. "Tell us the truth about what happened between you and Mr. Johnson."

Jim waited, unsure if Wilks would break. The man's will was already paper-thin, but when people were faced with an impossible situation, they could dig deep and pull themselves out. Thankfully, Wilks didn't have that kind of gumption.

Ralph Wilks took a breath and then nodded. "Natalie and I were having an affair." He wiped his nose and then cleared his throat. "We wanted to keep it a secret because of the divorce. She didn't want Tom to have any ammunition to use against her in the custody battle, because he's seeking sole custody of Amelia."

Jim studied Wilks, and after a few moments of analyzing his body language, Jim knew the man was telling the truth.

"So, the affair is more than a fling?" Kerry asked.

"Yes," Wilks answered. "It started out just as fun, but it turned into something more. I don't know when exactly it happened, but… it happened."

"When is the exact date that you and Mrs. Johnson became sexually active?" Jim asked.

Wilks paused and gave it some thought. "I'd say about eighteen months ago if I had to guess."

Jim tilted his head to the side. "Exactly eighteen months ago?"

Mr. Wilks nodded. "Yeah. I mean, we had always flirted with one another, but we didn't start sleeping together until about eighteen months ago."

"Did the girls know?" Kerry asked.

"What? No, of course not," Mr. Wilks answered. "We were very careful. Very discreet. I don't know how the hell Tom found out. Maybe Nat told him." He slouched then gingerly touched his busted lip.

"You're sure the girls didn't know?" Jim asked. "Because if they found out their parents were sleeping together—"

"I know how it looks, all right?" Wilks said. "But the girls didn't know. That's not why they left. Christ, I felt guilty enough about it before, no sense in piling it on."

"No," Kerry said, her voice stern. "We wouldn't want to hurt your feelings."

Wilks cast his one good eye toward Kerry. "This wasn't my fault."

"Clearly," Jim said. "Obviously, all of those times you had sex with Natalie Johnson were accidents."

Wilks didn't look up anymore, his head lowered in shame. "I'm trying. I mean, I'm really trying." He sniffled. "You know what life is like for an ex-addict with a record?" He finally lifted his gaze, but he didn't look either detective in the eye. "I did a lot of shady things when I was high. I was a bad father. A bad husband. A

bad person. But I have turned it around, and I just—"
He choked up again. "I just wanted a better life for my
little girl."

Jim stood. "You should have told us about the affair,
Mr. Wilks. Because you didn't just waste our time,
you've wasted your daughter's time." He walked behind
Wilks and lifted him up and then cuffed his arms
behind his back. "We're going to take you downtown
now, Mr. Wilks."

"What? Why?" Wilks shouted.

"Because you lied to investigators," Kerry said.

"I didn't lie—I was just trying to protect Natalie!"

"Yeah, well, you should have been protecting your
daughter," Jim said. "C'mon, let's go."

Jim walked Wilks out to another squad car, which
took Ralph downtown. Once Ralph was gone, Jim
turned his attention to Tom Johnson, who had kept his
head bowed in the backseat of the cruiser.

Kerry joined him outside. "Natalie won't come out
of the bathroom. I could hear her crying inside." Her
cheeks were flushed. "I can't believe that guy."

"Unfortunately, I can," Jim answered. "I saw guys
like that all the time when I was in the system. You'd be
amazed at how many people pretended to have their
shit together just so they could collect a check from the
government. I have zero sympathies for anyone who
puts themselves above their child." Jim clenched his jaw
and scuffed his right heel against the carpet as he
bowed his head. "Listen, why don't you take the lead

with Mr. Johnson. It'd be good for you to get some reps in leading an interrogation like this."

Kerry nodded. "Okay, yeah. I can do that."

The pair started toward the car, but a voice caused them to stop.

"Detectives?"

Jim and Kerry turned around and saw Natalie Johnson standing in the yard. Her eyes were red and puffy from crying, and she clutched a bunch of tissues in her hand.

"I need to speak with you," Natalie said.

Jim and Kerry exchanged a glance and then walked over toward Mrs. Johnson.

Natalie looked past the detectives to Tom in the car and then quickly lowered her eyes. "Do you mind if we speak inside?"

"No," Jim answered.

The trio returned inside the Wilks residence, and Natalie Johnson sat in the same chair Ralph had when he'd given his confession of infidelity.

Jim wasn't sure what more could be said about the matter but thought it best to listen to what the woman had to say. Both Jim and Kerry joined Natalie at the table and waited as the woman collected her thoughts.

"What do you need to talk to us about, Mrs. Johnson?" Kerry asked.

"I need to tell you something," Mrs. Johnson said. "Something I should have told you from the beginning."

JAMES HUNT

Jim had an idea of what she might confess to, but he remained quiet.

"You both know Tom and I are divorcing, but we didn't explain why." Natalie kept her head bowed, afraid or ashamed to look the detectives in the eyes. "I had an affair with Ralph."

The moment the confession came, Mrs. Johnson broke down into a stream of tears. Kerry handed her some tissues, and the woman dabbed at her face until she stopped crying.

"Mrs. Johnson, when did your husband find out about the affair?" Kerry asked.

Natalie blubbered something neither Jim or Kerry could understand, and when Jim asked her to repeat her answer, she said, "A few hours ago. It was why he rushed over here and started to beat up Ralph. I tried to stop him, but he was too strong."

"Why did you tell your husband now?" Kerry asked.

Natalie took a breath. "Because there's something that I only know about. Something I know about Amelia." She bowed her head. "Amelia isn't Tom's daughter."

Jim leaned forward. "What?"

"Who is her father?" Kerry asked.

"It's Ralph," Natalie answered. "Ralph is Amelia's biological father."

"Does he know?" Jim asked. "That Amelia is his daughter?"

Natalie shook her head. "It happened a long time ago. Back when he was still doing drugs. I got drunk

108

when he was high and…" She bowed her head. "Tom and I were engaged at the time, and the wedding was in a few months. I didn't want to ruin a good thing over one bad mistake, so I just kept it to myself."

"Did you ever have a DNA test done?" Kerry asked. "To confirm?"

Natalie nodded. "Yeah. I did it a few years ago, because I just couldn't take it anymore. I had to know the truth."

"Did Amelia know?" Kerry asked.

Natalie shook her head. "I made sure she didn't know." She scrunched up her face again as if she was going to cry and then looked away and managed to compose herself. "I know I should have said something sooner, but I was scared. There was just so much going on, and—"

Kerry reached for Natalie's hand, her emotions mixed. Knowing the parentage in a missing-person case involving children is pivotal information. "You kept quiet because of the custody battle for Amelia."

Natalie squeezed Kerry's hand. "I didn't want to give Tom's lawyers any ammunition to use against me. And Tom's been a good father to Amelia…" She broke down crying again, and this time Jim offered her the tissues.

"You should have told us," Kerry said, her voice stern as though she were speaking to one of her children. "And you're sure that the girls don't know?"

Natalie nodded. "I'm sure. I'm the only one who does."

But based on the note they'd found in Emily's sleeping bag, Kerry wasn't convinced. Kids were smarter than adults gave them credit for. "We're going to have an officer come in and take down your statement."

Natalie looked up from her tissue. "This is going on record?"

"It has to," Kerry answered.

Natalie groped at the air around the table for a moment, struggling to find anything to keep her afloat. She was a woman drowning in her own mistakes. Finally, she agreed, and Jim and Kerry stepped outside to process what they had just learned.

"The note Emily left must have been about the girls learning they were half sisters," Jim said.

Kerry nodded. "The only question is how? If Natalie is telling the truth, then there wasn't any way for the girls to know."

"We'll ask them when we find them," Jim said.

Kerry turned her attention to Tom Johnson in the back of the car. "We should talk to him. See if he has any revelations he'd like to share with us. He might even have something to do with the girls' disappearance."

"I don't think he had anything to do with this," Jim said. "If he just found out about the affair, he wouldn't have known Amelia wasn't his daughter."

"Unless he was lying too," Kerry said.

"It's possible," Jim said.

Kerry shut her eyes. "Christ, this is a mess."

Jim glanced behind him to Ralph's house. "We should take a look at Emily's room and see if we can't find anything." His phone buzzed in his pocket. It was the precinct. "This is Jim."

"Detective, it's Gary from IT," he said.

Jim perked up, hoping for some good news. "Did you get a location on Emily's phone?"

"Yes," Gary answered. "But before you get too excited, it's only the last known location before the phone was turned off. It's just off of Highway 137. I'll email you the exact grid."

"How big is the search field?" Jim asked.

"One square mile," Gary answered.

Unable to hear the other side of the conversation, Kerry raised her eyebrows, waiting for clarification.

"All right, thanks, Gary," Jim said and then hung up the call. "They traced the last known location on Emily's phone before it was shut off. We have a search grid of one square mile."

"That's good right?" Kerry asked, the pair moving quickly toward their cruiser.

"We'll know soon enough."

Jim handed Tom Johnson over to one of the uniforms, and instructed him to take him downtown to be detained for assault. They would talk to him again after they searched for Emily's phone.

Once Jim entered the coordinates into the GPS, Kerry activated the lights and siren and then floored the accelerator. Their path took them north of the city, up into the winding mountain roads of inner Washington State.

On the drive, Jim called the lieutenant, requesting a search team. "How soon until ETA?"

"I'll put any local resources there first to secure the area," Mullocks said. "K-9 units are already in route. Chopper takes off in fifteen."

"Copy that," Jim said. "I'll keep you updated on our progress."

Traffic subsided the further north they drove, and Jim noted the wilderness that surrounded them. "Plenty of places to hide out here."

"You think they camped?" Kerry asked.

Jim shook his head. "I don't know."

Local units were already on scene when they arrived just as the lieutenant promised, and Jim was impressed at how quickly their commander managed to move resources.

"I'll say this about the LT, she's efficient," Jim said.

Kerry flashed her badge when the patrolman handling traffic stopped her and then allowed her to pass through. She parked on the side of the road and unbuckled her seat belt.

Jim stared out the window, lost in a trance. He had been in woods like this before when he was a boy. And just as he had then, he now felt the same impending level of doom crawl over him.

Kerry examined the scene. "Secluded. Remote. What do you think?"

Jim unbuckled his seat belt. "If we find the girls out here, I don't think we'll find them alive."

Jim opened the door and got out of the vehicle, and Kerry followed suit. They found the officer in charge on the scene, a deputy from the King County Sheriff's Department.

"I'm Detective North," Jim said, quickly flashing his badge. "This is Detective Martin. Have you found anything?"

"Not yet." The deputy was tall, and his head was shaved bald. He pointed up the road a little way. "We've diverted traffic at a crossroads up ahead, which we're using as a border line for our search efforts."

The area was hilly, rocky terrain. It would be a long walk for them to come from the Montgomery's house. But Jim was beginning to think they might have hitched a ride.

"Jim," Kerry said.

"Huh?" Jim snapped out of his daydream.

"I asked if you're ready to take a look," Kerry said.

"Yes." Jim cleared his throat, hoping his partner didn't notice his hesitation. "Let's go." He walked forward first, climbing the short hill, praying they found something helpful.

The K-9 units arrived shortly after the search began, and everyone moved through the woods with hesitation. Never did hope and fear clash together than in a search party. Because while people hoped they found something, they feared their discovery wouldn't be alive.

Thirty minutes passed, and while they covered a lot of ground, no one found anything. Kerry walked next to Jim and glanced around to make sure they were alone. "What happens if this turns up empty?"

"Then the next time we get a lead, we'll get more pushback from the captain about the approval of the resources we need," Jim said.

Kerry crunched a twig and kicked a rock.

Jim glanced over. "Something wrong?"

"I just don't like wasting time," Kerry answered.

Jim stopped, and Kerry walked three paces ahead before she finally stopped too. "I didn't realize you had anywhere else better to be."

"C'mon, Jim," Kerry said. "Look around. I counted at least three dozen officers coming to these woods, and we have aerial surveillance, and nothing has been found. We need to explore other options. We could be looking at the girls' rooms, or talking to Tom Johnson back at the station."

Jim knew Kerry had a point. Cases like this were all about the allocation of resources. If they dried up too much too quickly, then they wouldn't have what they needed down the road. But the fact that the phone had been tracked to this location somehow felt significant. "We'll stay another ten minutes."

Jim traversed the rocky terrain, continuing his search when he heard the barks of the K-9 units. The animals were trained to search for bodies both alive and deceased, but Jim prayed they weren't too late in recovering Emily and Amelia.

The animals followed a scent deeper into the woods outside of the original search grid. Jim and Kerry followed the dogs until they stopped at a patch of dirt and dead leaves. They pawed at the ground, whining and whimpering, and the sight of the ground made Jim's blood turn cold.

"No," Kerry whispered.

Jim turned to the nearest officer. "We need shovels, and this area needs to be cordoned off. Now." He turned back to the ground, where the dogs continued to scratch and claw until their handlers pulled them back.

Officers returned with shovels and picks and carefully dug around the area. Jim and Kerry stood off to the side, and Jim's pulse started to race. He was suddenly a boy again, sprinting through the woods in the darkness, dirty and frightened out of his mind.

One of the shovels hit something, and the officer dropped to a knee, moving the rest of the dirt by hand until a small shoe emerged from the earth. "I've got remains!"

Jim turned away, shutting his eyes as he broke out in a cold sweat. He couldn't shake the memory from his past. Another child he couldn't save.

Somewhere in the distance, there was more barking, and Jim heard another voice, but it wasn't until a strong hand clamped around his arm that he was pulled from the past and thrust back into the present. He opened his eyes and saw the sorrow and pain on Kerry's face.

"What?" Jim asked.

But he knew the answer before Kerry spoke, because Jim heard the other K-9 unit barking wildly, pulling officers over to another area of the woods.

Another body had been found.

And then another.

10

*W*hen all was said and done, the K-9 units discovered three bodies, all of them within fifty yards of each other. Jim had taken a step back to allow the forensic team and medical examiners to work, but the exhuming was a painstakingly slow process.

Jim had feared they would find remains out here. The location was too perfect. It provided access to the main road but was still remote. There were plenty of trees to provide cover. It was a forgotten stretch of land in the middle of nowhere, the final resting place of lives taken far too soon.

The only saving grace Jim held onto was the fact that it was still too early to determine if any of the bodies they'd found were Emily or Amelia. But if it wasn't their missing girls, then that meant something even more sinister: a serial kidnapper.

"Hey," Kerry said, huffing on her climb back up the

hill. She took a moment to catch her breath when she finally reached Jim's side. "Lieutenant says the captain approved whatever resources we need. And the FBI is going to lend us additional help."

Jim nodded. "Nothing consolidates resources quicker than pulling dead kids out of the woods."

"Have they found anything yet?" Kerry asked, gazing out onto the three separate excavation sites.

"They're still working," Jim answered. "But we can check their progress."

A large white tent had been constructed in a clearing between trees. It was where the medical examiner and the forensic unit worked, sorting through the dirt to examine whatever remains had been found.

Jim stepped beneath the covered area and saw the three small bodies laid out on tables covered with tarps.

The ME on the scene was Jennifer Capone—no relation to the infamous gangster, as she was always quick to point out. Capone was hunched over one of the bodies, carefully examining the remains.

"Jennifer," Jim said.

Jennifer glanced up and flashed a friendly smile. She had thick red hair, which was pulled back in a ponytail, the curls bunched up together like a basket of springs, and a pair of glasses framed a pretty face. She wore a light green jacket, jeans, and work boots. "James. I wasn't aware you were the lead on this. I heard something about you being involved in IA?"

Jim cleared his throat. "I'm still on active duty for the time being. This is my partner, Kerry Martin."

Jennifer smiled and waved another friendly hello. She was oddly chipper considering the circumstances, but it was a trait that Jim had never noticed.

"Happy to be at work?" Kerry asked.

"Just trying to do my part," Jennifer answered.

Jim gestured to the bodies on the table. "What can you tell us?"

"Quite a bit," Jennifer said and then took a breath. "All three victims were between the ages of ten and twelve. Two females, one male." She pointed to each of the sexes respectively.

Each victim had been badly burned, the remains horribly disfigured, making the body unrecognizable. And the white tarp backdrop where the body lay contrasted against the blackened and charred flesh.

"The females," Kerry said. "Are they our missing girls?"

"No," Jennifer answered. "Theses remains have been out here for too long to be the girls who went missing last night."

"Well, that's some good news," Kerry said, sighing relief.

But judging off of the mangled bodies of the deceased, Jim wasn't sure he agreed. "What happened to them?"

Jennifer rubbed her gloved hands together, and paced around the tables, staring at the bodies. "Because of the burn marks, it'll be hard to give accurate and detailed information until we're able to bring the remains back to the lab, but from what I can tell so far, all three victims were killed the same way." She pointed to the necks. "Strangulation by affixation."

"They weren't burned alive?" Kerry asked.

"No, the victims were already deceased when the bodies were burned," Jennifer said but then picked up one of the hands of the victims. "And in all three victims, we see hole marks in both hands, and the ankles."

"Hole marks?" Jim asked.

"Yes, most likely by a nail," Jennifer answered.

Jim slowly connected the dots. "They were crucified?"

"Crucifixion is a means of death," Jennifer said. "But the injuries to the bodies were made post mortem."

"Are you telling me that our killer nailed their dead bodies to crosses and then set them on fire?" Kerry asked.

"It appears that way, yes," Jennifer answered. "I'll be able to analyze the accelerants that were used to burn the bodies, and perhaps even the wood the killer used to make the crosses."

"Sexual trauma?" Jim asked.

"From what I can tell, no," Jennifer replied. "But again, I'll be able to examine the remains more thoroughly when I return to the lab."

"How long have they been out here?" Kerry asked.

Jen walked to the table near the front of the tent. "This is our most recent victim. Male, between the ages of ten and twelve, I can approximate his death between six and seven months." She moved to the next table. "Female, same age range, time of death between twelve and thirteen months." She moved onto the last table. "This female, time of death around eighteen months ago."

"Every six months," Jim said. "Like clockwork."

"So if these kids aren't our victims, then who are they?" Kerry asked.

Jennifer led the detectives over to a separate table. "This is where we've started cataloging everything we found buried alongside the bodies."

Jim examined the contents of the table. There were three piles of clothes, each of them folded neatly on the table. "Did the forensic team put the clothes together like that?"

"No," Jennifer answered. "The clothes were already like that, and preserved in these plastic bags." She pointed to the bags marked as evidence.

Jim looked at the clothes, noting the care that had been used to bury the items. "Our killer took the time to bury the bodies, and then put together the clothes like that?"

"Yes," Jennifer answered. "It's very ritualistic."

"It's sick," Kerry said.

"Yes," Jennifer replied. "That too."

Jim walked the length of the table, studying the clothing carefully. "Any chance we'll be able to pull fibers or DNA off of these?"

"We'll test them at the lab," Jen said.

"Good." Jim paused when he reached the end of the table, and saw three pieces of paper that had been placed in evidence bags. "What's this?"

Jen joined Jim at the table. "I'm not quite sure yet. My initial thoughts were it was something that belonged to the children, but the paper was hard to read." She picked up the last one. "This is the paper that was buried with the boy, and you can see it's a letter."

Kerry walked over and joined Jim and Jennifer. "From the killer?"

"I think so," Jen answered.

Unlike the clothes, the letters had not been sealed in a bag, and their deteriorated condition made it difficult to read.

"I can't understand anything with it like this," Jim said.

"Well," Jen said, picking up another letter, and placing it side by side. "I did notice a pattern. I think the killer might have written the same letter for each child that was killed. I might be able to pull enough words, letters, and phrases from each of them and see what the killer might be trying to say."

"Any chance he signed his name?" Kerry asked.

Jim set the letter down on the table. "That would be too easy." He turned to Jen. "We appreciate the help."

"Of course," Jen said. "The moment I have the report finished, I'll contact you immediately. These cases are at the front of my queue."

Kerry cleared her throat. "Thank you, Doctor." She

spun around and then quickly walked past Jim and out of the tent.

Jim followed her, but Kerry was moving quickly. "Kerry. Kerry, wait." She wouldn't slow, so Jim jogged to catch up to her, but when he placed his hand on her arm to pull her back, she quickly jerked her arm free.

"Back off!" Kerry barked the words loudly enough for them to echo through the trees, turning a few heads in the process.

Jim held up his hands and stepped backward. "Okay. I'm back."

Kerry was breathing heavily, and Jim recognized the symptoms. Flushed. Sweating. Hyperventilating. Dilated pupils. She was having a panic attack.

"Sit down," Jim said.

"I'm fine," Kerry replied.

"No, you're not." Jim took one hesitant step toward her. "You need to sit down before you fall down."

Kerry staggered a step, and Jim lunged forward and caught her. He waited for her to jerk away like before, but she relaxed and slowly lowered herself to the ground.

Jim squatted in front of her. "Slow breaths. In through your nose and out through your mouth. Just take it easy. Slowly, there you go." Jim mirrored Kerry's breaths and waited for her to calm down. "How are you feeling now?"

Kerry cradled her head in her hands. "Like an idiot."

"Seeing something like that for the first time is overwhelming." Jim took a seat next to Kerry. The ground was cold against his bottom. "The first time I walked into a crime scene with a body, I immediately turned around and threw up outside."

Kerry glanced back to the tent with the children and then faced forward again, somber. "I can't believe we dug up three kids."

"As grim as it sounds and as horrible as it feels, this could help us," Jim said. "The information we gather from these victims could help us catch the perp before he does the same to Emily and Amelia."

"So you think they're connected," Kerry said.

"I don't see how they can't be," Jim replied. "We dig up three bodies the same age as our two missing girls in the same area where we traced the last coordinates for their phone? That's too much of a coincidence for it not to be connected."

Jim extended his hand to Kerry and then helped lift her off the ground.

"I think now is a good time to head back to the Wilks house, take a look in Emily's room," Jim said. "Then we can head over to the Johnsons' and look at Amelia's room."

Kerry dusted the dirt off of her backside. "Right. And we still need to talk to Tom Johnson back at the station." She looked to the tent still visible between the trees. "Hard to imagine he might do something like that though."

"You'd be surprised what people are capable of," Jim said.

The pair walked down the hill and back to the road

together. The media had already made camp just outside the police blockade that had been set up. There were at least a dozen news vans.

"Word spreads quickly," Kerry said as they approached the squad car.

"Yeah." Jim nodded as he opened the passenger-side door. He was glad Kerry sounded normal.

As they left the scene, Jim noticed the reporters risking life and limb to try and get Kerry to slow down and roll down her window to answer their questions, but she blew right on past.

11

*T*he inside of Ralph Wilks's house told the story of a bachelor pad. It was a small place with two bedrooms and only one bath. The kitchen and the living room were connected, and the décor was old. It was the house of a family that had just enough to survive.

"Her room is in the back," Jim said.

Kerry nodded and followed Jim into the second bedroom. Emily's room was easily identifiable by the posters of boy bands on the walls and the stuffed animals on the bed.

Emily was a girl caught between the two worlds of teenager and child. It was a phase all children experienced, but some were more willing to let go of their childhood than others.

Kerry thought of her own children and how her oldest would cross over into her teenage years sooner than Kerry would have liked. But Kerry couldn't stop them from growing up no matter how hard she tried.

The room was neat, tidy, which surprised Kerry. Her own daughter's room was a mess. But perhaps it only looked organized because Emily didn't have many things.

Kerry donned a pair of gloves as she walked to the bookshelf on the wall to the left of the door. Like the stuffed animals and boy-band posters, the literature was mixed with old picture books and Judy Blume.

Kerry removed a few of the books from the shelf, leafing through the pages, looking for any doodles, notes, or secret letters that might have been hidden between the pages, but she found nothing but a few earmarked pages from where Emily had left off.

"We need to see if we can find the journal Dr. Weathers was talking about," Jim said. "So long as she didn't take it with her."

Kerry then moved over to the small dresser in the corner. She opened the top drawer and saw that it was empty. She moved to the next drawer and the next, all of them empty. She walked to the closet and opened the doors. Only a few old coats hung inside. From the looks of things, Emily had taken nearly everything with her.

"She wasn't planning on coming back," Kerry said.

"What was that?" Jim asked.

Kerry pointed at the dresser. "She took all of her clothes with her to the slumber party. More than she needed just for one night."

Jim walked over and opened a few of the drawers. "So she had planned for the slumber party night to be the one where she ran." He spun around and looked at the rest of the room. "Amelia probably did the same."

"Probably, but we won't know for sure until we check." Kerry closed the closet doors.

She walked to the bed, placed her hand on the pink comforter, and ran her fingers from the foot of the bed to the headboard. Like everything else in the house, it was small, only a twin. Kerry flipped the covers off, finding nothing in the sheets. She checked beneath the small bedframe, finding nothing but dust bunnies.

"What are you looking for?" Jim asked.

"Every kid has secrets," Kerry answered, working her way up to the pillows. "And in a place this small, there aren't many spots to hide them. The dresser is empty, and so is the closet. The only thing left to put something anywhere would be—"

Kerry stopped when she heard the crinkle of paper inside one of the pillows. She carefully removed the pillowcase then opened the zipper on the pillow's side. She reached her hand inside and removed several sheets of folded papers, including a few envelopes.

"Jackpot," Jim said.

Kerry turned the envelopes over in her hands. "No address on it." She set the envelopes down and opened one of the letters. It was folded half a dozen times, and the lines that crinkled the pages made the words difficult to read.

Jim donned his own pair of gloves and picked up

one of the pieces of paper. "They're letters. Written to Emily. From Amelia."

Kerry frowned. "If Emily had her own secret phone, then why wouldn't the girls text one another?"

"Because Amelia's parents keep a close eye on her phone," Jim answered, quickly sifting through the letters. "If she were caught, Emily's phone would have been compromised, and she wouldn't have been able to call her mom."

Kerry glanced back at the letters. "There are dozens of these."

Jim rifled through them, trying to find anything useful, and then stopped. "Look at this." He pointed toward the paragraph for Kerry to read.

"My dad won't stop being angry," Kerry said, squinting as she struggled to read the handwriting. "He doesn't spend the night at home anymore. It's almost like I don't have a dad anymore." She looked to Jim, skeptical. "Angry enough to kill?"

"I don't know." Jim folded them back up. "We need to head over to Amelia's house, check to see if Emily wrote Amelia letters too."

Kerry nodded. "And we should have forensics take a look at these, see if we can pull anything useful off of the letters or envelopes."

"It's a stretch, but it might be worth it," Jim said.

Jim and Kerry walked out of the house and saw the reporters still waiting for them in the streets. Jim had discovered that when it came to missing children, two elements were inevitable. The longer it took him to find the kids, the less chance they would be returned. And the press would keep hounding them until another big story came along.

"Detectives! Detectives!" The reporter was a woman Jim recognized from Channel 6. Samantha something. "What can you tell us about the missing girls? Are any of the parents suspects?"

"We cannot comment on an ongoing investigation at this time," Kerry said as she opened the car door. "Now, please step back. For your own safety."

The reporter didn't step back, but she didn't press forward anymore.

Once both of them were in the car, Jim looked to Kerry. "You don't much like the press, do you?"

"Do you?" Kerry asked, her tone incredulous. "Those people don't care about anything other than making a splash in the ratings."

Jim shrugged. "Not all of them are bad. And they're just trying to do their jobs. Freedom of the press, remember?"

Kerry said nothing else as she started the car and then drove to the Johnsons' house in search of letters like those Amelia had written to Emily.

When they arrived at the house, they saw the squad car that had brought Mrs. Johnson back home from the Wilks residence.

More reporters tried to intercept them as Kerry parked in the driveway, but the uniform watching the house had set up a physical barrier, and the media didn't try to breach it.

Kerry and Jim got out of the car, and Natalie Johnson greeted them at the door.

Once everyone was inside, Natalie sheepishly approached Kerry. "I'm sorry I didn't tell you about the girls earlier. I was afraid."

Kerry knew berating the mother now was only going to make things worse. "Just remember to tell us anything else that might be useful, all right? No matter how the optics might look."

"Yes," Natalie said. "Can I get either of you something to drink?"

"Water will be fine for me," Jim answered.

"Same," Kerry replied.

"Okay," Natalie said and then smiled. "Amelia's room is down the hall on the left. I'll bring the water to you."

"Thank you," Kerry said.

The Johnson house was decidedly different than the Wilks home. It was larger, homier, but the outward appearance of a happy home was only a cover for the troubles inside.

"Never judge a book by its cover," Kerry said, leaning against Amelia's doorframe.

"What was that?" Jim asked, searching the girl's room.

"Nothing," Kerry answered. "Did you check the pillows?"

"I doubt both girls would hide the letters in the same place," Jim answered, walking around to the dresser, the desk, the closet, and the small vanity

Amelia had in her room. "There are more places for Amelia to hide her letters—if she even had any—in here than Emily had."

Kerry rolled her eyes and then crossed the room to the bed. She picked up one of the pillows and stuck her hands into the case.

Jim stopped searching through the middle dresser when he saw what she was doing. "Kerry, I really don't think that—"

"Found them." Kerry pulled out a stack of letters. "The girls are best friends and half sisters. It's not that far-fetched to think they would hide things in the same spot."

Jim and Kerry started to go through the letters. Jim read quickly, scanning the letters in hopes of finding anything that could lead them to where the girls might have gone.

"Jim, look," Kerry said, pointing to one of the letters. "In this one Emily talks about a man they met."

Jim took the letter from Kerry. Emily described an individual that both of them had met before, someone they both trusted. But it was one line that Jim latched onto more than the others. "He says we'll be free." Jim looked up to Kerry. "They mentioned that in their note."

Kerry nodded.

"What are those?"

Both Kerry and Jim snapped their heads up and found Natalie standing in the doorway with a glass of water in each hand.

Natalie stared down at the letters in Kerry's hands, and she began to tremble. "Where did you find those?"

Jim walked to Natalie before she could come any farther into the room. "Mrs. Johnson, why don't we go into the living room and sit down—"

"No!" Natalie shouldered past Jim, spilling water from both glasses as she set them on the dresser, and marched toward Kerry. "I want to know what those are! I want to know who they're from!"

"Mrs. Johnson," Jim said, intercepting the grief-stricken mother. "You need to let us do our job."

Natalie collapsed to the floor, sobbing quietly, her grip on reality slipping away. "I just want my little girl back. I just want her home."

Eventually, Jim and Kerry picked the mother up off the floor and helped her into the living room. They gave her some water, and after fifteen minutes, she finally stopped crying.

"The letters," Natalie said, her voice still shaky. "You think they were written by whoever took the girls?"

Kerry hesitated, unsure how much they should reveal, but Jim jumped right into it.

"We think the girls knew about being sisters," Jim said.

Mrs. Johnson was thrown off guard, shaking her head and stuttering to find the right words. "No. No, that's not…. That can't be right."

"Amelia and Emily wrote letters to one another," Kerry said. "And Emily left a note behind in her sleeping bag that said, 'We know.' Unless there is something else you haven't told us, I don't know what else it could be."

Natalie, still dumbstruck, sipped her water.

"What about her therapist?" Jim asked. "Has he ever been inappropriate with your daughter?"

Natalie looked up at them. "Gary? No. He is a good man. He's never had a record or—or—or had any hints at misconduct with children. And I would have known if he was inappropriate with Amelia."

"Thank you, Mrs. Johnson," Jim said.

"Did you find anything else?" Natalie asked.

Jim hesitated. He knew if he told the mother about the bodies they found it would only cause her more stress, more fear. He thought to spare her from that. "We'll be in touch if we find anything else."

Natalie nodded and then bowed her head as Jim and Kerry left the house. It wasn't until they were inside the car that Kerry spoke.

"You didn't want to tell her about the kids in the woods?" Kerry asked.

"None of them were her daughter," Jim answered, and then he clicked on his seat belt as he changed subjects. "We'll head back to the precinct, talk to Mr. Johnson one last time, see what he might know anything about the girls. And it'll give us more time to comb through these letters."

*J*im and Kerry immediately went to work at their desks when they returned to the precinct. They placed the pile of Emily and Amelia's letters between their desks, and went through each of them one at a time.

Kerry jotted any notes down she thought were pertinent about the case, including the continued mention of a mutual friend whom both girls admired.

But so far, the person wasn't named, though both girls described the individual as male, and someone they trusted, and the more Kerry read, the more she was convinced it was an adult.

Kerry set the letter down, adding it to the pile of ones that had been read, and then rubbed her eyes. "Have you found a name yet?"

"No," Jim answered, tossing one of his letters into the read pile. "But whoever it is, is someone who both girls are very familiar."

"Could be a parent, teacher—"

"Therapist," Jim said.

Kerry tilted her head to the side. "We don't have any evidence against the doctor. You said it yourself. His record his clean, except for that blackmail scandal, which he was proven innocent."

Jim grimaced. Kerry knew he didn't like Dr. Weathers, but they had no evidence to suggest the therapist was involved.

"I did find more instances of Amelia talking about her dad," Kerry said, returning to her notes. "Twice she says that she's afraid of him. That note coupled with Tom's outburst against Ralph, and I think we can confirm we're dealing with someone who is unstable."

Jim wrinkled his nose. "It's a stretch."

"It's not impossible that Tom uncovered the truth that Amelia wasn't his daughter," Kerry said. "The girls figured it out. And who's to say that a man with a temper like Tom Johnson couldn't go to extremes?"

Jim leaned forward. "The other figure in the letters describe someone who both of the girls seem infatuated with. That conflicts with Amelia's fear of her father."

"Maybe," Kerry said. "But until we hear back from the ME about the autopsy reports, these letters and Tom Johnson are our strongest leads. If he was angry about the fact that Amelia wasn't his daughter, then it gives him motive to do something about it."

Jim was quiet for a moment and then stood. "All right. You take lead."

Kerry smiled, glad Jim was taking her advice. They put in a request for Johnson to be brought from the holding cells and into the interrogation room. Once Tom was in the room, Kerry and Jim joined him.

Compared to Wilks, Johnson was primarily unharmed. He had some scrapes on his arm and a bruise on the left side of his neck, but that was the extent of his damages. The man was bigger than Wilks and not just by weight, but height too, all of it wrapped up in a trim and muscular physique.

Kerry sat where Jim usually sat during the interview, and for a moment, she blanked. Blood rushed to her cheeks, and she grew hot. All of her worst fears were coming to fruition, and she was going to choke on the first lead she was given. But she took a breath and forced the fog to clear.

"Mr. Johnson," Kerry said, "walk us through what happened today."

Johnson buttoned his lips and turned away. He flared his nostrils with every breath and bounced his right leg with nervous energy. "My wife—my ex-wife told me that she'd been sleeping with Ralph. She said that it had been happening for a long time and that she was sorry, but I didn't care about any of that shit."

"Why didn't you care?" Kerry asked.

Johnson shrugged. "We were already unhappy. Already getting divorced. Now I finally knew why."

"So you went over to Mr. Wilks's house and beat him up because you didn't care that he was sleeping with your wife?" Kerry asked.

Johnson sent a dagger-like stare at Kerry, but she didn't flinch at his response. "Far as I can tell, he was sleeping with her when we were still married. And I wanted to make sure he knew that I knew." He crossed his arms again over his chest and smirked. "I think he got the message."

"Did your wife—"

"Ex-wife."

"Right," Kerry said. "Did your ex-wife tell you anything else about the affair?"

Johnson chuckled. "What the hell else could she tell me? That she was sleeping with more than one person?"

"I just want to get all of the details I can from you," Kerry said.

"Details?" Johnson leaned forward. "You have me in here talking about nonsense when you should be out there looking for my daughter!"

"And how is your relationship with Amelia?" Kerry asked. "I understand that you're not living in the house anymore with her."

Tom frowned, thrown off guard by the question. "My relationship with my daughter is fine, and the only reason we don't live together anymore is because I can't stand to be in the same house with her mother."

Kerry studied Tom carefully, noting the reddening of his cheeks and his increase in volume as he spoke. He was agitated.

"Was your daughter afraid of you?" Kerry asked.

Tom laughed. "This is fucking ridiculous."

"It seems that you've had some anger issues recently," Kerry said.

"Yeah, because my wife is a slut!" Tom shouted. "God knows how many other people she's slept with during the course of our marriage!"

"Did your daughter know about your wife's affair?" Kerry asked.

"What? Of course not." Johnson huffed. "She couldn't have known."

Kerry tilted her head to the side. "I think there is a lot of things she knew. And I think there's a lot of things you know that you're not telling us."

Tom leaned forward. "The only thing I'd tell you is to find my daughter."

Kerry waited, unsure how far she should push the subject, but decided to place all of her chips on the table. "Did you know Amelia wasn't your biological daughter?"

Genuine shock spread over Tom Johnson's face. "What?"

With the trump card played, Kerry saw Tom had no idea about the news. And if he didn't know Amelia wasn't his daughter, then he wouldn't have motivation to hurt her.

Johnson shot up out of his chair, his cheeks burning bright red. "What the hell are you getting at? You think my girl ran away with that bastard's daughter because she found out that her mom was cheating on her dad? You think that this is our fault?"

The situation was escalating, and with Johnson's

temper rising, Kerry knew they were in a tinderbox that was ready to explode. "Mr. Johnson, I need you to sit down—"

"No!" Johnson kicked the table, and it slid forward a few inches. "Not until you tell me what the hell is going on! Where is my daughter?"

Jim went to the door and opened it. "I need officers down here to assist!"

"Fuck you!" Johnson screamed and then flipped the table over and charged at Kerry with full speed.

It all happened quickly, and Kerry knew the officers wouldn't arrive in time to help her, but she had worked the streets of the city for the past fourteen years. She had been forced to deal with individuals bigger, stronger, and faster than her, so when Johnson came barreling at her, she was ready.

Kerry pivoted left, evading the tackle, and then let his momentum do the rest of the work as she shoved his back hard and slammed him against the wall. She then reached for his arms and kicked the backs of his legs, forcing his knees to buckle.

Once Johnson was falling, Kerry had all the leverage she needed to keep him pinned until reinforcements arrived.

Johnson was swarmed by cops, and Kerry stepped back, catching her breath as her heart hammered in her chest. She stepped back and nearly tripped, but she felt a hand catch her before she went all the way down.

"Hey, let's get you in a chair," Jim said.

Kerry shook her head and took a few deep breaths.

"I'm fine. It's just the adrenaline." She raised her hand, which was trembling slightly. "It'll wear off in a minute."

Once Johnson was whisked away, Kerry and Jim returned to their desks. Kerry couldn't stop trembling, but her heart rate finally came down, and her breathing returned to normal.

"Here," Jim said, handing her a Coke. "It'll help take the edge off."

Kerry took the can, nodding her thanks, and sipped the soda. It was sharp and cold, but it did help. She forced herself to drink half of it and then set it down.

"You sure you're all right?" Jim asked.

"I'm fine," Kerry answered. "I used to deal with drunk guys like that all the time when I was a rookie on the night shift." She took another breath and then refocused on the case. "You think he's acting out because of something he did or because of grief?"

"He's hurting," Jim said. "And he's angry. I don't think the man is highly evolved enough to be capable of trying to fool us into thinking that was just a cover-up for something more sinister. It was worth the shot though."

Kerry nodded, and despite Jim's kind words, she still felt foolish. "Thanks."

Jim's desk phone rang, and he picked it up. "Yeah. Okay. Great, we'll be down." He hung up. "Jen's done with the reports at the morgue. Let's go."

13

At the morgue, Jim and Kerry found Jen, who still wore her scrubs, her face brightening into a smile when the detectives joined her.

"So, which one do you want to start with?" Jennifer asked, blinking with that bright-eyed look she always had whenever she got excited to share her results. Jim liked that she enjoyed her work.

"Does it really matter?" Kerry asked.

Jen paused to give Kerry's sarcastic comment some thought. "Well, it depends on the order you'd like to receive your information. If you'd like, I can—"

"Most recent to oldest is fine, Jennifer," Jim said. "Thanks."

Jen nodded, and the trio walked over to the first body.

"If you remember, the latest victim was male, aged between ten and twelve years, and I was able to determine he was Caucasian and so were our other victims,"

Jen said. "Now, cause of death was strangulation, and after further examination of the bodies, I narrowed down the murder weapon to an article of clothing, most likely a silk scarf." She pointed to what remained of the boy's throat. "I could tell from pulling off tiny burnt fragments that had been fused to the skin. I also found the same fibers on our other two victims."

"A silk scarf?" Kerry asked.

"Based off of the way the children were disposed of after the kill, it's probably another part of his ritual," Jim answered. "Any signs of sexual trauma?"

"No," Jen answered.

Jim was surprised. "You're sure?"

"Positive," Jen answered. "In fact, none of the victims were sexually assaulted prior to their death. Aside from the bodies being burnt, which again happened post mortem along with the faux crucifixion, it appears the children were killed very quickly, and by surprise." She pointed to the boy's throat. "The silk chose by the killer didn't allow for much bruising around the trachea."

"He wanted to keep the bodies pristine for his ritual." Jim nodded. "Anything you can tell us about the accelerant used to burn the bodies?"

"Lighter fluid," Jen answered. "And I've included the description of the nails the killer used to pin the bodies to the wood, which was cedar. But I'm afraid both could be purchased at any hardware store, so it doesn't narrow down the search field."

Jen moved onto to the next victim, noting the same

cause of death, same murder weapon, and same type of nails and accelerant used on the previous victim.

"He's consistent," Kerry said.

"And thorough," Jim replied. "Anything come back on the clothes that were set aside?"

"The clothes were washed prior to being buried with the victims," Jen answered. "He used Tide. Not my personal choice, but to each their own."

Kerry leaned closer to Jim. "Does she not realize the things she says sometimes?"

Jim kept his voice to a whisper. "She's very factual, and literal. You get used to it."

"Now," Jen said, moving to the last body. "I wasn't able to provide any specific identifications on the victims, but our last girl provides us the best chance."

"Find her driver's license on her?" Kerry asked.

Jen looked at Kerry, her face deadpan. "No, Detective, she wasn't old enough to drive."

Jim tossed Kerry a sheepish look and then shrugged. Jen was unable to pick up on sarcasm.

"My mistake," Kerry said.

"Happens all the time," Jen said, her voice chipper and cheery. "But what I did find was just as good." She removed a small flashlight from her pocket and then shone the light onto the victim's mouth. "See that?"

Both Jim and Kerry leaned closer as Jen opened the corpse's mouth, pointing inside.

"I wasn't sure what it was at first, but when I examined the residue on her teeth, I realized the victim had worn braces."

Jim and Kerry found each other's gaze, and Kerry smiled. It would help narrow the search field for at least one of the unknown victims. Jim didn't imagine there were too many missing kids in the area in the same time frame that were white, female, and wore braces, but he could be wrong.

"Anything else that you can tell us?" Kerry asked.

"All three victims had experience of untreated trauma," Jen answered.

"Physical abuse?" Jim asked.

"Yes, but not by the killer," Jen answered. "All of the fractures I found that were improperly healed on the victims were several years old."

"Can you tell what caused the injuries?" Jim asked.

"Blunt force trauma," Jen answered.

"Jesus," Kerry said.

"So all three kids were abused before our killer got to them," Jim said. "Sounds like he has a type he goes after."

"Yes, and I managed to compile all of the pieces of paper we found buried with the bodies," Jen said and then walked over to her computer, which was set up near some lab equipment. She typed in her password and then accessed one of her files. "Between the three pieces of evidence, I managed to compile what I believe is the full entirety of the letter." A few more keystrokes, and the recreated image appeared on the screen.

Jim leaned forward, eager to read the killer's message.

"Their pain is done," Jim said, reading the letter

aloud. "No more will they have to suffer from the fear of a broken home. No more will they be beaten and bruised. No more will they cry, and no more will they be forced into submission by violence. They are free."

Jim leaned back, the last line of the killer's note connecting to what Emily and Amelia had written in their own personal note at the Montgomery house.

"To be free," Kerry said, repeating the words.

"Can we get a copy of that?" Jim asked.

"Of course," Jen said and printed the document.

"Thank you so much for your help, Jen," Jim said.

"You're welcome," Jen replied. "I hope you catch him."

In addition to the document recreated from the three letters, Jen also provided Jim and Kerry with copies of her notes for the autopsy, and Jim re-read through all of it on the way back out to the car.

The car door slammed shut, and the pair settled into the vehicle. Jim reached for his seat belt and put it on, his mind racing with the next steps. He was so distracted that he didn't know how long he sat there before he realized that Kerry hadn't started the car, and they were still sitting in the parking lot.

Jim glanced over to his partner and saw Kerry staring at him. "What is it?"

Kerry hesitated, but she looked worried. "I've never been a part of a case like this before. The highest stakes I've ever had to deal with were making sure I filed the correct paperwork." She exhaled, rattled. "If we don't find Emily and Amelia, then they'll end up like those other kids."

"Hey," Jim said. "We stay focused. We still don't know what kind of timeline the killer's dealing with. Until we know the girls are dead, we operate under the premise that they're still alive. We need to get back to the station, see if we can identify those victims from the woods."

"Right." Kerry started the car and shifted into drive. But while she focused on the road, Jim glanced into the rearview mirror, staring at the hospital.

Jim had dealt with his fair share of sick pedophiles during his time with Missing Persons, but this was something different. They were chasing an experienced killer, a man who thought himself acting for some righteous cause. Someone who had mastered their craft. And if they didn't catch him now, then it wouldn't just mean the death of two more girls, but countless others.

The fact that their suspect had broken pattern and gone after two kids instead of one showed his confidence was growing. And a confident killer was a dangerous killer.

14

───────────

$\mathcal{K}$erry went to work on identifying the bodies they'd dug up based on what the ME had told them. The age range, physical description, and time frame of abduction and death helped narrow her search fields, but Kerry was both depressed and shocked at the number of children who had gone missing and were never recovered.

Kerry scrolled through hundreds of pictures, their families still wondering about the fate of their children, still clinging to the hope they would recover their children alive.

But for three families, Kerry would bring them the news all parents feared. And while it would provide the families closure, it would also break their hearts.

Kerry glanced across the desk to Jim, who was also sifting through Missing Person files. And all the while the clock ticked, the sands of time sifting toward the bottom of the hourglass, lowering their chances of successfully recovering Emily and Amelia.

Lieutenant Mullocks joined them at their desks, tossed a file onto Jim's desk, and planted her hands on her hips, finishing chewing something. "The profile put together by our friends at the FBI. What are you two working on?"

Jim didn't look away from his computer screen. "We're working on identifying the kids we pulled from the woods."

"What about the letters from the girls' rooms?" Mullocks asked. "Anything?"

Jim leaned back from the computer, sighing. "Nothing but vague mentions of someone they both admire. But we think the identity of that person is our abductor and killer."

Mullocks picked one off of the read pile and examined it silently for a moment before she returned it to the pile. "They're each other's confidants."

"They're best friends," Kerry said. "People called them M&M because they were so close."

"Cute name, sad situation," Mullocks said. "So chasing the girls isn't working. Maybe switch it up and chase the kidnapper." She tapped the folder.

"Maybe the other victims were runaways too," Jim said. "Maybe they were even in therapy. After all, that's a common connection between Emily and Amelia."

"That and they're related," Kerry said.

"It's worth pursuing," Mullocks said. "And that might help narrow down your search field of identifying the victims buried in the woods. Cross-reference any mention of therapy or runaway with your current results and see what you get."

Kerry turned to her computer and applied the search parameters, and to her surprise, they worked. "Holy shit. Twenty matches, all within the other parameters given to us by the ME's report."

Jim slapped his palm on the desk. "Now we're getting somewhere."

"See who they were in therapy with, and we might be able to establish a connection," Mullocks said. "Parents have all been ruled out?"

"I confirmed their alibis," Kerry said then reached for her notes. "Natalie Johnson was with a group of girlfriends during the disappearance, Tom was at a bar —CCTV footage put him there until two thirty in the morning, and he drove home—and Ralph Wilks attended an NA meeting," Kerry said.

"What about the druggie mother?" Mullocks asked.

"She was passed out in a ditch," Kerry answered. "Which, oddly enough, was also confirmed by CCTV footage. I couldn't believe how many people just walked past her and did nothing."

Mullocks nodded. "All right, then. Take a look at that profile. It'd be nice to tell Chief some good news when he calls me in the next twenty minutes for an update."

"We're working on it, LT," Kerry said.

"Work faster." Mullocks knocked on Jim's desk.

"Lieutenant," Jim said, standing up. "We should get warrants ready for the girls' therapist, Dr. Weathers."

"We don't have enough for a judge to approve that right now," Mullocks said. "Find me more, and then we'll pursue that lead."

Dejected, Jim sat down and returned to the letters. "He fits."

"We'll know soon enough," Kerry said. "But until then, the lieutenant's right. We don't have enough to serve him a warrant."

With Jim preoccupied with searching through the Missing Persons database, Kerry reached for the folder Mullocks had left behind and took a look.

"White male," Kerry said, flipping through the notes. "Mid to late twenties, most likely experienced trauma at a young age by parents or parental figures." She looked up from the pages, checking to see if Jim was paying attention. He wasn't. "Around six feet, brown hair, brown eyes, loner, doesn't pay attention to his partner."

Jim stopped typing and then glanced at Kerry. "Funny."

"I thought so." Kerry returned to the folder. "Ritualistic style of killings, and the lack of sexual release, point to a killer who is self-righteous. Killer would be a strong communicator and have a career that keeps him in close proximity with at-risk youth."

"Sounds like Dr. Weathers," Jim said.

"The abduction of two children suggest the killer's fantasies have intensified and will become more frequent if they are not caught." Kerry snapped the folder shut and then tossed it on the table.

Jim returned to the work of sifting through the screens, but stopped suddenly. "Whoa, I think I've got a match."

Kerry walked around to Jim's side of the desk and examined the picture of the girl on the screen. "Braces. White. Aged eleven. Reported missing eighteen months ago by her adopted mother." She looked to Jim. "I think Maisie Simmons was our killer's first victim."

15

_J_im brought the girls' letters, sifting through them again on the drive, but he could only read through so many before he was struck with car sickness. He set the letters aside and rubbed his eyes.

"Anything useful?" Kerry asked.

"Not unless Clark from biology abducted them," Jim answered and then blinked away the blackspots from his vision. "I never thought I would learn so much about a boy I never met."

Kerry smirked. "Mutual crush?"

"I don't know if 'crush' is the right word," Jim said. "'Obsession' probably works better."

Kerry laughed. "I remember those days."

Jim nodded along, but he didn't laugh. What childhood he'd known had been limited to survival. There were no crushes or secret notes passed during class. The only thing Jim had ever concerned himself with when he was in the foster system was getting out of it, and at any cost.

"You all right?" Kerry asked.

"Yeah," Jim answered quickly. "Fine."

Kerry was quiet for a moment, and when she spoke again, she trod lightly. "I imagine there's a lot of pressure on you right now." She shot him a quick glance. "Between this case and with the IA investigation."

Jim scoffed. "It's all bullshit."

"Did you tell IA that?" Kerry asked, her tone sarcastic.

Jim finally smirked, but it faded quickly. "I know what people say about me. I hear the whispers. I see the stares. I know I don't have a great reputation in the department."

"The first step is acceptance," Kerry said.

Jim ran his finger down the length of the scars on his left palm, thinking. "I knew turning Rich over was going to put me in hot water. I knew it the moment I found out he was dirty. I brought him down, and then he made all of these allegations against me, saying I was a part of his dealings all along." He closed his hand and shook his head. "All I've ever done is try to do the right thing. And I keep getting burned for it."

"My dad always told me people do what's right only when they think people are watching," Kerry said. "But it's when we're alone that we know our truest selves."

It was surprisingly insightful for a murderer, but Jim suspected Kerry's father had possessed some degree of intelligence for the amount of time he spent undercover. "Do you think that's true? That we only know our truest self when we're alone?"

Kerry shook her head, sighing. "I don't know. I hope not. I hope we're never really alone, and there are people who care about us and love us even when we're not there. I know I have that with my family."

When they arrived at the house, Kerry was the first up the drive, and Jim lagged behind. She rang the doorbell, and they waited until a short, middle-aged Asian woman opened the door.

"Mrs. Simmons?" Jim asked. "I'm Detective North, and this is my partner, Detective Martin. Do you have a moment to talk?"

The woman nodded gravely and let them inside.

It was dark in the house. All of the blinds had been pulled shut, and the only light came from the glow of the television, which was playing the Weather Channel. The house was small but clean and tidy. Jim saw the few pictures on the wall of Maisie Simmons, the girl they had identified.

Jim studied one of the pictures in particular. It was a picture of Maisie in her soccer uniform, posing with a ball and a small trophy. She was sweaty and sunburnt and sported a big smile. Judging by the age of Masie in the photograph, Jim suspected it might have been taken a few weeks before the girl disappeared. Before the young life was ended in the most brutal and horrible way imaginable.

Once everyone was settled in the living room, Jim

spoke. "Mrs. Simmons, I'm afraid we have some bad news. We found your daughter, Maisie. She's passed."

Jim had expected a flood of waterworks to pour out of Mrs. Simmons, but the mother only nodded and then took a breath.

"I thought she might be gone," Simmons said, and then she turned to look at the pictures on the wall. "I held out hope for a long time, but... a mother can sense those things."

"We're very sorry for your loss," Kerry said.

Jim leaned forward. "I understand that this is a difficult time and a lot to take in, but we had some questions we hoped you could answer about your daughter before she went missing."

"Is it about those two other girls?" Simmons asked.

Jim nodded. "We think the same person who killed your daughter might be involved."

Simmons straightened up. "I'll tell you whatever I can."

Jim opened his mouth but stopped, noticing the lack of a presence in the house. "Mrs. Simmons, do you know where Maisie's father is?"

Simmons cleared her throat. "No. I'm afraid we divorced after Maisie had gone missing."

"We understand that Maisie was adopted?" Jim asked.

"Yes," Simmons answered. "My ex-husband and I were unable to bear children, so we chose adoption. We knew there were so many kids looking for good homes."

"Did Maisie ever talk about her life in the system?" Jim asked.

"Not a lot," Simmons answered. "She had a rough time, and had been in several situations where she had been abused both emotionally and physically."

"Did you ever take her to therapy?" Jim asked.

"Yes," Simmons answered. "It was about three months before she disappeared."

Jim felt Kerry stiffen next to him, but he did his best to remain calm. "Do you remember the name of the therapist that treated your daughter?"

Simmons frowned, trying to think. "No. I couldn't afford one, but one of the teachers at her school was able to secure some services for her through a state program. I might have his information somewhere."

"If you could check to see if you still have it, that would be very helpful," Jim said.

"I'll be right back."

Once Simmons was out of the living room, Kerry leaned toward Jim. "You think it's Dr. Weathers?"

"If it is, I think we have cause for our warrant," Jim answered. "If we can identify the other kids and prove they were also patients of Dr. Weathers, then that's our silver bullet."

A few moments later, Mrs. Simmons returned, a piece of paper in hand. "Here you go. I had it filed away with my tax information."

Jim held the paper gingerly and scanned it until he came across the name he expected to find: Doctor Gary

Weathers. "Would you mind if I kept this, Mrs. Simmons?"

"No," she answered.

Jim knew he had more than enough to get his warrant, but there was something else tugging at him. "Is Maisie's room still here?"

A sad smile broke over Mrs. Simmons's face. "I was never able to clean it out. Come, I'll show you."

Jim and Kerry followed the grieving mother to the back bedroom. Maisie's room was similar to Emily's and Amelia's, that of a young girl caught between her childhood and adulthood, both fighting for her attention. He crossed the room to the pillow, donned a pair of gloves, and searched inside for any letters like the ones they'd found hidden by Emily and Amelia.

"Do you know if Maisie kept a journal or a diary?" Kerry asked, picking up on what Jim was searching for.

"No, not that I'm aware," Simmons answered.

Jim crossed the room to the dresser and opened the drawers, rifling through the girl's clothes. When that search yielded nothing, Jim turned his focus to the closet. He searched through boxes and looked inside shoes, pushed aside the winter coat, but still nothing. He was about to stop when he noticed that a section of the baseboard had been removed and replaced again.

It was almost impossible to see because it had been painted over, but Jim noticed the newer paint. He reached for the panel and then removed it, exposing a small hole. Jim reached inside and removed a small black journal.

"Oh my God," Simmons said. "I didn't even know that was there."

Jim opened the book, rifling through the pages, scanning them quickly, hoping to find something else, something incriminating, the nail in the coffin, something he hadn't been able to find in the letters between Amelia and Emily. Halfway through the journal, he found it.

Jim snapped the journal shut. "Mrs. Simmons, we appreciate your time, but we need to leave."

He left the room without another word and heard Kerry mumble something else to the mother as he stepped outside.

"Jim!" Kerry jogged after him, catching her breath when she reached the car. "What did you find?"

Jim flipped open to the page. "Maisie describes a relationship with a special person in this passage, an older man, someone who she trusts, someone who she loves." He pointed to the paragraph and then to the last sentence of the page. "Now, read that."

Kerry leaned closer to get a better look. "'I'm so thankful to have met Dr. Weathers.'" She paused, connecting the dots. "Oh my God."

"We need units sent to his house and to his office," Jim said, opening the car door. "We've got the son of a bitch."

16

$\mathcal{T}$he uniforms sent to Dr. Weathers's home and office found both of them empty, and that only confirmed Jim's fears.

"Have we tried calling him?" Kerry asked.

"His phone is turned off," Jim said. "We'll have tech search for a last known location. With any luck, it'll match up with the same area where we found Emily's phone."

Kerry nodded, typing away at her desk. "APB is out for the doctor. What do we need to complete for the warrant?"

"I'll fill it out," Jim answered. "I need to go and talk with the lieutenant for a sec. I'll be right back."

"Sure," Kerry said, returning to her work.

It was now late afternoon at the precinct, and the place was buzzing from their case. The three bodies they'd found in the mountains combined with the fact that both girls were still missing had lit a fire under everyone's ass, and it had been stoked by individuals high up in the chain of command.

Jim beelined down the hallway to the lieutenant's office, but he slowed down when he heard the lieutenant's voice coming through the cracked door. He noticed the stress in her tone. He glanced around, looking to see if anyone was nearby, but he was alone. Curious, he moved closer and listened.

"I understand your concern, Deputy Commissioner, but I can assure you my detectives are working very—" Lieutenant Mullocks was cut short, and Jim peeked through the crack and saw she had her cell phone glued to her ear. She was pacing behind her desk. "Yes, sir. Everyone here understands the urgency of the situation. Yes, sir."

Jim had seen that kind of body language before when he was at the academy. It was the same look and posture every recruit had when they were dressed down by one of the training officers in front of the rest of the class. The lieutenant was getting an earful.

"Sir, I just need—" Mullocks stopped again and then lowered her head, her left hand planted on her hip. "Yes, sir. It's understood."

The call ended, and the lieutenant tossed the phone on her desk and then raked her fingers through her hair. She hunched forward on the desk, and then Jim leaned away from the crack in the door. He wasn't sure if this was the right time to talk, but Jim pushed the fear aside, knowing that what was most important now was finding the girls. But he knocked first.

"Yeah, come in."

Jim opened the door, leaving it open behind him as Lieutenant Mullocks sat down. "Hey, LT, I need your final approval on some search warrants."

Mullocks reached for the papers and looked them over on her desk. "Judge Mathers?"

"He's one of the few judges that doesn't mind me," Jim answered.

Mullocks glanced up from the papers and cocked an eyebrow up. "Does it bother you, Detective?"

"Does what bother me, ma'am?" Jim asked.

"The fact that people don't like you."

"No, ma'am," Jim answered. "But I suspect that's one of the reasons people don't like me."

Mullocks smirked, and she scribbled her signature over the appropriate approval lines. "People worry too much." She finished and then handed the papers back to Jim. "Keep pushing, Detective."

Jim nodded as he grabbed the papers from her hand. "Yes, ma'am." With the approvals done for the warrants, Jim was heading for the fax machine when he was intercepted by Kerry.

"Hey," Kerry said, her demeanor and voice very hurried and excited. "I just got a response from Dr. Weathers's assistant. She said Dr. Weathers just left town."

Jim's eyes widened. One more piece of the puzzle was falling into place. "Did she have an address?"

"She had to email the old assistant, Lindsey, to get

it, but—" Kerry smirked and then flipped her phone around to show the email.

"That's up near where we found the bodies," Jim said.

"I managed to pull up images on Google Earth," Kerry said. "It's a cabin in the middle of nowhere. And get this: she said he goes on trips like this all the time."

Jim headed toward the desk, moving with purpose, and handed the warrants off to the nearest officer, instructing him to get them over to the judge for processing.

"What's the play?" Kerry asked.

"We'll need to mobilize a strike team for the cabin. Check to see who's on call for SWAT," Jim said, thinking out loud, then he raised his voice to the surrounding bullpen. "Listen up, everyone! We have a new suspect: Dr. Gary Weathers. I need a five-person strike team ready to go in five minutes. First five ready, come with me."

The bullpen erupted. Everyone wanted a chance to catch the bastard who was responsible for the abduction of two girls and the possible death of three kids.

Jim was on his way back to the lieutenant's office, but Mullocks had come back out after hearing the commotion from the floor.

"What do you have?" Mullocks asked.

"We might have the therapist's location," Jim asked. "A remote cabin near the dump site for the other bodies."

Mullocks removed her cell phone. "I'll put the Feds on standby in case we need a negotiator."

"Jim, let's go!" Kerry was already by the door, and he jogged to catch up with her.

Everyone was consumed with the rush of the moment, the burst of adrenaline that accompanied this kind of a bust, but the only thing that Jim was concerned about was mentally preparing for what they'd find when they arrived at the cabin.

Based on the condition of the bodies they found buried in the woods, Jim braced himself for the encounter. And despite the nagging doubt in the back of his mind, Jim allowed himself to hope that the girls were alive and unharmed.

17

*K*erry gripped the steering wheel so hard her knuckles were white. This was by far the biggest moment of her career, and she knew what was at stake. And while she hoped they would recover the girls alive and well, she also secretly hoped this would finally allow her to put the past behind her and erase the long shadow of her father.

"Look, things are going to happen fast once we're up there," Jim said. "SWAT will establish a perimeter, determine if there is anyone inside. They're going to be taking the lead on this one."

Kerry nodded and focused on her breathing. "Got it." She tossed Jim a quick glance. He was oddly calm. "Do you think they're alive?"

Jim was quiet for a moment. "I want them to be alive."

All of the units that arrived on the scene did so quietly and discreetly. No lights or sirens were used.

They didn't want to spook the man into running—or, worse, hurting the girls.

An access road led up to the property, where SWAT and the rest of the strike team had gathered, waiting for Jim and Kerry's arrival.

"Sergeant," Jim said, raising a hand.

Kerry followed Jim, but she noticed how the SWAT team stiffened when they saw Jim walk up to meet them.

Jim extended his hand to the SWAT sergeant, but the man didn't reciprocate, and Jim withdrew the offer. "Have you been given the details of the situation?"

"Your LT gave me the rundown." Sergeant Henry Jeffers was a big man who radiated the kind of stereotypical male machismo that one might find in the movies. "We'll head up the access road then keep to the woods once we're one hundred yards from the cabin." He gestured back to the van, where the rest of his team was set up. "You'll be able to view our body-cam footage from in there. Once we have the area secure, we'll notify you."

"We don't know if he has the girls or if they're still alive," Jim said.

"We understand what we're walking into," Jeffers replied. Then he turned around and rejoined his team.

Once he was gone, Jim turned to Kerry. "Now we wait."

Kerry followed Jim into the back of the van in which the support team was stationed and watched the body-cam monitors bounce up and down as the team made their way up the drive. The footage was jerky, and she had to look away so she wouldn't get motion sickness.

But when they neared the cabin, Kerry pushed past the feeling of nausea and gripped the back of one of the tech's chairs.

"In position," Jeffers said, his voice hushed over the radio. "One vehicle parked in the drive. Curtains are drawn across the front windows. Bravo team, status on back door?"

"Rear entrance covered," another voice replied. "Two windows, both north facing. Curtains also are drawn. No visible line on suspect."

"Hold position, Bravo," Jeffers said. He switched channels to command, where Lieutenant Mullocks and Captain Kierney were listening back at the precinct. "Command, waiting for final confirmation."

"Order approved," Mullocks said.

Jeffers switched back to the channel for his men. "We are mission go. Take assault positions."

The two teams converged on either door to the cabin and readied their entrance devices, each team using the kind of heavy metal battering ram that was held by two members and used to breach any door that wasn't military grade.

"Mark on three, two, one, breach, breach, breach," Jeffers said.

On the third "breach," the stealthy team exploded into action. Kerry jumped at the crash of both the front door and back door as they were knocked inward simultaneously, the teams charging inside.

Kerry's eyes darted around the screens as the SWAT team flooded the cabin. She squinted, struggling to see any details on the screen because of the officers' jerky movements and the fish-eye lenses of the body cameras.

And then, on Jeffers's feed, Kerry saw their suspect.

"On the ground! On the ground! Get on the ground!" Jeffers shouted, and the same orders were barked by every member of the SWAT team who had converged into the bedroom.

One of the SWAT officers pinned Dr. Weathers to the ground then quickly cuffed his hands behind his back. Kerry searched the screens for the girls but couldn't find them.

"Where are they?" Kerry asked. She turned to Jim and saw the solemn expression on his face. He was too calm. She looked back to the screens and saw the rest of the officers clearing the rooms.

"All clear," Bravo team said.

"All clear," Alpha team said.

Jim stepped toward the van's back doors. "We're up."

Kerry followed him out, and the pair walked up the long dirt road to the cabin. Kerry's heart was beating a mile a minute. She matched Jim's quick strides, looking to her partner for answers.

"Do you think he already dumped the bodies?" Kerry asked.

"I don't know," Jim answered.

"Christ, maybe we got here too late," Kerry said. "Shit."

"We'll see more when we have a closer look at the cabin," Jim said.

Kerry glanced around to the surrounding woods. "I mean, he could have put them anywhere out there. There's so much open space—"

"Kerry." Jim stopped in his tracks, and Kerry stopped with him. He locked eyes with her, still possessing that eerie calm. "We don't have any information other than the fact that we have our prime suspect in custody. Don't go running down paths we might not even need to pursue before we have all of the facts."

Kerry held onto that calm reason and nodded. "You're right. Sorry."

"It's fine," Jim said, and then he resumed his walk up the driveway.

Kerry followed, and while her mind was still racing with questions, she managed to keep a lid on it.

By the time they reached the cabin, Kerry's adrenaline had subsided, and the rattled nerves that came with it had calmed.

However, just before Kerry followed Jim through the broken door and into the cabin, she caught herself holding her breath as she finally crossed the barrier.

* * *

JIM BLINKED AWAY the sunspots when he stepped into the cabin. It was dark inside because of the shades that had been drawn. He paused in the foyer for a moment to get his bearings, and then Jeffers and two of his men stepped out of the hallway up ahead.

"He wants to know what the hell is going on," Jeffers said.

"Any sign of the children?" Jim asked.

"Nothing," Jeffers said.

"Have your men sweep the perimeter," Jim said. "He might have a shed or a secondary location that's nearby and on the property."

Jeffers hesitated but then realized now that their job was done, he was no longer the man in charge. "You want to talk to him in the bedroom or out here?"

Jim stepped from the foyer and went deeper into the cabin. It was old but well maintained. He could see a couch and two chairs in the living room, which connected to a small kitchen.

"Bring him out here," Jim said. "Put him on the couch."

Jeffers departed to fetch their suspect, and Jim turned to find Kerry glancing around with wide eyes.

"You ready?" Jim asked.

Kerry nodded and then clenched her hands into fists. "Ready."

The pair sat in the chairs as Jeffers brought out Dr. Weathers, who was still dressed in his pajamas and barefoot, tripping over his feet. Out of his professional attire, Jim noticed how thin he was, his legs and arms almost too long for his frame. The officer pushed Dr. Weathers onto the couch, his arms pinned behind his back. Out of his office clothes he looked older, his small belly exposed on his thin frame.

Jim and the doctor locked eyes as Jeffers's men shoved him onto the couch, and the doctor sank into the cushions without resistance.

"What the hell is going on?" Dr. Weathers asked, aiming his dark, focused, beady eyes at Jim.

"It's good to see you again, Doc," Jim said. "You're a hard man to locate when you don't want to be found."

"I'm on vacation," Dr. Weathers replied. "I come up here every six months for some peace and quiet, and I demand to know why the hell all of that has been disturbed!" He stomped his feet on the rug and triggered a dull thud through the wood flooring.

"Emily Wilks and Amelia Johnson," Jim said.

Dr. Weathers was dumbfounded. He paused and glanced around the room before he aimed his beady eyes at Jim once more. "Is this some kind of a joke? You break into my cabin, tie me up, and point guns in my face because you think I kidnapped those girls?"

"When was the last time you spoke with Emily and Amelia?" Jim asked, switching gears and hoping to throw the therapist off his game. Jim figured the man would be smart, and if they didn't find the girls here, there was no reason for him to admit to any wrongdoing. Right now, he was holding all of the cards.

Dr. Weathers bowed his head, slumped, and acquiesced to the line of questioning. "God, I don't know…

Emily was probably last Tuesday, and Amelia was the Thursday before that."

"So the girls never had therapy sessions on the same day?" Jim asked.

Dr. Weathers kept his head bowed. "Not that I can remember."

"What did you talk to them about?" Jim asked.

"Whatever they wanted to talk about," Weathers answered.

"And what did they want to talk about?"

Dr. Weathers flung his head up, anger flashing over his face. "Is all of this really necessary? If you want to know more about the girls, then I can just show you the files at my office—"

"We already have a team searching the files at your office, Dr. Weathers," Jim said. "I'm more interested in your personal relationship with the girls and how you connected with them."

Dr. Weathers frowned, his eyebrows pinching together. "My personal relationship with them?" He looked around and shook his head, the loose skin of his jowls trembling. "No. I didn't have a personal relationship with them."

"You're sure about that?" Jim asked.

"I maintain the strictest professional standards," Dr. Weathers said. "I don't know what you're talking about."

Jim leaned forward in his chair. "Where are they?"

And then Jim watched it happen, almost as if it was in slow motion. The man's breathing became shallow, and his forehead dampened with sweat. His pupils dilated, and he started to cry. He was breaking. "I don't know what the hell is going on."

Jim stood, and Kerry mirrored his movements. "We're going to find those girls. Now, you can make it easier on yourself and tell us, or we can go down to the station and do this the hard way."

Dr. Weathers's mouth hung open. He gaped like a fish gasping for air. "I didn't do anything wrong. I swear it!"

Jim found Jeffers and then motioned for the sergeant to take the doctor away. A pair of men plucked Dr. Weathers from the couch and carried him out, the man screaming, "I didn't do anything! I didn't do anything!"

18

The entire way back to the precinct, Kerry thought she would have felt better now that they had someone in custody, but the longer she sat behind the wheel and the longer the silence stretched between herself and Jim, the more uneasy she became. She glanced over at her partner a few times, checking to see if his expression had changed at all from the time they had left the cabin. He was as still as a statue.

"We caught the guy," Kerry said, but even when she finally spoke the words aloud after repeating them in her head so many times, she noticed the uncertainty in her voice.

Jim finally shifted in his seat, the first sign of movement, and then stared down at the scars on his palms.

Kerry remembered the story that he had told her about the time he was abducted, and she frowned. "What is it?"

Jim closed his hands into fists and then took a deep breath. "If the kids weren't at the cabin, then they're most likely dead."

Kerry flinched. "They're still looking at his house and his office. Something else could turn up."

Jim nodded, conceding the point, but there was still something bothering him about what they had seen at the cabin. "I've been around enough pedophiles and kiddie snatchers to think that I had a pretty good idea of how they react to being caught." He shook his head. "Either that guy is the best actor I've ever seen, or we've missed something."

When they finally arrived at the precinct, the news hordes had already set up camp, transforming their small precinct into a circus. Officers were stationed out front, making sure the reporters didn't overstep their boundaries, and they made a hole for Kerry to drive through as she entered the parking lot.

A few moments later, the SWAT van carrying their suspect arrived, and again the horde of reporters swarmed the scene.

Kerry glanced behind them at the media circus. "It was a good idea having him ride in the van. No windows means no one will be able to see who is inside."

"And covers our asses if we're wrong," Jim said.

Kerry turned to her partner. She didn't like all of the doubt circling his thoughts. "You're making me nervous."

Jim sighed. "Sorry. I just need—"

"More data?" Kerry asked, finishing his thought for him.

Jim cracked a smile, and she thought it might have been the first time she'd actually seen him lighten up a little. "I suppose I should start taking my own advice and not travel down a road until I know where we're going."

"Probably a good idea," Kerry said.

Jim reached for the door handle and then paused, turning back to Kerry. "What did you think of him?"

Kerry hesitated. "I think he's involved, whether he knows it or not."

Jim held her gaze for a moment longer and then nodded. "Let's go find out."

The pair entered the station together, and both of them watched as Dr. Gary Weathers was escorted in by the SWAT team.

Every officer in the precinct stopped what they were doing, and the building fell quiet as the man was brought into interrogation room one. It wasn't until the suspect was locked inside that everyone returned to work. Kerry had never seen anything like it since she'd joined the force.

Sergeant Jeffers walked over to Jim. "He's all yours."

"How was he on the trip down?" Jim asked.

"Quiet," Jeffers answered.

"We appreciate your help, Sergeant." Jim again tried to shake the man's hand, and again the sergeant denied him.

Kerry grimaced as the man walked away, resenting the fact that Jim didn't get the respect that he deserved. Neither of them did. "What an asshole."

"It's fine," Jim said, turning his attention to the monitor showing Dr. Weathers. "We'll let him sweat for a while. That'll give forensics time to finish their sweep of the office and his house."

"Get as much ammunition as we can," Kerry said. "It's a good idea."

The pair lingered in front of the monitors for a moment, a crowd gathering behind them, everyone wanting to take a look at the man they believed was responsible for five abductions and three murders.

"Guy looks guilty," a voice said.

"Nail that sucker," another replied.

Kerry knew how much was riding on their interrogation, because they could only hold the man for twenty-four hours before they had to charge him or let him go.

Kerry and Jim turned, and the cluster of cops gathered behind them made a hole for them to cut through, all of their eyes glued to the screen. It was like watching a monkey at the zoo. *No, not a monkey*, Kerry thought. *A predator.*

An hour passed as Jim and Kerry detailed their notes and spoke with the forensic techs charged with collecting evidence. Nothing of significance was found in the house, but the office was a different story.

"Jim," Kerry said, slamming the phone down. "Jim!"

"Hmm?" Jim glanced away from his computer screen.

"We got it," Kerry said.

"The scarf?" Jim asked, growing hopeful. "The silk one Jen told us about?"

"No, but it's just as good. Forensics found photographs at Dr. Weathers's office," Kerry said then flipped her screen around to face her partner. "Emily and Amelia tied up."

Jim's eyes widened at the pictures.

"Locked away in his filing cabinet." Kerry pounded her fist on the desk. This was their smoking gun. This was the leverage they needed to get Dr. Weathers to talk.

"Have forensics do a full workup on the photographs," Jim said. "Prints, fibers, where they were printed, everything they can tell us. And print out copies for us so we can take them into the interrogation room."

"Already done," Kerry said, turning her screen back around. "We have him. We have the bastard."

And depending on when the pictures had been taken, there was still a chance that the girls were alive. But Jim and Kerry needed to get Dr. Weathers to talk.

The pair gathered up all of their resources and then headed to the interrogation room. And just like the officers had done when Dr. Weathers had been marched through the precinct, once again, everything came to a standstill as they crossed the room.

The pressure was on to push for a confession, and while Kerry knew her mind should be focused on the interrogation, she couldn't help but think of the girls. No one knew if they were still alive. But if they were, they were going to bring them home.

19

*J*im pretended this interrogation was just like all the others he'd performed over his career, but as he took a seat and opened the case file, which contained all of the information that they had managed to put together for Emily and Amelia, Jim knew it was folly.

Two factors were working against him. The first was the clock, because if the girls were still alive, time was running out to save them. The second was his suspect, because Jim had never seen a guilty man act as innocent as Dr. Weathers.

But Jim and Kerry's investigation had led to the discovery of very damning evidence against Dr. Weathers. A man who had been entrusted with the care of minors. A man who had used his position to manipulate the young minds he was supposed to heal.

"You need to let me go," Dr. Weathers said. "Don't I get a phone call, or—"

"Dr. Weathers, detail your last forty-eight hours for us," Jim said. "You can start on Thursday night."

Dr. Weathers, now calmed a little bit from the manic episode that he had gone through just moments before, took a breath and stared at the table between them while he answered. "Thursday night I left my office after my last appointment, which was at 6:45—"

"That's when your last appointment started, or that was when you left your office?" Jim asked.

Dr. Weathers sighed. "That was when I left my office." He took another breath and then restarted. "I drove home. Finished packing."

"For your trip to the cabin," Jim said.

"That's right," Dr. Weathers replied.

"Do you always pack that early?" Jim asked.

"I like to be prepared."

Jim nodded along. The man was cooler under pressure now. "Please, continue."

"I made dinner, watched a little television, and then went to bed," Dr. Weathers said.

Jim listened as the man went through the rest of his Friday, and according to the therapist, he had done the same routine on Saturday as well, but when Jim asked him if anyone could confirm his alibi, he had no one.

"Do you have a security system at your house?" Jim asked.

"No," Dr. Weathers answered. "I live in a very safe neighborhood."

Jim double-checked their timeline for when the girls had disappeared from the Montgomerys' home.

"So no one can confirm your whereabouts between midnight Friday and six o'clock Saturday morning?"

"No one but me," Dr. Weathers answered.

Jim tapped his finger on his knee. "Tell me about the cabin."

"What do you want to know?" Dr. Weathers asked.

"Do you ever bring people up there?"

"No."

"Does anyone else know of its location?"

"Just my assistant."

"What time did you leave your home to head up to the cabin today?" Jim asked.

"It was shortly after your visit, Detective."

Jim smiled. "Feel the need to get out of town?"

Dr. Weathers remained quiet.

"And what time did you arrive at your cabin?"

"Mid-afternoon," Dr. Weathers said. "A few hours before you broke down my door."

"Did you make any stops on your way up to the cabin?" Jim asked.

"No."

"You're sure?"

"Yes."

Jim paused, tapping his fingers on the top-right corner of the case file. He was waiting for the right time to reveal the pictures. He wanted to make sure that he crossed all of his T's and dotted all of his I's. And he had a few more surprises up his sleeve. He removed a sheet of paper that he had printed out, which showed a map with a route from the doctor's house to his cabin.

"We pulled this route off of your car's GPS," Jim said, placing the sheet of paper on the table and then sliding it across so the doctor could see it. "It looks like you did make a stop along Highway 137."

Jim studied the doctor's expression while the man examined the sheet of paper. He searched for the most subtle hint or sign of recognition. Even the best liar couldn't deny the facts when they were shoved directly into his face. But the old doctor surprised him.

"This isn't right," Dr. Weathers said. "It must have been from some older route."

"The route was time-stamped on your GPS," Jim said. "It was the same time that you just told me you drove up to the cabin, and you said you didn't make any stops."

Dr. Weathers frowned, and Jim saw the walls closing in on the man. "It must have been some kind of mistake. Maybe traffic slowed down long enough for me to actually stop. Maybe I saw something... I don't know."

"What would you have seen that made you stop?" Jim asked, knowing the bodies had been found along that same route.

Dr. Weathers leaned back into his chair, and his chains gave the slightest rattle from his movement, causing the doctor to glance down at his restraints as if he had forgotten they were there in the first place. "I don't know, I don't remember—" He popped his eyes open wide, so wide Jim thought the eyeballs would roll out of their sockets and splatter on the table. "Something had happened. There was a traffic jam. Something was happening in the woods."

Jim wasn't sure if Weathers was willingly playing into the scenario, but only time would tell. "Enough to be happening for you to pull over and stop the car."

"Yes," Weathers replied.

"But you just said you didn't stop." Jim tilted his head to the side, studying Weathers closely.

Weathers grew more frazzled. "I must have misremembered."

Jim nodded and opened the file, staring down at the pictures of the charred bodies. "Do you know what was happening in those woods along that route, Dr. Weathers?"

Weathers shook his head, dumbfounded.

"Maybe these will jog your memory," Jim said.

Jim placed the photographs of the remains of the three children onto the table for Dr. Weathers to see, and the man immediately recoiled.

"We found those bodies in the woods today," Jim said. "And one of them was Maisie Simmons, a girl you treated two years ago. She happened to be going through a rough time. Parents divorced. Just like Emily and Amelia."

Dr. Weathers continued to look away, refusing to stare at the pictures. "Get those away, please." He trembled, his breathing shallow and quick.

"Having trouble looking at your handiwork?" Jim asked.

Weathers snapped his attention back to Jim. "I didn't do any of this!"

Jim kept the photographs on the table and allowed the doctor's words to linger in the conference room until Weathers finally dropped his gaze back to the pictures of the burned corpses of the children, and then whimpered as he quickly looked away again.

An interrogation was all about power, and the person who wielded that power the most effectively was the individual who would win the battle of wills. And Jim was determined not to lose that battle at any cost.

Jim paused for a moment, studying the doctor's facial expressions. This tactic gave the person being interrogated a chance to jumble their own thoughts up like balls of yarn.

Jim tapped his finger onto the picture of the most recent victim. The boy. "Tell me about him."

Weathers kept his face turned away. "I don't know him."

Jim leaned forward and rested his forearms on the table. He clasped his hands together. "Sure you do."

"I told you I don't know him!" Weathers's complexion flushed red, his jowls shaking.

"Why'd you pick him?" Jim asked. "Was it because of the trauma of his past? Like the others? We know you strangled him to death."

"Jesus Christ." Weathers blurted the words out with a sob.

"Why did you want to set them free?" Jim asked.

Weathers continued to whimper, looking away from Jim and the pictures, shaking his head. "You've got the wrong man."

"I don't think so," Jim said and then reached for the photograph they found in Weathers's office. He placed it over the top of the others, front and center, the girls bound and gagged. "Where are Amelia and Emily, Dr. Weathers?"

"I don't know," Weathers answered.

"We know you took them," Jim replied. "We know that you buried the bodies close to the cabin you visit every six months, which is also when you decide to go after your next victim. Like clockwork. Tell me where they are, Gary."

"I didn't take them!" Dr. Weathers jumped against his restraints, screaming at the top of his lungs. "I didn't do anything to those girls! I don't know why you think I did, but I had nothing to do with them! I swear to God!"

Jim's tone stiffened, and the longer Weathers sat there sniveling and crying, the more he felt himself lose control. "This photograph of Emily and Amelia was found locked away in a filing cabinet in your office. Where are the girls?"

Dr. Weathers's face twitched with small spasms of shock, and he recoiled from the photographs. "No, I— NO! This isn't what happened! I didn't do that!"

Jim stood, moving closer into Weathers's personal space. "Where are the girls, Doctor?"

"I don't know why these were in my office!" The doctor cried, sinking deeper into his chair. "Please. You have to believe me."

"Where are they?" Jim asked, ending each question with a pound of his fist. "Are they still alive? Did you kill them? Where are they? WHERE ARE THEY?"

Jim's face had gone beet red, and a little spittle had fallen from his lower lip. He quickly wiped it away and then leaned out of the doctor's personal space. The man had broke, and the waterworks were in full effect. It was pathetic.

Jim collected all the paperwork except for the pictures of the bound and gagged girls. He made sure to leave them for Weathers to see.

Jim pressed his finger onto the photograph, waiting until the doctor looked up with tears filling his red-rimmed eyes. "You look at them. Take a moment. Maybe it will come back to you when we speak again." Jim turned toward the door, and Kerry lingered behind for a moment.

"Wait, please," Dr. Weathers called out to them before they left. He opened his mouth, his fear and grief causing it to open like a large oval. He tried to talk, but nothing came out for the first few seconds, and then his voice crawled out of the dark cavern of his mouth. "I didn't do this."

Jim flared his nostrils. "We'll talk soon, Doctor." He then left, Kerry following, and the doctor started screaming again and kept screaming until the door was sealed shut.

Jim and Kerry didn't stop as they passed the officers who had been watching the video feed of the interrogation. He didn't care what they thought of his techniques. He would get the confession in time, but for now, he needed to check for any holes in the doctor's story.

Before Jim and Kerry returned to their desks, Lieutenant Mullocks intercepted them and pulled them both into her office. "I need a word."

Jim didn't like the LT's tone, and he certainly didn't like the way she was looking at them. She looked worried and pale—more pale than normal, at least from what he could tell based on the few interactions they'd had.

Jim looked to Kerry, who shrugged.

"Maybe we get a 'good job' sticker?" Kerry suggested.

Jim doubted it. He stepped toward the lieutenant's office, bracing himself for whatever storm they were about to weather.

20

*K*erry saw the worry on Jim's face, and his worry made her worry. It wasn't surprising for the LT to want to talk to them after the interrogation, but when they entered her office and saw both the captain and the deputy chief waiting for them, she knew that wasn't the regular procedure.

It was an ambush.

"Kerry, shut the door for me, will you?" Mullocks asked.

Kerry nodded and then closed the door, praying she wasn't sealing herself in her own tomb. The door clicked, and when she turned around, she saw Jim was still standing. She decided to stand too.

"The captain and the deputy chief would like an update on the case," Mullocks said. "They wanted to make the trip down in person."

Captain Kierney had been captain of Seattle's fifth precinct for the past seven years. He had risen through the ranks quickly, and everyone knew he was being groomed to become chief one day. Apparently he had the "right look" for the job.

"We wanted both of you to understand how committed we are to providing you the resources to get this job done," Captain Kierney said.

And to make sure they hadn't ruined anything in the process, Kerry thought.

Deputy Chief Mark Winston was older, nearing retirement. The man had reached the pinnacle of his career, and many believed he would retire when the current chief stepped down. The chief happened to be Winston's closest friend and was the reason many believed he had originally been appointed to the position.

"What can you tell us so far, Detectives?" Winston asked.

"The suspect we have in custody was also the therapist for both girls," Jim said. "We're backtracking his movements for the past forty-eight hours, and so far, he hasn't been able to provide a witness to corroborate his alibi."

"I'm still waiting to hear the nail in the coffin, Detective," Captain Kierney said, a hint of warning in his tone.

"The forensic team found photographs in a locked drawer in the doctor's office," Jim said. "The photographs pictured both Emily Wilks and Amelia Johnson, bound and gagged."

"Jesus." Deputy Chief Winston let the word escape

through an exhale that deflated his shoulders. "Are the girls still alive?"

"We're not sure yet, sir," Jim said. "We haven't been able to find any other evidence suggesting that our suspect in custody possessed and/or disposed of the bodies of the girls."

"What about the three kids you found up in the mountains?" Captain Kierney asked. "Have you been able to tie any of those remains to the suspect?"

"One of the girls we found was a client of his, but we haven't been able to identify the other two bodies yet, sir," Jim said. "But we're combing through the names of the patients in the doctor's files to see if they match up with any of the missing-person cases that remain open or unsolved. We're hoping that will give us some more evidence and allow us to identify the remains we discovered."

"I don't have to tell either of you that the press is eating all of this up," Deputy Chief Winston said, a tinge of disgust in his voice. "And the mayor's office has been swamped with calls requesting updates. People are worried we have a serial kidnapper out on the loose, killing our city's children. I want to be able to tell them that we caught the bastard."

"We're working on it, sir," Jim said.

"Well, work harder and work faster," Winston said. "I want a confession before the twenty-four-hour holding period is up. I want the lawyers handling this case after we're done discussing how long he'll be locked up instead of whether he'll be locked up at all. Build the case, Detectives."

"Yes, sir," Jim said.

"Yes, sir," Kerry echoed Jim's words and then nodded as the deputy chief walked out, escorted by Captain Kierney, who was whispering in the deputy chief's ear as if they were spies.

They had left the door open, exposing the office to the noise of the precinct, and again Lieutenant Mullocks nodded for Kerry to shut the door.

Once it was just the three of them, their lieutenant spoke more candidly. "I hope you two understood the message."

Jim sighed. "We don't close the case, and they pin the blame on our ineptitude. It's our fault instead of the department's fault. And with both of our histories, we're easy targets."

Kerry bowed her head. "Shit."

Mullocks leaned forward on the desk, clasping her hands. "You two might have histories, but despite what people think, it's not bad for the department. I wouldn't have paired you two together if I believed that." She turned her attention to Jim. "How confident are you that he is our guy?"

"Right now, I'd put our odds at seventy percent," Jim answered without hesitating. "If we can't get him to crack and confess, then we're going to need to prove that no one can confirm his location during the time frame the girls disappeared from the Montgomery home."

"If we don't get him to confess, we get dragged through the press," Kerry said, stepping next to Jim. "We need to get back in there and press him."

"We already pulled out our ace in the hole with the pictures," Jim said. "If he didn't crack at that, then we'll need to find something bigger."

"What the hell is bigger than having pictures of missing kids bound and gagged locked away in a drawer in your office?" Kerry shouted, raising her arms. "Because that sounds pretty fucking damning to me." She caught herself and then turned to her lieutenant. "Sorry."

"We need to find the murder weapon used on the other children," Mullocks said.

"So far forensics hasn't been able to locate the silk scarf the ME said was used on the other children," Jim said.

Mullocks shook her head. "If you have doubt that the man in custody right now isn't our guy, then you're running out of time to bring back those girls alive and catch the real killer." She turned to Kerry. "So get your ass in gear."

"We'll get this done, Lieutenant," Jim said.

Kerry knew the lieutenant was trying to light a fire under her ass, but all Kerry could think about was losing her shield.

21

*R*eports. More reports. Data points. Reports. Kerry buried herself into everything they knew and didn't know about the case, focusing primarily on identifying the two other victims they found in the woods. And so far Kerry hadn't been able to find a match in the Missing Person database with any of the names from Dr. Weathers's patient files.

"Maybe he's working with someone?" Kerry asked, thinking out loud. Even before she spoke, she knew that it was ridiculous to say. Whoever was responsible for the crimes had a solo mentality, and they had already established it would be one individual. Kerry held up her hand, silencing Jim before he had a chance to rebuke her thought. "I know, I know. Don't bother."

"Where are we at with identifying the other bodies?" Jim asked.

"The patient files haven't been any help, but—" Kerry rocked forward in her chair and then opened up the few files she had narrowed down. "I've got two possible matches for the one-year girl and three possible matches for the boy." She flipped the screen around so Jim could view all of the profiles. "I've contacted the families, but no one has returned my calls just yet."

Jim studied the screen for a moment and then nodded, seeming to approve of the matches. "Keep reaching out to them."

Kerry watched Jim return to his work and then got up and walked over to his side of the desk. She had gotten to know him enough to realize that if she wanted to see what he was up to, she would have to go to him. It was a man thing.

"What are you looking at?" Kerry asked.

"The techs finished most of their reports on the house," Jim answered, still studying the papers. "They did find some unknown fibers, but the preliminary analysis didn't show any matches for the fibers we found for our current missing girls."

Kerry plucked the papers from Jim's hands. "Maybe we can get a match with the bodies at the morgue. Jen did say that she had some hair fibers she managed to pull off."

"Maybe," Jim said. "Maybe, maybe, maybe." He quickly stood and paced around their paired desks. "Too many maybes for my liking. Maybe the guy we have in the interrogation room is the kidnapper and killer? Maybe he's not? Maybe someone else is still out there? Maybe not? Maybe the girls are alive? Maybe not?" He stopped and kicked the side of the desk, the outburst garnering attention.

Kerry walked over to him and grabbed his arm, moving close enough to smell the coffee he'd just drunk on his breath. "Hey. We need to keep it together. Watching eyes, remember?"

Jim glanced around, noting the glares. "Right. Sorry."

Kerry let him go. "It's all right." She returned to the forensic reports on his desk and picked them back up. "So right now, all we have are the pictures in his office."

"And any fibers they find there won't be able to be used in court," Jim said. "The girls were there at least once a week."

"What about reaching back out to the assistant?" Kerry asked. "The one Dr. Weathers had before the old lady. She might be able to tell us something."

"I tried reaching out to her again, but haven't heard back," Jim replied.

It was the first time in their investigation together that Kerry had seen Jim at the point of exhaustion.

"It's been a long day," Kerry said.

"And it'll most likely be a long night." Jim rubbed his face. "We need to find a way to tie Weathers to the other kids. Until we identify them, I don't know if the DA will have enough evidence to convict. Too many holes are starting to appear. Too much doubt."

Kerry knew what she was about to say wasn't what Jim wanted to hear, but she spoke her mind. "Why don't we just book him now?"

"Because we don't know if he did it," Jim answered.

Kerry sat on Jim's desk. "Jim, you heard what Mullocks said. We need to charge the guy before this gets out of hand. If we pass this off to the DA now, it'll create such a media circus that we'll fade to the background. And I don't know about you, but I'd like to keep being a detective."

The moment Kerry saw Jim's reaction, she knew he was angry.

"You can't be serious," Jim said.

But a part of Kerry was. "We're good cops, and we've both been through shit to get where we are. Why not give ourselves a break? We found the photos in his office. He has no alibi. We've already connected him to at least one of the bodies we found, and the graveyard happened to be within five miles of his cabin which he visits every six months, which is the time gap between the kids being taken." She took a breath. "It has to be him."

Jim was quiet for a moment, and Kerry braced herself for a lecture, or a shouting contest, but for the first time since this case started she saw the cracks in his face. He suddenly looked older, exhausted.

"You know how many times that's crossed my mind?" Jim asked. "More than it should have." He bowed his head and then opened his hand, revealing his scarred palm. "But every time those thoughts creep into my head I can't help but remember that time when I was locked in that cage. And I see that boy's face."

"That wasn't your fault, Jim," Kerry said. "You were

a kid for Christ's sake. There was nothing you could have done."

Jim touched his palm. "There is always something to be done." He made a fist and then looked up at Kerry. "I don't blame you for wanting to throw it in. I can't imagine what it has been like for you here for the past fourteen years. Your father left you with a terrible burden. But I need to see this through. No matter the cost."

Of all the rumors that Kerry had heard about Jim, the one about his dedication to the job seemed to be the only one with any shred of truth to it.

"You're a good man, Jim," Kerry said.

Jim blushed, dismissing the comment, but Kerry could tell it meant something to him. She walked back over to her own desk and sat down.

"What are you doing?" Jim asked.

"We still need to identify those other kids, right?" Kerry asked, reaching for the phone, and then cast him a glance. "You don't have to see everything through to the end by yourself, Jim."

The calls still didn't yield any results, but Kerry continued to leave messages in hopes of a return call first thing in the morning. She tried not to glance at the clock, but after another hour she saw it was nearly midnight.

"Go home," Jim said.

"I told you I'm not letting you go through this alone," Kerry said. "That's not what partners do."

"You have a family," Jim said. "The only thing

waiting for me at home is a twin mattress with dirty sheets. I'll be fine. Go."

Kerry opened her mouth to object, but it transformed into a yawn. She was too tired to fight him on it. "All right." She stood, shutting down her station. "I had my desk phone forward me my calls should any of the parents get back to me. If I hear something, you'll be my first call."

"Sounds good," Jim said.

Kerry stepped toward the door, but only made it a few steps before she turned around. "You sure you'll be all right?"

"Yes," Jim said. "I'm fine."

Kerry walked away again and then paused once more, turning around. "You know, he's a trained manipulator."

Jim looked away from his computer screen. "Dr. Weathers?"

"Yeah," Kerry answered. "He's spent his whole life dedicated to the idea of understanding people's minds. That kind of knowledge can be leveraged into a powerful weapon, which he used on the most vulnerable of victims. He might even be good enough to pull one over on the great Jim North. So remember that as you're slowly torturing yourself by replaying the same conversation over and over again in your head." She tapped her left temple. "That's what he wants."

Jim folded his hands in his lap as he leaned back into his chair, wearing an expression of surprise. "I thought I was supposed to be the one who was mentoring you?"

Kerry gestured to herself. "Age before beauty, sweetheart."

Jim nodded, again that hint of a smile stretching across his face. "Thank you."

"You're welcome," Kerry said. "See you in the morning?"

"Yes," Jim answered. "We'll press him hard, give it our best shot, and then see what we can come up with. He's going to have a restless night inside there, and I want to use that to our advantage. He'll be weak, and we might get the confession we need."

Kerry nodded. "Sounds like a plan to me." She turned and headed for the door. "See ya."

"Good night," Jim said.

The parking lot was practically empty, but Kerry saw the reporters still hanging around out front. She made sure to avoid them as she left, resisting the urge to run them over on her way home.

The last mile of Kerry's drive home was the hardest. She was exhausted. Her eyelids remained half closed, and twice she caught herself drifting off the road, alerted by the heavy bumps from the indentations placed on the roadside to alert drowsy drivers such as herself.

Traffic was still surprisingly busy on her drive home, but when she pulled into her neighborhood, all was quiet and calm.

Kerry shut off the headlights before she pulled into

the drive. Both of her kids were shallow sleepers, awoken by even the slightest change in their environment. They had inherited that quality from her.

Brian could sleep like a log anywhere, anyplace. Kerry never understood how he could do that, but he always told her it was because he came from a big family. Too many siblings and not enough space and beds growing up, so he'd had to make do.

Parked in the driveway, Kerry shut off the engine, and the soft rumbling was replaced with the silence inside the car.

Kerry sat behind the wheel for a little while and found herself hesitant to go inside the house. She simply stared at the front door, the darkened windows, and the still quiet of the home, and she wondered if these were the kinds of cases that she would always work.

Throughout her career in law enforcement, Kerry had seen her fair share of bad. It was inevitable, and it came with the job. And up until today, she had always been able to process all of those bad images and criminal activities that she had seen on the job and separate them from everything she loved about coming home.

But each time she closed her eyes now, she saw the bodies they'd found in the woods. She saw those burned and charred remains on the cold steel of the examining table.

Kerry rested her forehead on the crest of the wheel. She knew she needed to take a page out of Jim's book and not allow herself to become so emotionally invested. But she had kids, and Jim didn't. He might be able to understand, but he couldn't experience the same thing that she felt. It wasn't possible to know the mind of a parent until you became one yourself.

Kerry sat in the darkened driveway for another ten minutes and then finally managed to step out and head toward the door. She entered quietly, shutting and locking the door behind her then disarming and resetting the alarm.

The house was neat and tidy. Brian always kept an orderly home, and she was glad, because organization wasn't as important to her as it was to him. She saw a note on the table and recognized her husband's hasty, scribbled handwriting that informed her dinner was covered and in the fridge whenever she wanted to eat.

Kerry smiled and set the note down. She wasn't hungry, but she knew she should eat. She preheated the oven and then made a detour to her kids' rooms.

Her son's door was still ajar. She entered like a shadow, the only sound she created coming from the cracks and groans of the door.

Kerry approached the bed carefully and stared down at her boy. She'd always loved watching her kids sleep when they were little. It was incredibly peaceful, and she particularly enjoyed watching them sleep after she had a bad day like today.

Raising children was a mixed bag of emotions. There were days when she never thought she could love anything more, and there were days when she thought she had made some terrible miscalculation of her abilities to raise a child.

The tantrums, the talking back, the screaming and crying, the disobedience, and the sheer frustration that came with raising children had caused her to question herself more than she'd ever thought possible. But all of those doubts melted away when she came into their rooms and watched them sleep.

The smallest moment of peace could trigger reflection for Kerry. She had always been like that, and she knew how lucky she was for it. Because life didn't hand out a large slice of peace daily. She had to take what she was given, and she was beyond grateful for her tiny sliver of happiness.

Kerry kissed his head and then left his room and walked down to her oldest. Unlike her son, Kerry's daughter was a bit more like her. She was messy and at times moody, and she rarely pulled back the curtain to show people who she really was.

Her daughter was a tangled mess of limbs and hair spread over a bare mattress, her blankets bunched up in a ball at the foot of her bed, and she was snoring.

Kerry repressed her smirk and calmly walked over and picked up the blankets and placed one of them over her daughter's body.

The girl twitched, and there was a brief lull in her snoring, but she didn't wake.

Kerry brushed her daughter's hair back, kissed the top of her head, and then walked back to the kitchen, where the oven had already preheated.

Dinner was steak, mashed potatoes, and green beans. While the meal heated, Kerry checked her phone to see if Jim had received any updates, but there was nothing.

Kerry knew Jim was a grown man, and he was well equipped to handle his own decision-making, but she still found herself worried about him. They might have been recently paired, but she thought that they had worked well so far, at least from what she could tell. But the way he obsessed about a case could backfire on him one day. And she wasn't sure if he was equipped to handle that disaster.

Kerry eventually pushed the thought aside as her stomach grumbled at the smell of the food heating up in the oven. She retrieved her dinner, devoured it faster than she should, and then sat back in her chair with her hands over her protruding belly as she stared at her empty plate.

She remained like that for a little while but finally forced herself up and out of the chair. She made her way to her own bedroom, where she found her husband fast asleep.

Almost too tired and full to even make it to the bed, Kerry only kicked off her shoes as she climbed into bed next to her husband.

She lay down, and her body sank like a lead weight into the mattress. She closed her eyes and then rolled over to Brian, whose back was to her. She rested her nose in the small curve in the nape of his neck and slipped one arm around his waist.

He reacted by squeezing her arm tight, and Kerry smiled. He was so warm that all she had to do was close her eyes, and she drifted off to sleep. She only hoped that whatever dreams came her way would be free of the horrors from her day. But as she squeezed her husband tighter, she wasn't sure if those wishes would come true.

---

22

*J*im didn't look at the clock. He didn't know what time it was, but he knew that it was late. Probably early-morning late. Aside from the skeleton crew that had been left behind to work the night shift, the precinct was practically deserted.

No new information had come his way since Kerry had gone home for the night, and even after Jim requested a second sweep of the house, cabin, and office, no silk scarves were found.

Jim's stomach grumbled, and he made his way over to the vending machine. He removed a crisp five-dollar bill from his wallet and inserted the money. The machine ate it up, and Jim took a step back to consider his options.

It was all junk food. All of it was bad for his health and would provide him with a very miserable night's sleep. But since his sleep was always shit, he hit the K7 button, and the vending machine pushed out a Snickers bar from its metal coils. It hit the bottom of the vending machine, and Jim reached inside to pick it up.

Half of the candy bar was gone by the time he returned to his desk, and he sat there and chewed the caramel and nougat, letting his mind sift through the jumbled mess that was this case.

Jim had worked a lot of cases during his career. The majority of them were straightforward, simple, and followed all of the normal guidelines of a missing-persons case. Most of the time, it was a father or mother or grandparent who snatched the kids, a loved one who believed they were doing the right thing by taking the kid out of a situation.

Sometimes they were right in making the moral choice, and sometimes they were wrong. But Jim did his best not to get tangled up in the morality of his work. There was too much gray area, too much room for interpretation.

It was one of the reasons he relied so heavily on the evidence of a case and why he worked so hard to collect so much of it and to do it quickly. But in this scenario, all of the evidence was conflicting.

Jim popped the rest of the Snickers bar into his mouth and tossed the wrapper into the waste bucket near his desk. He picked up a folder and set it in his lap.

Jim had been spending most of his time going through Dr. Weathers's old files, searching for anything they might have overlooked. And he was going through

Dr. Weathers's schedule when he noticed there was a recurring lunch every Friday with a Dr. Peppercorn.

Jim jotted down the name, and after a little digging discovered Dr. Peppercorn had been Maisie Simmons's therapist before working with Weathers.

Jim did a background check on Peppercorn, found he was clean, and then made a mental note to speak to him first thing in the morning. He entered the address in his phone and would swing by and talk to Peppercorn before they interviewed Weathers for the final time.

Jim then turned back to the letters between Emily and Amelia, along with Maisie Simmons's diary. He had already combed through all three, but he continued to double-check everything.

Jim stared at the letters long after the last bits of candy bar had been swallowed, and eventually, the words and letters blurred together on the page in blues and blacks, and all he could see were smears. His brain was toast.

Jim tossed the letters back into the folder and then placed it on the desk with the rest of his materials. "Maybe we just got the wrong therapist."

He stood, took a few more sips of water from his cup, and then headed for the interrogation rooms. Jim stopped in front of the monitors that recorded the insides of rooms, and he turned his gaze to the man in room three, who currently had his head down on the table.

Nothing about his interaction with the therapist

gave Jim any useful information as he tried to make sense of how the doctor was involved in the kidnapping. It was almost as if he had been framed. But Jim knew that until they had another suspect that fit the bill, this was still their best chance.

Jim headed for the door, making one last pit stop to the sergeant's desk before he left.

"Hey," Jim said, tapping the watch sergeant on the shoulder and interrupting his reading (more observing really) of a swimsuit model magazine. "My guy is in room three, and he's asleep. Make sure he wakes up about every thirty minutes. I want him nice and groggy for our conversation in the morning."

The desk sergeant, a man who had grown comfortable in his chair, flashed a grin as he turned his gaze back to the magazine. "For that dirtbag? My pleasure."

Jim nodded and then stepped out into the cool spring air.

The ride back to his house was slow, not because of traffic but because he couldn't stop thinking about the case. The roads might have been empty, but his mind was alive with several theories.

But the late hour had sapped his energy, and by the time he reached his house, he couldn't connect two thoughts to save his life.

Without even knowing it, Jim did the same thing Kerry had done when he pulled into the drive and shut off the engine. He rested his head on the crest of the wheel as he shut his eyes.

But unlike Kerry, Jim had no one waiting for him

on the other side of his front door. When he finally lifted his head off of the steering wheel and made the short walk inside, there would be no children to check on. No wife to climb into bed beside and hold onto.

Jim was alone.

Jim lifted his head and then rubbed his eyes, knowing that throwing himself a pity party wasn't going to change the facts. He just needed some sleep, and then he would be up first thing in the morning, and they would go hard on Weathers. Hopefully, they would have more evidence from forensics by then as well. But until then, all he could do now was wait. And hope.

Jim chuckled at the last bit. It had been a long time since he had asked for any kind of hope because he knew how quickly it could burn out.

Hope was fleeting and manipulative. It could alter your way of thinking, forcing you to chase down leads and ideas and theories that weren't helpful to the root of the problem. Most of all, hope was a distraction.

Jim rolled his head to the left and glanced out the window. The rest of the neighborhood was dead asleep. Not so much as even a car engine rumbling on the horizon. It seemed the whole world was asleep at that moment except for him.

When Jim had been a boy, he would often lie awake on nights like these, his mind swirling with thoughts and questions, nearly all of them centered around a single thought: How am I going to survive tomorrow?

It was a question that no child should have to ask

himself. But growing up in the foster-care system, spending years bouncing around from house to house with grown-ups taking care of him that couldn't even take care of themselves, had created doubt and mistrust of those in a position of authority.

But Jim found solace in the fact that he knew he wouldn't be a child forever. One day, he would grow into an adult, and he would be able to make his own choices and decide his own fate. He clung to the prospect of his future with all of his might on those nights when he was afraid and alone.

Jim had also vowed that when he was finally aged out of the system, he wouldn't forget the kids he saw fall to the wayside. He wouldn't forget the boy in the cage and the expression he had seen plastered across the boy's face, which begged for him to be put out of his misery.

No child should ever, under any circumstances, wish for death. But even so, Jim knew many, many childhoods were stolen and cast aside every day, all over the world.

Jim rubbed his eyes one more time then sighed and opened his car door. He climbed out of his sedan, his body and mind heavy. He swayed left and right and then staggered forward when he reached the door, nearly bumping his head against the frame, but he managed to insert his key in the lock and push the door open.

Normally, Jim would have turned on the lights when he entered his home, but the exhaustion of the day, coupled with the stress of the case, had stolen most of his faculties, and the only thing he was concerned with in that moment was getting to bed.

But he never made it.

Because waiting for him inside his own house was a cluster of masked men who ambushed him the moment he closed the door behind him.

The first blow came to the back of the head and knocked Jim forward, where he lay on the cool floor of his foyer, his belly scraping against the tile. His mind was swimming with questions and confusion, and he didn't understand what was happening to him. He frowned, glancing up, his vision blurred.

But in the fuzzy darkness, which was growing even darker, Jim saw silhouettes hover above him, and one of them kicked his spine. Jim bucked from the pain, and only when it subsided was he kicked again, this time in the stomach.

Jim gasped for breath, the wind knocked out of him, a din filling his ears. The silhouettes spoke, but the voices were muffled. But when they were finished speaking, they brought down another rain of fists over his body, each one triggering a moan or groan.

More than once, Jim tried to pick himself up, and each time he was shoved back down onto his back. It was all he could do but to curl himself into a ball and try to protect his face, though the damage had already been done.

Jim wasn't sure when the beating stopped, because even when the fists stopped raining down over him, the pulse beating through his body made each of the contact points where he had been struck feel like he was being hit again.

Unsure if his attackers were gone, Jim slowly lowered his arm and saw five masked men circled around him.

One of them pointed a finger down at Jim, his lips surprisingly pink in the black slit of the ski mask, and spoke. "You have two options, North. You either do the honorable thing and quit the force, or you can expect more visits just like this one. And don't bother going to the chief about this one, because no matter what you do and no matter what you say, you are no longer one of us. You're a rat, and we'll kill you if we have to."

Jim flinched at the last word and then felt something warm smack him in the face as the man spit on him.

The final act of disgust triggered the rest of the group to depart, each of them leaving behind their own little snickering phrases and warnings. Jim couldn't hear all of them, but he understood the tone, and he understood the message that had been sent.

Cops don't talk to IA. Cops don't turn in other cops. Partners don't rat out partners.

Jim lay there on the cold tile of the foyer long after the goons had left, and he wondered what would be waiting for him on the other side if he just let himself die. What kind of life would be waiting for a man who had done nothing but be alone his entire life? Would his actions in this world mirror what came next? Was there anything at all?

Jim didn't know the answers, but he knew he didn't want to find out yet. He waited until he gathered enough strength to sit up. He took another break and remained where he was until he could move to his feet.

The moment Jim was up on two feet, he swayed left and collapsed back to the tile and had to start the process all over again. But he finally did manage to stand again, and he made his way to the hallway bathroom.

Jim flicked on the light and then held onto the sink with both hands as he examined himself in the mirror. It wasn't too bad aside from the blood, but he knew the red marks on his face would swell up by morning and make him look even worse.

Jim removed his bloodstained shirt and cast it aside, examining the similar bumps and bruises along his backside and abdomen. The men had pulled no punches when they were beating him down. But he took a few deep breaths and slowly and carefully rotated his trunk. He was sore, but there were no immediate pinches and pains associated with broken ribs.

Jim leaned forward and took a closer look at his pupils, which weren't dilated. He wasn't queasy or nauseous, so he ruled out a concussion. All in all, the beating had been painful and might leave a few scars but no real permanent damage.

But what this would bring, and what Jim had been

trying to avoid this entire time, was attention. In his line of work, some form of attention would always come his way, but he had always been able to deflect it toward the case.

None of this was about the case, though. This was the vindictive response of people who believed rumors over truth. And as he stared at his bruised and bloodied reflection, Jim wondered how much longer he would be able to wait before the truth had its day.

23

The alarm blared loud and early. Kerry reached her left arm across the bed and smacked the snooze button. She had been in a very deep sleep, and the sudden departure from her rest had made her feel foggy and slow. She lay in bed, tangled in the sheets, and glanced down at her body and saw she was still in the same clothes as the night before.

"Gross." Kerry flung the sheets off of her, her mind slowly catching up to the movement of her body. She sat on the edge of the bed for a few moments, taking stock of the morning. She needed coffee.

Kerry nodded and then stood, walking carefully down the stairs as she made her way toward the kitchen. She smelled breakfast cooking before she saw her husband at the frying pan, bacon sizzling in grease. "Morning."

"Hey." Brian offered a sleepy smile, his scruff peppered with black and white along his face. He gestured to the pan. "I thought you might like some breakfast before you go charging headfirst into battle." He pumped his hand into a fist and then scowled, but the gesture was lackluster because of the yawn that followed.

Still, Kerry couldn't suppress her chuckle and walked over to her husband and gave him a tender kiss on the lips. "You are the best, most caring person I've ever met in my entire life. I don't deserve you."

Brian playfully waved it off. "Stop it. I mean, it's true. But stop it."

Kerry poured herself some coffee from the carafe and took a seat at the kitchen table, trying to get into the necessary headspace she needed for the interrogation, but she couldn't break through the fog.

Brian had his back to the table and to Kerry, but when he turned around to look at her, he raised an eyebrow. "Got in pretty late last night."

"Yeah," Kerry answered in mid-yawn and then cupped both of her palms around the mug of warm coffee. "We pulled in a suspect."

Brian again turned, raising both eyebrows this time. "Really."

Kerry nodded. "Jim and I were pressing him pretty hard, but the man just wouldn't break. I mean, the evidence we found against him… it's pretty damning."

Brian remained half turned to Kerry, still keeping an eye on the bacon. "What makes you think he's guilty?"

Kerry and Brian had come to a mutual understanding about Kerry's job. If she didn't want to talk about it or couldn't talk about it, she would say so, but until she raised that flag, Brian was going to keep asking questions, and for the moment, she was okay with that.

"We found some pictures," Kerry said, trying to bring up the photographs without actually picturing them in her head. "They were... graphic."

Brian transferred the bacon from the pan onto a plate, adding it to the eggs and toast that were already made, then brought it over and placed it in front of Kerry. "How bad?" Brian took a seat next to his wife, hands clasped together, his shoulders bunched up nervously as he braced himself for the unwanted answer.

"Worse than you can imagine." Kerry picked up the fork on her plate and picked at the food, but she didn't have much success at eating anything, and she just pushed the food around. It was rare that she wasn't hungry in the morning, and Brian noticed.

"Is it just the case that's bothering you?" Brian asked. "Or is it something else?"

Kerry snickered and shook her head. "I don't think you want to open Pandora's box."

Brian reached for her left hand and cupped it in both of his own. "I'll open it if I must." He leaned closer. "That's our job, you know. To take care of each other." He frowned and then looked away. "At least I think that's what our vows said."

A genuine smile broke over Kerry's face, and she

squeezed his hand back. "I don't know how I got so lucky with you."

"I always thought I was the lucky one," Brian replied.

Kerry took a deep breath and then sighed. "It's Jim. My new partner. And even though he's younger than me, he's smart, and driven, and has loads of experience. He's a good cop."

Brian raised an eyebrow. "But?"

"But he comes with baggage," Kerry answered. "And he's in a different frame of mind than I am. He's twenty-five, single, no kids, and all about the job. If I was ten years younger it might be a different story, but I'm not sure I can keep up with him. It might be better for me in the long term if I just... worked with someone my own speed."

"First of all, you're not that old," Brian said. "Second, what's this baggage he's coming with?"

Kerry dropped her voice an octave, not even realizing she had done so, as if someone might hear her talking about it at their own dinner table. "He turned his last partner over to IA, and then the partner he turned over said Jim was involved. It's a bit of a mess." She poked at her eggs, and she finally shoveled a bite into her mouth. "I mean, everybody has the potential to be paired with someone that goes dirty. Sad to say, the odds are higher than they should be." She chewed on the eggs, the first bite triggering her appetite, and she started to go full throttle. "But this guy has a reputation for not playing nice with others. He's had more partner transfers than any other detective in the past three years." Kerry shoveled another bite into her mouth. "And I know with my father's past and how people treated me it's hypocritical for me to judge just based off of rumors, but I'm not going to get another shot at this." She pointed to the shield on her belt. "I worked too hard for it to be taken away from me."

Brian took a moment to process her thoughts and then crossed his arms, setting his brows in a flat line. He looked the way he did whenever he was about to discipline their kids. "Do you think that I'm a good person?"

Kerry was taken aback. Unsure of how to react, she could only laugh as she waited for further explanation, but Brian only stared at her, waiting.

"Yes," Kerry said. "You're the best person I know."

"Do you remember how I told you when I was in college I was the editor for Stanford's student newspaper?"

Kerry's cheeks were stuffed with breakfast now as she rolled her eyes. "You wrote for a scientific journal. You once told me that you wrote a ten-page piece on the bacteria in your stomach."

Brian laughed. "It was really interesting! Do you know how much the bacteria in your gut affects your overall diet—I'm getting off track. My point is that when I was working on an article, I came across some professors who were in my own degree program, people who I respected and looked up to... doing some not-so-professional things."

Kerry frowned. "You never told me any of this."

"Well, it hasn't been very pertinent until now," Brian said. "But I can tell you that I was in a very precarious position, because the people I needed to report were directly linked to my personal and professional success. If they went away, then the funding for my thesis project might be in jeopardy."

Kerry set the fork down, taking a break between bites. She had an inkling of where this was going, but she wasn't sure where he would finally land. After all, Kerry already knew that Brian had never lost his funding when he was at Stanford. "And?"

"And I told the dean." Brian tapped his fingers on the table as he did so. "I didn't hesitate, because I knew it was the right thing to do."

Kerry stuttered, still not completely following what her husband was trying to tell her. "So, the professors who were doing these 'not so good things' were reprimanded."

"Nope," Brian answered, shaking his head. "It was immediately swept under the rug, and then they kicked me off of the paper."

Kerry shook her head in disbelief. "How could they do that?"

Brian shrugged. "I don't know. Because after I got kicked off the paper, I didn't push my luck." He bowed his head, his cheeks reddening with embarrassment, which eventually spread to his ears. "I just focused on my work in the lab and kept quiet. But it always ate at me, just gnawed away at me until I graduated. Because I felt like a coward."

"But you told the dean," Kerry said.

"And when the dean didn't do anything, and after I was kicked off of the journal, what did I do?" Brian leaned back in his chair and then placed two fingers on the table, mimicking legs. "I just ran to the lab and prayed that they didn't take anything else away from me."

Kerry stared at her husband and then stared down at her now empty plate. She considered what her husband was trying to tell her and then nodded. "So the bad guys got away with it."

"Yup," Brian said. "And granted, what I found wasn't anything life-threatening or really dangerous. My professors were taking kickbacks from businesses to do speeches based on university-funded research that hadn't been completely finished yet. I think the reason the dean never reported it was because he was getting some of those kickbacks too."

Brian leaned forward again and then placed his hand on Kerry's arm. His touch was warm and gentle, and it brought her back from the ledge of stress that currently plagued her.

"The point I'm trying to make is that I still wish I would have had the courage to keep pushing the issue," Brian said. "The world has never been kind to whistle-blowers or people who upset the status quo. But the world does need those people. And those people need help too."

Kerry nodded, looking at him with a smile. "You're a smart man."

Brian smirked. "I have my moments." He held her hand and then squeezed. "Just get to know him a little more." Brian kissed her cheek and grabbed her empty plate as he returned to the sink. "You should get going before the kids wake up and you get sucked into Sunday-morning madness."

Kerry smiled, her gaze lingering on her husband. Before she had met him, she hadn't had much luck in love. She'd dated a lot, had a few flings, but nothing stuck. And then one day, grabbing coffee after an all-night stint on the job, she had bumped into a man after turning around and picking up her order, spilling coffee all down the front side of her shirt and his.

Kerry had always been clumsy, and even though it was her fault, the long night coupled with the reaming she'd received from her superior for misfiling some evidence had made her so angry she started screaming at him.

And even though she was in the wrong, he was the first to apologize and had even offered to buy her a new coffee and a T-shirt to go with it.

But it came on the condition of going on a date with him.

Kerry thought it was odd for a man to ask her out on a date after just being completely berated by her. But she took a chance, and it had ended up being the best decision of her entire life. She stood and walked behind her husband, put her arms around him, and squeezed.

"Thank you," Kerry said.

Brian reciprocated the hug. "You're welcome."

Kerry kissed him one more time before she headed out the door and greeted the rising morning sun with renewed confidence. She climbed into her car and started the engine. But just before she managed to put it into reverse, her phone buzzed, and Kerry answered. It was Jim.

"Hey, I'm just leaving the house now," Kerry said. "Are you already at the precinct?" She checked the time. "We've still got a few hours before we have to charge him."

Silence lingered, and Kerry checked the phone to make sure they hadn't been disconnected.

"Jim? Are you still there?"

"Hey," Jim answered. "Yeah."

Kerry frowned. He sounded weak, tired. "Did you not go home last night?"

"I went home," Jim said. "But it didn't really help me feel better."

"I know what you mean," Kerry said.

"Yeah, listen, I have another lead," Jim replied.

Kerry perked up. "Another suspect?"

"Not sure yet," Jim answered. "But it's something I want both of us to check out. I'll text you the address. It shouldn't take us very long."

"Sounds good," Kerry said. "Anything I should know beforehand?"

Again a silence fell between the two of them, and Kerry wondered if the call had become disconnected. But this time it was Jim who finally spoke up first.

"Just come with an open mind," Jim said. "I'll see you in a little bit."

The call ended before Kerry could say goodbye, and Kerry paused before she left the house. She thought of her conversation with Brian and knew that she would need to make a decision about what to do with Jim soon, before it was too late.

24

*J*im was already at the address he had given Kerry during the call. He had been there after a long, slow, agonizing night of piecing himself back together.

The morning light had revealed a beaten and bruised man, and what short time had passed since his attack had only worsened the pain throughout his body.

The encounter the previous night had been meant to send him a message, not to kill him. The other cops were hoping that Jim would be too embarrassed to show up to work. But they didn't know him very well.

All Jim had ever concerned himself with the moment he put on the badge was doing the right thing. The right thing was rarely easy, and it often came with unexpected consequences, but Jim clung to that single idea that if enough people did enough good things, then slowly but surely, the world would get better.

That was Jim's endgame. But change wasn't without consequences.

Jim caught his reflection in the rearview mirror and grimaced. He wished he had been more aware during the beating so he would have been able to gather more information about his attackers, but the men had come after him like a Blitzkrieg.

Jim had replayed the scenario over and over in his head throughout the rest of the morning, but he still couldn't identify his attackers. But he knew who might.

Kerry's car pulled up next to the house, and Jim checked himself in the mirror one last time before he got out of the vehicle.

"Hey," Kerry said, stepping out of her car as Jim crossed the street toward her. "So who are we looking at?"

Jim kept his face down, trying to conceal the extent of the damage, but his efforts to conceal the wounds didn't last very long. "I found the other therapist who—"

"Jesus Christ, what the hell happened to your face?" Kerry slammed her door shut. She lifted Jim's chin so she could get a better look at the damage his visitors had caused the night before.

Jim moved his chin out of her grip and then scowled, feeling like a child who didn't want to tell his mother who had beaten him up on the playground. "It's nothing."

"Bullshit 'it's nothing,'" Kerry said. "What the hell happened last night after I left?"

Jim had wanted to tell her, and he had already resigned himself to that truth before he called her up. But now that he was standing in front of her in the middle of the day, his desire to be forthright suddenly disappeared.

"Jim," Kerry said. "Tell me what's going on."

Jim pursed his lips. He had always struggled to speak up on his own behalf, a habit he'd developed when he was in the foster-care system. Jim learned quickly that sometimes keeping his mouth shut was the easiest way to avoid being put in a situation that was even worse than the one before it. A lot of kids felt that way in the system. You just learned to deal with it. Grind through it. Find a way to cope.

Most of the time, kids didn't cope with their horrible situations in healthy ways. Some fell into drugs and alcohol. Others grew violent and angry. Some shut down completely and just accepted their fate. But Jim had his own way.

Jim had learned quickly that even though he was a child, he had a voice. And he was careful only to use that voice when he was completely sure and confident that he could trust someone. Because trust was the most important trait to him. Without it, there could be nothing else.

But Jim still wasn't sure if he could trust Kerry.

"What did you think of me?" Jim asked.

Kerry frowned. "What? Jim, this isn't the time or the place. Are you hurt? Do we need to take you to the hospital?"

Jim waved her hands away from him. "Just listen to me for a minute, all right? Answer the question. What was your first reaction when you saw me and realized that I was the person who was going to be your partner?"

He studied Kerry's facial expressions closely. He remembered the way she had looked at him when they first made eye contact. He knew she'd looked disappointed, but he wanted to hear her say it out loud. He genuinely wanted to know what she thought.

"Jim, this isn't the time to talk about that kind of stuff," Kerry said. "You're hurt, you're tired—"

"Oh, you think this is bad?" Jim asked, pointing to his face. "This is nothing compared to the beating I took when I was ten at the hands of my foster father. The man had a wicked right hook. But I thought it was better for him to beat me instead of the other four kids he had stuffed in a room in his two-bedroom apartment, which was falling apart. I'm no stranger to getting beaten, Kerry. So answer my question. What did you think when you found out I was your partner?" Jim clenched his hands into fists, his nails digging into his palms because he was squeezing so hard.

Kerry opened her mouth to speak more than once, but each time Jim believed she would give him an answer, she stuttered and pressed her lips together, sealing the answers in.

Jim laughed, the tone desperate and angry. "Okay, Kerry. All right. You don't want to tell me? Fine. I'm a pretty good detective. Let me paint the picture for you.

The moment you saw me, the first question you asked yourself was, 'What's he going to rat on me about?'" He raised his eyebrows. "Tell me I'm wrong."

Kerry held Jim's gaze. "I didn't know you. Not the real you." She studied him for a moment and then shut her eyes, shaking her head. "How many people did this to you?"

Jim gently touched his forehead. "I don't know. Five or six guys. They all wore ski masks. And it was dark. They broke into my house. I should have seen this coming."

"It's not your fault, Jim," Kerry said.

"Yeah, well it's someone's fault," Jim said, growing bitter. "Everybody always thinks that I'm some sort of career killer!" He leaned closer to Kerry, and he felt all of the rage that he had been holding back start to build up inside of him, reaching a tipping point he had always done his best to avoid reaching. But now that he was so close, he couldn't help but try and peek over the edge. "No one ever stops to think that maybe, just maybe, I was right!"

Jim spun around, his complexion flushed and his head pounding from the adrenaline and the anger and the beating. He shut his eyes and gently massaged his temples as he kept his back to Kerry.

"You're right," Kerry said. "That's exactly what I thought when I first saw you. But you have no idea how long it took for me to earn my badge."

Jim turned and saw Kerry's own complexion had flushed red.

Kerry pointed at the badge on her belt, her eyes reddening. "I worked my ass off to get this badge." She wiped the snot from her upper lip. "So don't even talk to me about crooked cops, all right? You have no right to tell me anything about that shit, do you hear me?" She waited and then lunged forward again. "I said do you fucking hear me?"

"Yeah," Jim said. "I hear you."

Kerry walked over to Jim's car and leaned her back against the warm metal. The pair remained quiet for a little while longer, the sun rising higher in the sky and the neighborhood slowly waking from its sleepy Sunday-morning slumber.

"I was wrong about you," Kerry said, breaking the silence. "Everyone is wrong about you. You're a good cop. The best, really."

Jim wiped a tear from his eye before it fell, hoping Kerry didn't notice. "It doesn't matter now." He glanced to the house they had come to see. "I found this guy's address looking through some of Weathers's old contacts. Of all the therapists that he keeps in contact, he talks to this guy the most. Turns out Maisie Simmons had a therapist before Dr. Weathers."

"You think he might know something?" Kerry asked.

"I hope so."

erry studied the inside of Dr. Peppercorn's house. It was modestly decorated and possessed a minimalistic style. It was very masculine though, and Kerry knew the moment she walked in that this was a house that had gone without a woman's touch.

Dr. Peppercorn sat in a forest-green armchair that had matching green buttons running along the armrests and the top part of the back. He crossed his legs, wearing a bathrobe, and sipped coffee from a mug. Aside from the white hair and wrinkles, he looked younger than his sixty-seven years.

Kerry and Jim shared a love seat positioned across from the therapist. Everything in the house was clean but well-worn and dated. Judging from the style of the furniture and the house itself, Kerry suspected that the doctor had bought everything new around the time when disco had peaked on America's radio charts.

"We appreciate the time, Dr. Peppercorn," Jim said.

"Of course." Dr. Peppercorn maintained a friendly disposition, though his smile was still tired from the early morning. He pointed to Jim's face, concerned. "Are you all right?"

"I'm fine," Jim answered. "I assume you know why we're here?"

Peppercorn nodded. "I've been watching the news, and I think what's happening is just terrible."

Kerry jotted down her initial reactions about the doctor. He was confident but not arrogant. The tidy house signaled an organized mind, and the fresh scent of lemon and cleaner suggested that he regularly cleaned the house.

"Do you live alone, Doctor?" Kerry asked, hitching onto a thought she'd had.

"Yes," Dr. Peppercorn answered. "I do have some goldfish, but they don't take up much space." He laughed on cue as if this was a joke he told to people who asked him the question, which they probably did frequently. Kerry didn't see him wearing a wedding band.

"What can you tell us about Maisie Simmons?" Jim asked.

"I looked up her file when you called me," Dr. Peppercorn answered. "Just to refresh the memory, and it all came back quick enough." He chuckled again and then sipped from the mug once more before he continued. "She had been through a rough childhood. Product of the foster system, unfortunately, which is very overtaxed. She had been through several abusive homes but finally managed to be in a safe place with the foster parents who brought her to me."

"What can you tell us about her past?" Kerry asked.

"The abuse Maisie suffered at the hands of her previous foster parents had been both physical and emotional," Peppercorn answered, keeping the rim of his mug close to his lips. "No sexual abuse, so she was lucky on that front, but unlucky in about every other department. She had suffered a dozen skeletal fractures by the time she was nine, and the kinds of things she told me her foster parents used to tell her…" He shook his head and stared into the blackness of his coffee. "A child shouldn't have to hear those things."

"And why did you stop treating her?" Kerry asked.

"I had to change the type of insurances I accepted for my practice, and the Simmons were no longer covered under my new policy," Dr. Peppercorn replied. "They asked me for a few recommendations based on who their insurance would pay for, and I circled some names for them."

"And Doctor Weathers was one of those names," Jim said.

"Yes."

"What can you tell us about him?"

Dr. Peppercorn smiled but hid it quickly. "Gary is a good man. And an even better therapist. He has a way of getting a child to open up that I've never seen before. He's gotten so good that he often teaches seminars on the subject at colleges and retreats. It hasn't hurt his bank account either."

Jim shuffled through some of his papers and then removed a single sheet. "What kind of trouble has he gotten into in regard to working with his patients?"

Dr. Peppercorn frowned. "Gary's never been in any kind of trouble before."

"We found a complaint filed against him ten years prior about a case of abusive touching—"

"Ah, yes." Dr. Peppercorn nodded, still sporting his grimace. "I remember that. It nearly sank Gary's entire career. The parents were found to be fraudulent. Apparently, they had run that kind of scam before in a few other states and had finally worked their way out west. They threatened to file the charges unless the doctor paid them. Supposedly, until Gary, the parents had been very successful in getting therapists to fork over the dough. But Gary didn't stand for it. He called their bluff, and the parents were arrested."

"And you don't believe Dr. Weathers is capable of having an inappropriate relationship with a child?" Jim asked.

"No," Peppercorn answered. "Absolutely not."

"What do you remember around the time Maisie went missing?" Kerry asked.

Dr. Peppercorn's face sagged at the mention of the abduction. "I'm afraid not much more than what I saw on the news. Maisie was Gary's patient by that time."

"What about when Maisie was your patient," Jim asked. "Did you note any strange behavior? Did she mention any adults she had been close with? Any new friends she had made?"

Dr. Peppercorn shook his head. "Most of our conversations revolved around the abusive nature of her previous homes. But if you need the names of those individuals, I can provide you copies of her file."

"What about during her therapy sessions?" Jim asked. "Was she overly happy? Did she seem to be looking forward to something?"

Dr. Peppercorn paused as he thought the question over and finally nodded when he came to his conclusion. "Actually, yes." He leaned forward and set the coffee down. "I even notated it in the file, but I didn't mention it because I thought it was because we were making strides in our sessions together."

Both Kerry and Jim eagerly leaned forward.

Peppercorn shut his eyes and thought hard. "She mentioned something to me right before she left. She said…" He pressed his lips together, forming a thin, pink line, and then opened his eyes and leaned back into his chair. "I'm sorry. I don't remember."

"Did you happen to scribble it down in your notes?" Jim asked.

Peppercorn shook his head. "I'm sorry, Detectives. I wish I could have been more helpful."

Jim forced a smile, which caused his face to ache. "We appreciate the time."

But while Jim stood up to leave, Kerry remained sitting. "Can you tell us more about your relationship with Dr. Weathers?"

Jim paused and glanced back at her, intrigued. He then returned to his seat and listened to Peppercorn's response.

"Gary and I had known each other for many years," Peppercorn replied, smiling fondly at the mention of his friend and colleague. "Like I mentioned to you before, he was very talented. He was the brightest student in our class."

"The two of you went to college together?" Kerry asked.

Peppercorn nodded. "Even roomed together for our senior year. Fun times. Though I'm glad we didn't have all of the social media cameras back then like we do today." He winked at Jim, who nodded politely at the attempt at male camaraderie.

"And aside from that allegation ten years ago, you never witnessed Gary do anything inappropriate? Cross the line? Lead into any moral gray area?" Kerry tilted her head side to side, trying to measure Peppercorn's reactions.

"No," Peppercorn answered. "Not once. His dedication and care for his patients and to his craft is unparalleled by any of his peers, me included."

Peppercorn paused for a moment, almost as if he wanted to add something at the end, but then thought better of it. But Kerry noticed, picking up on the missed cue.

"What is it, Dr. Peppercorn?" Kerry asked.

"Nothing," Peppercorn answered, trying to dismiss the idea he was holding back, but this time Jim noticed it as well.

"Doctor, if there is something you want to tell us, then now is the time," Jim said.

Peppercorn squirmed uncomfortably in his chair. Finally, he calmed himself and then cleared his throat. "Gary had a bit of a reputation as a ladies' man. Something he never really outgrew."

"What do you mean by ladies' man, Doctor?" Kerry asked, wanting Peppercorn's interpretation of the phrase before she jumped to conclusions.

"Oh, you know, dating around," Peppercorn answered, being dismissive of his colleague's promiscuity. "But as he got older, his girlfriends stayed the same age, and it started to raise some eyebrows."

"Was he ever with anyone that was underage?" Kerry asked.

"Oh, God no!" Peppercorn was aghast. "Nothing like that. He never went below twenty-one, but..." He fiddled with his fingers, keeping his eyes on his lap as he spoke. "He had a tendency to hire attractive young women as his secretary, and those professional relationships often evolved into more personal ones." He continued picking at his fingers but looked up to Kerry and Jim.

"Did Dr. Weathers get himself into any kind of trouble with these office romances?" Kerry asked.

"Once—well, almost," Peppercorn answered. "He managed to calm things down. I only bring it up because, well, it rattled him a little bit."

Kerry jotted the information down. It wasn't much,

but it was a new avenue they could pursue during their final interrogation. But Dr. Weathers's affinity for beautiful adult women who happened to be in their twenties was a stark counterpoint to the serial pedophile predator they were looking to catch.

Kerry and Jim waited for more, but when Peppercorn didn't offer up any more details, they thanked the doctor for his time once more, and Peppercorn walked them to the door.

"Listen, aside from his libido, Gary is a fine man," Peppercorn said. "Though I have to say that I haven't forgiven him since he took Lindsey."

"Did she ever mention anything to you about Dr. Weathers's behavior?" Jim asked.

Peppercorn laughed, catching both Jim and Kerry's attention. "He, Detective. Not she."

Kerry and Jim both frowned, repeating the same question at the same time. "What?"

Peppercorn glanced between the pair of puzzled detectives on his porch and then frowned. "Lindsey is a man. He used to be my secretary, but after the scare Gary had with the last woman he hired, I referred him over to Gary."

"Did Lindsey happen to be your secretary when Maisie Williams was still your patient?" Jim asked.

"Um, yes, I believe he was," Dr. Peppercorn answered.

Kerry and Jim stared at one another for a moment and then made a beeline for the car, talking amongst themselves.

"Do you still have Lindsey's home address?" Kerry asked.

"And phone number," Jim answered.

"We'll get a team over to his house and a judge to approve the warrant." Jim stopped at his car and checked the time on his phone. "Just leave your car here, and we'll be back for it." He reached into his pocket and tossed her the keys. "I'll be able to work faster if I don't have to drive."

Kerry snatched the keys out of the air and quickly got into the car. She started the engine and pulled on her seat belt as Jim sat down beside her.

"I never considered the secretary could have been a man," Jim said, staring at his phone. "We only corresponded over email."

"It was the way he probably wanted it," Kerry said then flipped the sirens and lights as she sped forward. "Put the address into the GPS."

Jim inputted the information into the computer and then struck the dashboard with his palm. "I can't believe I didn't look at him more closely."

"It's fine," Kerry said. "And we still might be able to catch him before he hurts the girls."

26

The small neighborhood where Lindsey lived was old. The street was nothing but rows of short, run-down apartment buildings that had been originally constructed as affordable housing units in the late seventies.

But the funds to maintain the homes had long since dried up, and the landlords who'd bought the buildings from the U.S. government had done little to maintain or update any of the structures. They simply milked the units for all that they were worth, and since most of the buildings didn't have any debts, the people who owned them still made a nice profit even after taxes, if they paid any at all.

And while the government got its money back and the landlords were making profits, the tenants of the buildings received the short end of the stick, and it created the perfect breeding ground for crime and drugs to proliferate.

But what made the situation even more tragic was the children, kids whose only crime was being born into poverty, like the three Kerry saw unsupervised in the front yard.

None of them could have been older than three, and the youngest couldn't even walk. All of them wore diapers but nothing else. No shoes, pants, or shirts. They were exposed to the elements, one of them crying as he sat in the dirt, while the other two kids simply looked on, unsure of what to do.

Kerry had seen plenty of places like these when she was working the streets. It was heartbreaking.

"Hey," Jim said, calling out to her from the front porch steps. "You coming?"

Kerry turned away from the dilapidated structures and nodded to her partner. "Yeah." But just before she entered the building, she stole one last glance at the children in the front yard and then called back to one of the uniforms on the street. "Hey! Someone find those kids' parents!"

One of the uniforms raised his hand and jogged over to the building as Kerry followed Jim inside the complex.

"We pulled the address off of this place from the files on Weathers's computer," Jim said as they ascended the staircase, his voice muffled by the loud television, music, and screaming that penetrated the paper-thin walls.

"You really think our guy lives in a place like this?" Kerry asked.

"It could be a decoy," Jim answered. "Our guy is smart."

Kerry huffed up the stairs, the bulky Kevlar she wore making it difficult to breathe and move. She normally didn't wear a vest on the job, but these were abnormal circumstances.

Jim and Kerry slowed when they reached the fifth floor, and they drew their weapons, silently clearing the hallway of any bystanders, waving everyone to head back into their own apartments, where they would be safe from any potential gunfire. Most of the people already had their bias against the police, and they cleared out quickly the moment they saw the badges.

With the hallway empty, Jim took the lead on the approach to the front door. He moved toward the handle, and Kerry took second position. It had been a long time since she had drawn her weapon on duty and even longer since she had fired it on the job. The best-case scenario in this situation was to have their suspect on the other side with the two girls and to rescue everyone without gunfire.

Jim locked eyes with Kerry and then nodded. He counted down, and on zero, he kicked the door down, rocketing inside and clearing his corner while Kerry followed and made sure that his backside was in the clear.

"Seattle Police Department!" Jim screamed his arrival as the pair settled into the living room.

But as Kerry cleared her section without incident,

she examined the entirety of her surroundings. "It's empty." She lowered her gun slightly, but Jim kept his guard up.

Jim glanced around the empty room, and then he quickly moved into the adjacent bedroom, which was also empty.

Kerry holstered the weapon as Jim stepped back out into the dusty living room and kitchen area. "Place looks like it's been empty for a long time." Kerry walked carefully over the floorboards as if it was cursed ground. "Do you think he ever lived here?" She was walking toward the window when she turned around after Jim didn't answer her. "Jim?"

Jim stood in the middle of the apartment, gun still in his hand, his head bowed. His posture was one of defeat. "He never lived here."

Kerry stepped toward her partner, but she didn't get too close. Something about the way Jim looked at that moment frightened her. "How do you know?"

Jim lifted his head and then gestured to the surrounding apartment. "It might as well be a PO box." He pointed to the floor with this gun. "There's no marks on the ground from furniture being moved." He walked over to the kitchen and turned on the faucet. The pipes groaned, but no water ejected from the tap. "Water shut off. No power. It takes at least two months before utilities shut off after no payments. It's all a front." He finally holstered the weapon and then headed out the door.

Kerry followed him, the pair catching a few more

stares through cracked front doors as they returned downstairs. "We'll find him. At least now we know who we're looking for."

Jim stopped halfway down the stairs and then spun around. "And what good will that do? We're well past the twenty-four-hour mark, and right now, we have the wrong man in custody." He turned back around and restarted his trek down the stairs.

Kerry followed. "Jim, we're going to catch this guy—"

"It's not just about catching the perp!" Jim stopped and aggressively spun around, his face twisted in a snarl. "It's about the girls!"

Kerry raised her hands, surprised by the sudden turn by her partner. "I know." She joined him on his step. "And we'll get them back."

Jim's cheeks were still flushed, but he realized he was acting rash and calmed down. He averted his gaze, embarrassed by the sudden outburst. "I'm sorry."

Kerry walked down a few more steps and then turned back up to look at Jim when she realized he was still standing there. "C'mon. You said it yourself; we're running out of time. Let's go."

Once outside, Kerry glanced over to the neighboring building where the kids had been playing in the front yard and saw none of them were outside anymore. She found the officer who had gone over and requested an update.

The officer was young, maybe not even old enough to drink, and the creases on his uniform were as fresh as the dew on his face. "A woman came and collected the kids after I walked over. She didn't say anything to me."

Kerry looked to the building and the dirt yard where the kids had been playing. "Do a follow-up with child services."

The young cop nodded but then winced. "You know, it's not likely that anyone will come back out to check on the kids. DCF is always swamped with these types of calls."

"File the report anyway," Kerry said. "At least we gave it a try."

Before Kerry rejoined Jim by their car, she took a quick picture of the building and then jotted down the address, making a note in her calendar to check on the family the next day.

Jim was on the phone when she approached, and while he had his head down, listening to the person on the other end, the rest of his body language had changed. Kerry was glad he had managed to pull himself out of his pity party.

Kerry waited on the other side, resting her arms on the roof of the car as Jim finished his call.

"Okay, thanks," Jim said and hung up.

"What'd you find?" Kerry asked.

"APB has been put out, but one of the uniforms back at the station managed to pull some old files on Lindsey," Jim answered. "Apparently, his father had done some time for possession of child pornography."

Kerry slapped the hood of the car. "Son of a bitch."

Kerry knew, as did Jim, that most pedophiles were abused when they were little kids too. "Do we have a location on the parents?"

"Dad was killed a few years back, but the team found an address for the mother," Jim answered.

Kerry waited for something more, sensing Jim was holding something back. "What?"

"The house is less than a mile from where we found the bodies," Jim answered.

27

*J*im scrolled through the notes sent to him by one of the officers on the phone, and he shook his head in disbelief. "One of the officers we sent out to canvass the neighborhood even interviewed Lindsey's mother after we found the bodies." He closed the notes on his phone and then rubbed his eyes. "He was right under our nose the entire time."

"It's probably doubtful that Lindsey lives with her, isn't it?" Kerry asked.

"I don't know," Jim answered. "I guess we'll find out when we get there."

Jim was silent for the rest of the trip, trying to go over everything they knew about this guy, anything that he could use to his advantage.

"He's smart," Jim said.

"Lindsey?" Kerry asked.

"Yeah," Jim answered. "He wanted a position where

he could be close to kids, but didn't have to be directly in charge of them. As a therapist's secretary it would have been easy for him to gain access to the notes made about the children. And if he's moved around from different therapists, it could keep the heat off of him."

Kerry shook her head, disgusted. "He used children's own trauma against them."

Jim took a deep breath and shifted in his seat. "He didn't even have to be a good manipulator. All he had to do was read the therapist's notes. It must have been like painting by numbers for him." He wiped his face, grunting. "Son of a bitch."

"No one could have known," Kerry said. "Hell, he managed to trick two therapists, people who spent their entire lives and dedicated their careers to the understanding of the human mind." She glanced at him. "I think you can cut yourself a break."

A pain formed on the side of his head where he had been kicked, and he winced, turning his face away from Kerry, who still noticed.

"You all right?" Kerry asked.

Jim held his grimace, gritting his teeth. "Yeah. Fine."

"Jim, if something is wrong, then we need to get you to the hospital," Kerry said. "I should have taken you there the moment I saw what happened."

Jim shut his eyes and forced the headache into submission as he turned back to his partner. "If you had done that, then we never would have had the conversation with Dr. Peppercorn, and we wouldn't have figured out who Lindsey was."

"Well, if you're going to be stubborn about it, at least take some medicine. Do you have anything in the glove box?" Kerry asked.

Jim opened the glove box and retrieved a bottle of Excedrin. He opened the cap and then popped two, chewing them instead of swallowing, knowing that the drug would dissolve into his bloodstream faster that way. The pills tasted bitter, but he made sure to swallow all of the particles, because he wanted a clear mind for his conversation with Lindsey's mother.

It wouldn't be the first conversation of the kind Jim had had, speaking with the parent of a person of interest, but he'd never had a conversation with the parent of a pedophile and murderer.

Jim and Kerry arrived at the mother's house alone, foregoing any backup. Neither of them wanted to cause a stir in case the son wasn't hiding out inside. And in poor places like this, everyone tended to have a preconceived notion about who law enforcement protected.

"There," Jim said, pointing to a rusted Airstream. "That's hers."

Lindsey's mother, Doris Shuckle, lived in a small, rusted trailer in a community of similar housing. The area was poverty-stricken, and the only difference between this poor community and the one they had left in the city was geographical location.

Kerry parked the cruiser in front of the Airstream. No secondary vehicle was in the area, so there was no indication that Lindsey was at the residence and no possibility for Mrs. Shuckle to try and make a run for it.

Kerry shut off the engine, and she caught sight of the growing sets of eyes watching them. "People really don't like the police, do they?"

"Not until they need help," Jim answered.

Kerry turned toward her partner. "How do you want to play this one?"

Jim had given it considerable thought on the drive over. "Talking to a parent like this is tricky, because there's no way to know how much the parent knows about what their child has done. And even the most neglectful parents can be protective about their own offspring." Jim had seen it time and time again. It was like there was an unwritten rule for parents and authorities. The moment Jim and Kerry flashed their badge to Doris inside that trailer and told them they had a few questions about her son, her guard would immediately go up. "We'll start with the premise of her not knowing anything. See how she responds to us. Go from there."

"I can't imagine she's going to be much help," Kerry said then gestured to the couple staring at them from the inside of their small camper. "Just look at those two over there. You think they have a shotgun waiting for us with some shells inside?"

Jim regarded the pair Kerry had seen. They were middle-aged, and both of them were scowling. "This kind of people don't like outsiders."

Jim was the first to the door, Kerry walking up

beside him, keeping an eye on their surroundings. If Lindsey was here, and if he made a run for it, the surrounding woods would provide plenty of opportunities to hide.

Jim knocked, the old Airstream's door rattling, and after a few minutes, they heard footsteps and ragged breaths until the door opened. A shriveled old woman appeared, wearing a scowl and cannula.

"What?"

"Mrs. Shuckle?" Jim asked.

The old woman stared at them for a moment, her expression never changing to anything nicer. "What do you want?"

Jim quickly flashed his badge. "I'm Detective North, and this is my partner, Detective Martin. We would like to ask you some questions about your son."

Doris Shuckle was quiet for a moment save for her raspy breathing, which was aided by the faded green oxygen tank in the wheeled cart at her side. She had bloodshot eyes and wide pupils. She might have been hopped up on pain meds, but there was a clarity to her gaze.

"Fine," Doris said and then opened the door. "But I get to keep watching my shows."

"Of course." Jim cast Kerry a glance, and then the pair entered.

It was the stench Jim recognized first, and it was one he was familiar with, the stale scent of tobacco which covered the walls like a second coating of paint.

The lingering stench of smoke, combined with the

old furniture, musty carpet, and decay of the very woman who inhabited the Airstream, made for a potent combination.

Doris pulled her oxygen tank cart to the only chair in what Jim assumed was the living room. They waited until the old woman had settled into a more comfortable position.

"Mrs. Shuckle—"

Doris groaned. "Oh, God. Drop the formalities. I don't need to be reminded that I'm married to that son of a bitch every time you ask a question. Just get to the point of it."

Jim cleared his throat. "Okay, Doris. When was the last time you saw your son?"

"I don't know," Doris said. "A couple of weeks ago. He doesn't stop by very often. The little bastard doesn't like me." She blew a raspberry and yelled at the TV. "You need to buy a goddamn vowel!"

"Doris, can you tell me about your son?" Jim said.

"What do you want to know?" Doris asked, her gaze glued to the television screen.

"Do you know where he hangs out, what he does for work or in his spare time?"

Doris reached for a cup of something and sipped from it. She coughed and spilled a little bit onto her chest. She wiped her mouth and set the cup down. "I don't know what the boy does. He was always a strange one."

"Strange how?" Jim asked.

"He never had friends." Doris grimaced. "What kind

of boy never has any friends? He just locked himself into his room all day, never came out." She shivered, shaking her head, which caused the loose jowls to wiggle even after she stopped moving. "Boy wasn't right."

"Doris," Jim said, changing his tone to a more serious one. "Your son Lindsey is in trouble—"

Doris chuckled. "Stupid name." She finally turned away from the television and looked up at the pair of them. "Do you know how much I hated when he told me he was changing his name to that? It's a woman's name. I asked him if he was getting a sex change, but he told me that he didn't like his old name."

"What was his old name, Doris?" Jim asked.

"Terrance Shuckle," Doris said. "Granted, it's not the best, but it's damn better than some girl's name. I never understood that boy."

"Do you know where he lives?" Jim asked.

"No," Doris answered, all of her attention focused on Pat Sajak and *Wheel of Fortune*. She sipped from the cup again, this time making sure she got all of it into her mouth.

"Doris, your son is in trouble," Jim answered. "A lot of trouble."

Doris scoffed. "Figures."

Jim stepped between Doris and the television, forcing the old woman to look at him. "He's in the kind of trouble that's caught the attention of federal authorities."

"Get out of the way!" Doris vigorously waved her

arm, but the gesture did nothing. Jim stood his ground. "I don't want any part of whatever he did!"

"Then you need to give us something we can use, Doris," Jim said. "Because if you don't, then you're going to have a team of agents and local police going through your property."

Doris wiggled and squirmed in her chair. "Any kind of reward that goes with useful information?"

Kerry muttered under her breath, catching another glare from the old woman, but she said nothing as she waited for Jim to respond.

"It depends on how useful the information is," Jim said.

Doris grunted and then leaned back in her chair again, trying to relax. "That's the trick, isn't it? If it's useful." She coughed and then adjusted the screw cap on her oxygen tank. "Damn thing's empty. Hand me a new one, will you?" She pointed to a corner of the room to the left of the television, where three tanks were propped against the wall.

Jim retrieved the tank for the old woman and then placed the old one in the opposite corner per Doris's instructions as she put together the new tank.

Once the fresh air was flowing to her lungs again, Doris closed her eyes and nodded. "All right, Detective. I'll give you some information."

Both Jim and Kerry were eager, but Jim wasn't going to get his hopes up until he was sure the information he got was actually useful. The world was chock-full of people like Doris Shuckle, and every single one of them was always on the lookout to milk something from the establishment.

"His daddy wasn't a good man," Doris said. "Used to beat me, and do worse to the boy." She grimaced at the last part. "I tried to do something about it, but when you're poor with a baby, you have to take what you can get. So we both muddled through it. I always thought he might have come out the other side all right, that maybe all those times he was quiet in his room was just his way of working through all of the shit that happened to him... I don't know. Maybe that's just something I tell myself so I don't have to think about it very hard."

Kerry grimaced. "What kind of a mother lets her child be abused like that?"

Jim braced for an outburst, but to his surprise, Doris had no rebuke.

"A shitty kind," Doris said. "That's who. And I was as shitty as they come." She coughed, the noise rattling and shaking her lungs, and then she grabbed a cloth and hacked something into it. When she removed the cloth from her lips, she stared at the contents for a second, her expression stoic, and then she folded it up and set it on her armrest. "Anyway. Terrance's father, or Lindsey, or whatever the hell he's calling himself these days, left him a small piece of land with a cabin on it. It was purchased off the books, so there isn't much of a paper trail. But I suspect that if the boy was in trouble of some kind, then that's where he would go."

Jim stared down at the old woman, who reminded him of so many of the foster parents he'd had growing up. It never ceased to amaze him what happened to the kids from broken homes, and he wondered how much nurturing really helped with certain people. "Where is it?"

Doris scribbled the cabin's location down for them, and Jim thanked the old woman one last time before he headed for the door. But just before they stepped out, she called out to him, her voice hoarse, broken, and tired. "Is it bad? The trouble he's in?"

Jim knew she would find out soon enough on the news, and while he was supposed to keep all information locked up tight, he didn't think the old woman would be able to reach the boy in time, even if she wanted to do that in the first place.

"He's a serial killer," Jim said. "And a pedophile."

Jim searched for any sign of recognition on Doris Shuckle's face that she had known what her son was, but her expression never betrayed her thoughts.

Doris only nodded and then turned back to her television.

Jim joined Kerry outside, and the pair checked the address on the computer. They waited anxiously as the laptop searched for service, and then the map loaded on the screen.

"Okay, I got it," Kerry said.

Jim studied the screen then reached for the radio on the dashboard. "This is Detective Jim North. I need all available units to Highway Thirty-Nine, mile marker

—" Jim squinted down at the screen. "Seventy-one. There is a dirt path that veers off the highway." He took his hand off the receiver and listened to dispatch confirm and then go into detail over the radio.

Kerry shook her head and then glanced back to the trailer. "How many situations like this are there in the world? You know? How many people turn into bad people because they had shitty childhoods? How much could we avoid if we just took the time to take care of our kids?"

Jim had pondered the same question for many nights, and while he still didn't have an answer, he did find something that helped him feel better. "People are nothing more than a collection of experiences. But you never know how a person is going to react until you press them one way or another and then watch how they respond to that pressure."

Jim turned back to Kerry and recognized the sympathy on her face.

"I could have turned out different than what I am now," Jim said. "I would have had plenty of excuses for it. But somewhere along the way, I made things better for myself because I knew that I could."

"Not everyone is like that, Jim," Kerry said.

"No, they're not," Jim answered. "But that's why we do what we do. To help those who can't."

28

---

*T*he nerves fluttering through Kerry's system were wreaking havoc on her concentration, but thankfully, traffic wasn't bad. But she did keep flexing her hands as she drove, squeezing the steering wheel so tightly it made her hands ache.

The chatter over the radio had intensified from the news spreading about Lindsey's location. She wouldn't be surprised if every cop in the state showed up to knock on that door.

"We might be the first ones on the scene," Jim said, still glancing out the window. His voice was calm and deeper than it normally was. "If that's the case, we'll need to decide how quickly we want to act, and if we want to handle this without backup."

"What are the chances the girls are still alive?" Kerry asked.

Jim weighed the options. "The bodies of the other victims suggested Lindsey enjoyed taking his time with the kids before he killed them." He swallowed and fidgeted with his hands, the first break in his stoic demeanor. "They might be alive, but they probably wish they weren't at this point."

A sharp pain rippled through Kerry's left hand, and she relaxed her grip again, which had tightened to a viselike hold on the wheel. "So we go in."

Jim reciprocated the nod. "We go in."

A rush of nerves rattled Kerry's stomach. She drew in deep breaths to try and calm herself down, but the breathing exercises did little to stop the butterflies from jangling her system.

"ETA?" Jim asked.

Kerry's breathing was labored as she checked the GPS on the screen. "Ten minutes." She cleared her throat and slowed her breaths, but it did little to calm her heart rate. Heat radiated from her cheeks, and sweat soaked her undershirt.

"What did you think of the mom?" Jim asked.

"What?" Kerry was taken aback by the question. "Doris?"

"Yeah," Jim answered.

"Oh," Kerry said then swallowed, trying to gather enough spit in her mouth so she could answer. "She's obviously had a hard life."

Jim waited. "But?"

Kerry took a breath, once again relaxing her hands on the wheel, which were starting to ache again. "But people are presented with challenges every day." She shrugged. "When you talk about how hard life is, it's all relative. What's hard for me might be easy for you and vice versa."

Jim looked at her, arching his left eyebrow. "Would you have given up one of your kids if they had done something like this?"

Kerry opened her mouth and then shut it rather quickly. She had asked herself those types of questions before, but it had always been in theory. Both of her kids were good, neither of them ever getting into trouble, at least not more than the normal amount for a kid. But those thoughts had crept into her mind more than she would have liked over the past few years, and the more she saw on the job, the more those thoughts festered into fears that could transform into reality.

"I don't know what I would do," Kerry said. "And that's the honest truth."

Jim leaned back into his seat but remained sitting upright. Kerry's hands ached from the tight grip on the wheel, she didn't let up. She bore down, feeding off of the adrenaline funneling through her veins. Being so close to the perp only focused her rage.

Kerry had kept her eyes on the road for the majority of the drive, but when she glanced over to Jim, his eyes wide and attentive. "How close are we?"

Jim averted his gaze to the monitor, tracking their progress to the location. "Two minutes." He faced forward again. "Kevlar is still in the trunk?"

"Yes," Kerry answered. "Do you think we'll need it?"

Jim nodded. "He'll be ready. And we need to be ready too."

When they arrived at the dirt road next to the mile marker off of Highway 37, Kerry veered from the highway and onto the pathway to the cabin, where they would hopefully find Lindsey and the girls still alive.

They were the first on the scene, and knowing they had already made the decision to go in if that was the case, Jim still radioed dispatch to get an ETA on any backup.

"SWAT is still ten minutes out," dispatch said. "There was a delay in transportation, but we have a few other officers only seven minutes away."

Jim had gone in alone before, but the numbers suggested that if they waited they would have a higher chance of surviving, but with the amount of time the girls had been gone, Jim knew the window was closing on being able to bring them home alive.

Kerry pulled the car over, and both of them exited the vehicle. They headed around to the trunk, which Kerry had popped open.

"It's a three-minute hike up the road," Jim said, glancing ahead and trying to get a lay of the land, but the trees were too thick for him to see through. "I don't know what he'll have waiting for us when we get up there, but we need to move quickly and quietly."

Kerry nodded, readjusting the Velcro strips on her Kevlar vest. "Standard two-man formation. You take the lead, unless you don't feel up to it." She then stored a few magazines of ammunition in her belt and unholstered her weapon.

Jim was glad to see her in go mode. "I'll be fine." He

adjusted his own vest, added a few more magazines to his own collection, and closed the trunk. "We get the girls. No matter what."

Kerry nodded. "No matter what."

It had been a long time since Jim had been with a partner he could trust, even longer with one that he actually liked.

Jim headed up the dirt road and unholstered his weapon. He remained hunched forward, padding his feet lightly against the gravel. The road twisted and curved through the thick brush, and the longer Jim hurried along the path without actually seeing the cabin, the more worried he became that he had missed something along the way or that the mother had lied to them about the cabin's location.

After another minute of moving up the road, Jim spied the outline of a building through the trees. He held up his hand, slowing to a stop as Kerry followed suit. He hunched lower, hoping the trees would provide adequate cover on their approach.

Jim was also mindful of any traps that might have been set for intruders. The guy was smart, and if he had gone this long without being caught, then it stood to reason he would have security measures in place if his location and his identity had been compromised.

The road curved on one final bend, and Jim dropped to one knee.

The cabin was a traditional log cabin and very old. Two windows could be seen from Jim's vantage point. They were small and dirty, and Jim saw no movement inside. A car was parked off to the side of the cabin, matching the vehicle registered to Lindsey. Their suspect was inside.

Jim turned around and met Kerry's gaze, the pair still hunched low. "I only see one front entrance. I imagine he has a back door, but we won't know until we move."

Kerry nodded. "So what's the play?"

"Unless his mother tipped him off, which I don't think is possible, the suspect won't have any idea that we're about to bust down his door," Jim answered. "I think the smartest play would be for both of us to go through the front entrance to make sure we can still watch each other's backs." He paused, hoping he could hear the noise of sirens in the distance, but there was only the rush of wind from the trees. "Priority is the girls. But if we see the suspect first, we secure him and then search for the girls. Sound good?"

Kerry nodded.

Jim faced forward again and resumed his trek up the gravel road. Exposed on the final approach to the cabin, Jim double-timed it. He positioned himself on the left side of the door while Kerry took the right.

Both detectives panted to catch their breath, sweat beading on their faces, but their concentration was laser focused, and Jim felt everything slow down.

Jim repositioned himself in front of the door. With all of the might he had in his system, he kicked it, and the old wooden frame splintered off as the door swung inward. Jim rushed inside, aiming into the darkness.

The contrast between the morning light outside and the darkened interior made it difficult to see, but Jim's eyes adjusted quickly. The front entryway to the house opened up into a living room and kitchen area, and there was a hallway directly in front of the door, which led to a back exit.

Jim kept his weapon at the ready, but when he performed a quick sweep of the living room, he found only furniture and an old television with antennas.

The black-and-white static on the screen combined with the white noise distracted him for only half a second, but that was more than enough time for Jim to miss the quick-moving figure in the hallway.

"Jim!" Kerry was the first one down the hall, the back door already closed by the time she arrived.

The pair bottlenecked by the back door then stopped, finding closed doors on either side of them. Jim turned to the room on the left and opened it, the pair of detectives flooding inside.

The room was barren save for a twin mattress shoved up against the wall with a stain in the center of the padding. But it was the pair of discarded handcuffs and the rope that caught Jim's attention.

Kerry shook her head, her knuckles blanched from the tight grip on her weapon. "It's empty."

Muffled screams echoed behind them, and Jim and Kerry spun around, moving quickly toward the second room.

Jim entered first, leading with his gun, and forced himself to keep moving to clear the room even though he saw Amelia tied up and gagged on her own mattress in the corner. Kerry was the first to reach the girl and quickly removed the gag.

Amelia cried, her words incoherent.

"It's all right, sweetheart," Kerry said, reaching for the blade in her pocket to cut the zip ties around Amelia's ankles and wrists. "We're here to help you."

With Kerry taking care of the girl, Jim returned to the hallway and opened the back door through which the perp had fled. More dense woods spread from the back of the cabin, the brush so thick Jim couldn't see where the fugitive might have gone.

Kerry's voice drifted from the back of the building. "Amelia, where is Emily?"

Jim turned back to the empty room then to the rear door, and he knew where Emily had been taken. Without a word, Jim sprinted into the backyard.

Jim knew Lindsey's impulse to kill his victims was reaching the highest point of intensity. The interruption of his ritual combined with the prospect of his life being over, since he was about to be caught, might push him over the edge.

Tree branches smacked Jim's face as he pushed deeper into the woods. The terrain was hilly and rocky, and after a few marches up and down, he started to lose his breath.

Jim stopped when he reached the top of a hill, his lungs burning along with his muscles, as he struggled to remain upright. The long night combined with the beating he had taken early that morning had sapped his strength.

Jim turned, searching for any sign of where Lindsey might have taken the girl, but all he saw were trees and rocks and dirt. But as he continued to scan the horizon, Jim caught sight of a flash in his peripheral vision to his left.

Jim pivoted in the direction of the flash, leading with his weapon in the process, and then caught another flash ahead through the trees.

Jim hurried after the suspect. The world around him blurred into nothing but trees, and he grew disoriented the further he trudged into the woods. Memories of his escape from the cage he was held from his own abduction inserted themselves into the present.

The shrubbery and foliage thickened the deeper Jim penetrated the woods, but he kept a line of sight on his target. Jim pushed past the pain plaguing his body, the bruises and welts left behind by the cops who jumped him beckoning him to stop. But he was on the scent now, like a prized bloodhound tracking its prey through the backwoods. It was only a matter of time before he found what he was searching for, and he was closing the gap.

But just when Jim thought he could stand his ground and fire off a shot, the yellow and green of the shirt suddenly vanished, and Jim skidded to a stop, his heels sliding across a patch of dead leaves. He turned left then right then faced forward again. He slowed his breathing and listened for any noise that would give away Lindsey's location.

But there was nothing.

Carefully, Jim pressed forward, stepping beneath a large tree branch. A few more feet and the brush cleared, and Jim found himself in a small clearing. He immediately dropped his gaze to the ground in search of tracks, which was a mistake, because the moment he dropped his guard, Lindsey bum-rushed him from the side and tackled him to the ground.

Jim attempted to twist to the left from where he was hit, but the moment he hit the ground with Lindsey on top of him, Jim knew that something was wrong.

A sharp pain, very hot and pinpointed just below his ribs, had sent a shock through him. When Lindsey finally stood, he hovered over Jim with a bloodied knife in his right hand.

Jim glanced down to the source of the pain and saw blood darkening his shirt. The knife had entered just below the Kevlar, near the waist on his left side, and he pressed his palm against the wound to try and staunch the bleeding. But Lindsey had yanked across his stomach, opening up a six-inch gash over his belly.

"You shouldn't have come," Lindsey said, panting and out of breath. "You should have just let me continue to do my work."

The blood was coming out of Jim quickly now, and the pain grew more intense, paralyzing him on the ground.

Lindsey glanced behind him, his body still tense, waiting for the cavalry to appear, but when no one burst through the trees, he turned back to Jim. "I've almost saved these girls." He glanced down at the bloodied knife and then wiped it off on his jeans. "I've almost freed them from their pain and their broken homes." He sheathed the knife and then wiped sweat from his upper lip.

Jim stared up at the perp, but in his peripheral vision, he saw his gun, which he had dropped when he was tackled. It was concealed by some grass, and Jim didn't think Lindsey saw it yet.

Jim knew reaching for the weapon would require speed, and he wasn't sure if his reflexes were up to par for the moment. Still, it might be his only shot.

Jim reached for the pistol, his hand slick with blood, but before his fingers even reached the grip, Lindsey swooped in and picked up the weapon.

"You can't stop me, Detective," Lindsey said. "My work is too important."

"Your work of killing kids?" Jim asked, the color draining from his face.

"Of saving them!" Lindsey barked. "Do you know how many kids I saw coming through the offices of the therapists I worked for? How many files I read? How much horror I saw them endure?"

"That's how you moved around," Jim replied, doing whatever he could to keep the man talking. "You became an assistant because it put you close to the children, without being too close. And it gave you access to their files. Everything you needed to know about them was right at your fingertips."

"And for good reason," Lindsey said. "I know what it was like to be those kids. I was one of those kids! Do you have any idea what I would have given so I could have been free from the torture of my father?"

"It's never too late," Jim said, gesturing to the gun in Lindsey's hands. "Go ahead. Set yourself free."

Lindsey stared down at the weapon and shook his head. "No. There are others to save."

"No, it's over, Lindsey," Jim said.

Lindsey grimaced, and then stomped away and out of sight. Jim rolled onto his back, gingerly placing his hand over the knife wound again, but he had lost feeling in his fingertips. He wasn't even sure if he had his hand over the wound anymore.

Jim opened his mouth to try and yell so he could alert Kerry to his whereabouts, but the only sound he could muster was a few wisps of air. He rested his head back, closing his eyes. His pulse pounded in his head, which hurt something awful.

It was the commotion of a muffled voice and Lindsey's grunting that pulled Jim's attention back to the present moment, and he found Lindsey with Emily Wilks pressed up against him, the gun still in his hand.

"Look at her, Detective," Lindsey said. "Look at how much pain she was in."

Emily winced, her eyes wide with fear. She could barely stand up on her own, and her wrists and ankles were bound together.

"She came to me," Lindsey said. "She wanted a way to escape all of the horrible things that her parents had done to her. And I told her I could give her that freedom. For her and her friend."

"Let her go," Jim said.

"I will, Detective," Lindsey said, his voice growing eerily calm. "And you will be witness to her freedom."

Jim watched as Lindsey put the gun away and then removed the silk scarf from his back pocket. The same scarf Jen told him was used in the killing of the other children.

"You'll see, Detective," Lindsey said. "I'll show you how I save these broken children."

* * *

By the time Kerry finished freeing Amelia from her restraints, Jim was already sprinting into the woods, but his partner didn't notice until he was already out of sight. "Jim, we need to—" She turned, finding nothing but an empty doorway. "Jim?"

Amelia whimpered, leaning into Kerry and squeezing tight. "I just w-wanna go home."

Kerry placed gentle hands on the girl's shoulders and then lifted Amelia's chin. Kerry stared down into those red, watery eyes and wondered what kind of horrors the girl had experienced. "You will go home. I promise you. But right now, I need you to be brave for me. And I know that you're brave because you're still here. You're alive, Amelia. And that's all that matters right now." Kerry glanced behind her, hoping that backup would arrive soon. "I have to go and find my partner."

Amelia's eyes popped open, and she clawed at the Kevlar over Kerry's chest, her nails raking down the vest. "No! Please! Don't leave me here!"

Kerry snatched the girl's wrists in her hands and held them with a firm strength. "You're going to be fine. But I need to find Emily, okay? I need to make sure that Emily's okay. So I need you to stay right here. More help is coming, and when they show up, I need you to tell them that I went outside into the woods behind the cabin, okay? Can you do that for me? Amelia?"

Amelia whimpered and trembled, holding back tears, and nodded.

Kerry kissed the top of Amelia's head. "Good girl." She stood and then retreated toward the back door. "Just stay here, okay? Help is on the way."

Amelia nodded, remaining huddled on the bare hardwood floor instead of the dirty mattress.

Kerry stepped out into the backyard, searching the tree line for any sign of her partner. She wasn't sure what kind of situation he was in and knew the moment she started screaming, whatever element of surprise either of them hoped to achieve would fly right out the window.

"C'mon, Jim, talk to me," Kerry spoke through clenched teeth, squeezing her pistol tighter as her frustration grew. She stomped the ground with her left foot and then charged forward. If Jim was chasing someone, then it stood to reason the person he was chasing was trying to get away from the road, which was to her south, so north would be the best bet. And as she sprinted deeper into the wilderness behind the cabin, she hoped that she wouldn't be too late to save her partner and Emily.

* * *

BLACK SPOTS BEGAN to form over Jim's vision. The combination of the knife wound and the beating from last night had taken its toll on him. But he knew that the moment he passed out, Emily was a goner. The only reason the girl wasn't dead now was that Lindsey wanted Jim to watch.

"Your mother," Jim said, trying to keep Lindsey from placing the scarf around Emily's neck. "She told us about you."

Lindsey paused at the mention of his mother, the silk still in his hands and not around Emily's throat. He shut his eyes, shaking his head. "That's how you found me."

"That's right," Jim said. "We know about your father too."

"Then you know why I'm doing this good work!" Lindsey said. "You understand!" He looked down to Emily and gently caressed her cheek. "Just like you will understand."

Emily whimpered. Her hands were bound behind her

back, and she was dirty all over. She looked at Jim just as that boy in the cage had done. She wanted him to save her.

But no matter his will to try and push through the pain, his body was too far gone. The desire was there, but the ability had vanished. It was all Jim could do to keep the guy talking.

"I never knew my mother," Jim said, keeping his voice as strong as possible, and while it felt like he was shouting, his volume was just above a whisper.

Lindsey scowled. "You're lying."

Jim shook his head, coughing. "No, it's true. She dumped me the day I was born." And then, through the clouded fog of his mind, an idea struck him, something that he could use to keep Lindsey preoccupied. "I was a foster kid, beaten and abused just like the kids you're trying to save."

Slowly, Lindsey realized that this wasn't a game and that Jim was serious about his past, and he slowly loosened his grip on the girl. "So you really do understand."

"I do," Jim answered. "But I'm still hurting, Lindsey."

"How bad was it?" Lindsey asked. "Your childhood."

"Worse than you can imagine," Jim answered. "And I know you can imagine quite a lot."

Lindsey nodded. "I can." His eyes watered, but he continued to loosen his grip on Emily. "People don't understand what it's like to live in a dangerous place when you're a child. Because when you grow up you're supposed to be safe. Your parents are supposed to protect you, not hurt you!"

Emily flinched when Lindsey shouted.

"Do you think you could help me?" Jim asked.

Excitement sparked in Lindsey's eyes.

"I don't want to carry the burden of my past anymore," Jim said, goading Lindsey into letting Emily go, at least for the moment. If he could just get the man close enough, he might be able to steal the gun back. "I don't want to be afraid anymore."

Jim watched Lindsey's desire grow stronger. He knew he had struck a chord. Lindsey couldn't help himself. He was a man who believed he was doing righteous work.

"I understand your burden," Lindsey said, finally letting Emily go as he stepped closer to Jim. "I understand your pain."

Jim thought he saw something in his peripheral vision in the woods, but then a black spot covered it, and he wasn't sure if he had only imagined it. "I knew you would. So you'll help me?"

Lindsey nodded. "Yes, Detective."

More movement to Jim's left, but he kept his eyes focused on Lindsey, luring the man closer. "Thank you, Lindsey."

Lindsey pocketed the scarf, and then removed the gun, aiming it at Jim's head. "It'll all be over soon."

"Yes," Jim said. "It will be."

Jim's eyes betrayed him at the last second, and it caused Lindsey to turn just as Kerry broke through the tree line.

Kerry tackled Lindsey to the ground, disarming the perp and then securing him.

"No!" Lindsey said, his voice screaming. "No! You need to let me finish my work! I need to help them!"

"Shut up!" Kerry barked and then tightened the steel cuffs.

With the job done, Jim's remaining strength ran out of him, and he lay flat and still on the ground. His vision and hearing started to fade in and out more frequently now.

"Jim!" Kerry shouted at him, her voice sounding like it was underwater. "Jim, stay with me!"

Jim tried to hang on to the words, but he was slipping away, disappearing into a cold, black hole, and as the darkness consumed him, he was once again plagued by the sight of the boy in the cage, begging him to be let out. But Jim was too tired. Way too tired.

* * *

THE MOMENT JIM PASSED OUT, Kerry knew the situation was dire. She glanced back to Lindsey, who was still flat on his stomach, both arms and legs restrained but now wearing a smile.

"He's home now," Lindsey said, and then he spread his smile even wider. "He's free."

The rage that overtook Kerry's senses started slow, and it wasn't until she had her hand on her weapon that she realized what she was doing. "You're a monster."

Lindsey spit laughter in her face. "I'm the savior! I'm the one who protects our children from more harm! I free them from their pain."

Kerry had heard something similar to those words before, back when she had listened to her father try to explain why he had committed all of those crimes and why he had betrayed the very community he had sworn to protect.

Lindsey had no remorse about what he had done. Kerry could see that in his eyes. He wasn't going to admit that he was wrong, and he wasn't going to be rehabilitated, and Kerry knew every breath Lindsey drew moving forward was one too many. Kerry's father had told her once that the only thing a man like Lindsey understood was the violence he enacted on others.

Kerry slowly aimed the weapon at Lindsey's head.

A glint of fear registered on Lindsey's face, but it vanished quickly. "You won't do it. You're a cop. You don't have it in you."

"That's because you don't know about my nature," Kerry said. "You don't know who my father was. But he was a killer. Like you."

Kerry knew she would be crossing a line, and once she stepped over it, there was no turning back. But Lindsey would receive no tears of sympathy if he died, probably not even from his own mother. The world would be a better place without this creature breathing.

Lindsey squirmed on the ground, his belly slithering over the dirt and rocks with his feeble attempts to escape. "You don't have the guts!" His cheeks reddened, spittle flying from his lips. "You don't have the balls to shoot me because you're afraid of what will happen to you!"

And he was right.

Conflicting voices raged in Kerry's mind. On one side was her conscience, the other her father. Both were strong willed, and slowly but surely, Kerry felt her restraint slip. Her father's voice grew stronger. He could hear him tell her that she was right to kill the villain.

All she had to do was squeeze the trigger, and one bullet through Lindsey's brain would give the sick killer the only justice he deserved and the only punishment he would understand.

"Please," Lindsey said, his voice was stripped of the arrogant superiority he had displayed only moments ago and was now petulant and whimpering. "Please, I-I can't control myself. I don't know what I'm doing sometimes. It's just like my mind goes blank and... And I'm not myself."

"But you allow yourself to be that way," Kerry said. "You want to be that way. That's the problem."

And was this what Kerry wanted? Had she always wanted to be her father? To push beyond the limits of the law? Did she want to cross the moral boundary that had been the single guiding light of her career?

The answered frightened her. Because deep down, no matter how much good she tried to do, no matter how many procedural manuals she read, she couldn't escape the voice in her head.

Lindsey only grew more pathetic and petulant the longer Kerry deliberated on ending his life. And she grew even more concerned about what she was doing, because she knew it was a slippery slope to the corrupt side of the law.

And suddenly Kerry knew she wanted to kill the man. The doubt had disappeared, and now all she had to do was pull the trigger.

Hand shaking, Kerry was moments away from squeezing the trigger when she heard the sirens in the distance. It was the sound of the authorities, of her brothers and sisters in arms, that broke her trance.

Kerry glanced down at the pistol and then holstered the weapon, turning back to her partner, who was still bleeding to death on the ground. She dropped to his aid, listening to Lindsey's screaming laughter behind her.

"You should have killed me!"

Kerry ignored the psychopath and placed her hand back over Jim's wound to stop the bleeding. She checked for a pulse, and a slight bump pressed against her fingers. "Thank God."

Kerry glanced over to where Emily lay on the ground, still bound by her restraints. "Everything's okay now." She smiled, but it was forced. "Help is on the way." She turned back to Jim, the sirens growing louder now. "Everything's going to be okay."

29

The ambulance sped down the highway, the medics in the back hovering over Jim with a pair of paddles on his exposed chest. His heart had stopped by the time they arrived in the woods.

"Three-two-one-clear!" The medic applied the paddles, and electricity coursed through Jim's body, the current so strong it caused his body to buckle on the board he'd been strapped to for transportation. The team worked to keep Jim alive, stopping the bleeding and popping an IV line into his arm.

Kerry sat off in the corner, away from the group and doing her best not to get in everyone's way. She watched Jim's lifeless body jerk and twist on the board, the medics continuing to place the paddles over his chest to jump-start his heart.

Kerry found her gaze shifting from Jim and his life-less body to the bloodied clothes that the medics had peeled off of him and discarded on the floor. She then stared at her palms, which were also covered in Jim's blood.

She gently rubbed the tips of her fingers together, mesmerized by the blood that had dried on her skin. She had never seen an officer go down in the line of duty before. But as she stared at her bloodstained hands, one of the medic's voice snapped her from her daze.

"I've got a pulse! He's going to need a transfusion when he gets to the ER. Tell the hospital that it'll be two units," the medic spoke to his partner, and then turned to Kerry. "Do you know his blood type?"

Kerry hesitated. "What? Um, no, I don't."

"What's your relationship to the detective?" he asked.

"I'm his partner," Kerry answered.

"Well, call your boss. See if you can get his information from his file," the medic said. "He's going to need help, and he's going to need it quickly."

Kerry nodded and then fumbled with bloodied fingers for her phone. She couldn't remember the phone number for the precinct, but she had Lieutenant Mullocks's number programmed into her phone, and she scrolled down her contacts until she found it.

Kerry's heart thundered in her chest, blood rushing to her head. The situation—the blood, the smell, the sounds, the chaos of the moment—was starting to overwhelm her. She shut her eyes as she pressed the phone to her ear, and she focused on the ringing.

"Kerry, the news just came through to the precinct,"

Mullocks said, some chatter and general noise in the background. "Where are you?"

Kerry struggled to find her voice. "I'm in the ambulance with Jim. The hospital needs to know his blood type, and I don't know—"

"Kerry, breathe," Mullocks said. "We're sending Jim's medical file to the hospital. It's standard procedure when an officer is injured in the line of duty."

Kerry took a breath and then opened her eyes, feeding off of the lieutenant's strength. "Right. Procedure."

Mullocks was quiet for a moment. "Lindsey should be arriving at the precinct soon. I don't know if I'll be able to keep the chief's dogs from taking over the interrogation and processing if you're not here to do it yourself, but I'll see what I can do."

Kerry looked back to her partner, who was on the bed, dried blood all over him, the medics working tirelessly to keep him alive, and she suddenly no longer cared about what happened or what credit she received on the case. "It doesn't matter. The sooner he gets into a prison cell, the better. I'll call you when I have an update on Jim."

"Good work, Detective."

Kerry ended the call and returned her phone to her pocket then remembered what the medic had asked her to do. "They're sending his medical records to the hospital. The doctors should have everything on his background when we arrive."

"That's good," the medic said.

"Is he going to make it?" Kerry asked.

"It's hard to tell," the medic answered.

Kerry nodded, and then the ambulance hit a pothole, rattling everyone inside. Kerry braced herself before she fell out of her seat but noticed that Jim's hand had fallen off the cot. She reached for it to place it back on his chest, but instead, she inched closer to him, holding his hand for the rest of the trip.

Jim's vitals were barely hanging on when they finally arrived at the hospital, and when the doors opened, there were four nurses ready to receive him on the loading dock.

Kerry released Jim's hand as he was rocketed out of the ambulance and hurried to follow them into the building.

The staff was shouting orders as they wheeled Jim to the nearest operating room, and when one of the staff tried to block her, she flashed her badge, and they granted her entry.

Kerry followed Jim and his gurney all the way to the operating room, but there, she was finally stopped for good. Even her badge wouldn't gain her access to the OR.

"I need to be updated the moment he's out of surgery," Kerry said. "The moment he's done. Okay?"

The nurse assured her that she would be notified, but until then, Kerry would need to wait like everyone else.

Kerry nodded, glancing one last time at the closed

door, and whispered a prayer to the big guy upstairs that Jim would be all right.

Kerry returned back to the central waiting room for the ER and checked in with the nurse's station to get a status update on the girls they had pulled out of the cabin.

Neither Emily or Amelia had any obvious wounds, but both girls had been brought to the hospital to be examined for any injuries they might have sustained at Lindsey's hands. She had just gotten the room number when she heard several frantic voices behind her.

"Where's my daughter? Where is she?"

Kerry turned to find Tom Johnson, Natalie Johnson, and Ralph Wilks bursting through the automatic ER doors, their expressions ranging from angry to apprehensive.

Kerry intercepted the parents before any of them made too big a scene. "We have your girls. They're alive, and they're being examined by a doctor right now."

Natalie Johnson's face was red and puffy from crying. In the twenty-four hours since Kerry had seen the woman, she seemed to have aged years.

"When can we see her?" Natalie asked.

Kerry wasn't sure how soon the doctor would be finished, and she wasn't sure what kind of news they would receive, but Kerry needed a distraction from Jim's situation. She also knew the parents needed time to process what had happened, and they needed to do it in a place that wasn't so public.

Kerry spoke to one of the nurses and explained the situation. From there, they were escorted to a separate waiting room, but the confined space made it feel more like a cage.

No one spoke, but nearly everyone paced nervously. Kerry sat in the chair right next to the door, watching the new family dynamics.

The anger over the affair had died down, but Kerry could tell that not all was forgiven. But with the news of the recovery of their children, Kerry figured the parents had set aside their feuds in good faith.

Watching those parents wait and wallow in uncertainty only made Kerry more thankful than ever to know that her children were safe and sound with their father.

Kerry's phone buzzed. It was a text from Lieutenant Mullocks.

Lindsey just copped to the bodies we found. DA is getting his statement in writing. He's going to enter a guilty plea. It's done.

Kerry clutched the phone tighter in her hand and then leaned her head back as she closed her eyes. She exhaled a slow breath, letting the tension leave her body. She knew they still faced several weeks, perhaps even months, of legal proceedings even with Lindsey's admission of guilt, and it wasn't as if he couldn't change his mind on his final day in court.

But Kerry had faith in the forensic teams gathering evidence at the cabin, and she and Jim had done a good job cataloging their evidence, creating a time-

JAMES HUNT

line, and filing paperwork. Still, Kerry counted it as
a win.

"Detective?"

Kerry lifted her head, opening her eyes, and saw
Natalie Johnson standing in front of her. "Mrs. Johnson, please sit down."

Natalie sat and leaned forward, her shoulders
sloped, her hands collected in her lap, the chair swallowing her up.

Kerry waited for a question, and when none came,
she placed a gentle hand on Natalie's arm and felt the
woman jolt from her touch. "Mrs. Johnson, are you—"

"What did you see?" Natalie asked, blurting the
words out quickly and lifting her gaze to look Kerry in
the eye. "When you found them?" She was tearing up,
her eyes reddening.

Kerry knew what Natalie wanted to know. But they
weren't details she could offer the grieving mother.
"Mrs. Johnson, even though we caught the man
responsible, the investigation is still considered open,
and there are certain details—"

"Please." Natalie spoke through clenched teeth and
squeezed her hands into fists as she shut her eyes. Her
entire body thrummed with the adrenaline and anger
Kerry had only seen in the most desperate of people.

"Leave her alone, Natalie," Tom Johnson said.

"No!" Mrs. Johnson stood, raising her voice to
frantic volume. "I need to know what happened to my
little girl!"

Kerry stood, no one else coming to the aid of the

mother, and tried to calm her down. "Mrs. Johnson, the doctors are with Amelia now. She's getting the best of care, and—"

"Was she raped?" Mrs. Johnson blurted the words out, and she quickly covered her mouth with trembling hands as if she had said something unspeakable. She slowly lowered her hands, her fingers twitching. "Was she?"

Kerry knew the doctors were performing a rape kit on both girls. Girls who were no older than twelve and eleven. Girls who should have spent the past two days gossiping and playing and dreaming about the day when they would finally be old enough to make their own choices. The kind of things that all kids think about when they're young.

But Kerry knew that both Emily and Amelia had experienced something that no one, at any age, should ever be forced to go through. And the tragedy that they had experienced by the cruel and vicious acts of a selfish man had forever tainted their childhood.

And while Kerry knew none of Lindsey's previous victims had been sexually assaulted, she also knew how pedophile's fantasies grew more intense. They wouldn't know for sure until the examination was complete.

Kerry's silence triggered Natalie into tears, and she collapsed to the floor, hugging herself and screaming at the top of her lungs.

Kerry dropped to the floor with the mother, trying to pick her up, but she wouldn't budge. And with no one else in the room offering a hand or saying a word, Kerry let the mother work through her grief. Because while she might have had her daughter back, there were going to be some missing pieces.

Natalie eventually cried herself into a stoic gaze, and when she was finished, Kerry helped her into a chair. Unsure of what else she could do or say, Kerry simply reached for the woman's hand and held it in her own. And they stayed that way until the doctor arrived.

All at once, the parents rose, each of them approaching with the same frightened, curious expression of wanting to know the truth about their daughters, and all the while, Natalie kept hold of Kerry's hand.

"We've finished the examination on both girls."

The doctor was a middle-aged man with thinning brown hair on top. He was tall, the long white medical coat he wore small enough to fit him like a regular jacket. His thin, wire-rimmed glasses rested halfway down the bridge of his nose, and he adjusted them frequently while he spoke. He had a mild manner, and his sallow cheeks suggested he had seen more trauma working at the hospital in one day than most people experienced in a lifetime.

"They're dehydrated and sleep deprived, but from a medical standpoint, they seem to be healthy. We tested their blood for any STDs and—"

Natalie whimpered.

"Are you saying that they were..." Tom Johnson swallowed, unable to speak the words aloud, and then shut his eyes before he found the courage to speak. "Raped? Were they raped?"

Natalie, Tom, and Ralph leaned forward, and the air in the room seemed to have been sucked up in a vacuum while they waited for the news.

"No," the doctor said. "We found no signs of forced penetration on either girl."

Natalie broke down in tears again, and a collective sigh escaped from Ralph and Tom. Kerry squeezed Natalie's hand, thankful they had gotten there in time, and prayed that she would be able to give the good news to Jim should he survive.

* * *

WHEN JIM finally stirred awake in his hospital bed, the first thing he noticed was the rotten taste in his mouth. It was hot and sour, and caused him to grimace. But the smell was immediately overpowered by the dull ache in his side and the subsequent wave of pain that washed over his body as he regained control of his faculties.

The room was bright and whitewashed for a moment until Jim's vision cleared. He was enclosed in a section of a room that had been walled off by privacy curtains. He lowered his gaze to his own body, which was stiff and sore beneath the crisp white hospital sheet, and he saw the tubes and lines running from his body to the machines to his right.

The light cadence of beeps and bops mixed into the dull chatter of voices somewhere beyond the curtain. A voice echoed over an intercom system, a nurse paging a doctor for counsel.

Jim shut his eyes again, taking a few deep breaths. Even the small stint of consciousness had made him weak and dizzy again. His eyes remained shut until he gathered another burst of energy.

This time, when he opened his eyes, the room was clearer from the start. He opened his mouth to try and call for someone, but his voice was hoarse and scratchy. He rolled his tongue around the inside of his mouth, the organ like sandpaper, until he gathered enough spit to smooth the roughness and tried again.

"Hello?" Jim asked, his voice rising from the curtained tomb he had been placed in.

When no one answered, Jim tried again, this time raising his volume, but the exertion caused black spots to form over his vision, and he grew tired again.

Jim shut his eyes, taking a moment to gather his strength. Then he heard the quick rush of his curtain moving, followed by a calm and gentle voice.

"Detective North," she said. "How are you feeling?"

Jim opened his eyes and saw the woman in front of him. She was young, short, and very pretty. When he didn't answer, she picked up his chart from the foot of the bed and then checked on his vitals.

"Looks like your vitals are coming back strong," she said, her tone brightening with the good news as she turned back to face Jim. "Is there anything I can get you?"

Jim wasn't sure why he had called for help other

than the fact that he was alone. But as he remained conscious, and as his mind slowly caught up with his present predicament, he knew there was only one person that could give him the answers he wanted. "Kerry. I need—" He shut his eyes, grimacing from another shot of pain through his stomach. "I need to speak with Detective Kerry Martin."

The nurse nodded. "I'll see if she's still here."

Jim rested his head back on the pillow as the nurse stepped outside the wall of curtains, which once again sealed him inside, and closed his eyes.

But while Jim knew rest was important, he couldn't stop his mind from racing with questions. He struggled to remember the last images of what had happened. He remembered arriving at Lindsey's cabin, but after they approached the front door, his mind grew hazy.

Had they saved the girls? Did they find Lindsey? Was Kerry injured too?

"Hey," Kerry said, approaching Jim's bedside. "How are you feeling?"

"Bad," Jim answered, and before she could respond further, he asked, "Did we save them?"

Kerry was hesitant for a moment but finally nodded. "They're safe."

Jim relaxed, taking a deep breath. He shut his eyes, thankful they had succeeded. "Good." But when he opened them again, he saw Kerry's saddened expression. "What?"

Kerry avoided Jim's eyes, tilting her head down, and

shook her head. "Nothing. I'm just glad that you're all right."

Jim glanced down at the bandages over his abdomen. "I think that remains to be seen."

"The doctors said no vital organs were hit," Kerry said. "Some of your small intestines were removed, but you should recover fine."

"How long have I been out?" Jim asked.

"A couple of days," Kerry answered. "Lindsey already pled guilty to abduction and murder charges. The brass is happy, and as far as I know, we still have our jobs."

"I'm sure they're soaking up the good press," Jim said.

"Oh, you know they are," Kerry answered. "But our names were redacted from any public statements. The chief said the success of the case was the benefit of interdepartmental communication and dozens of officers. So they're classifying this as a departmental win."

Jim studied Kerry to see how it affected her. She didn't strike him as someone who needed the attention, but he knew her response mattered to him in a way that it didn't matter to him before. "And does that bother you?"

"No," Kerry answered with no hesitation. "It's all about the job, right?"

Jim agreed, but he sensed that there was something else bothering her, something else that she was keeping from him. "What happened after I blacked out?"

Kerry was quiet for a moment, averting her gaze

quickly before looking Jim in the eye again. "I restrained Lindsey, and then kept an eye on your vitals until backup arrived."

Growing up in the foster-care system, Jim had been forced to learn how to read people quickly, and he had prided himself on being accurate. But while he knew something else was bothering Kerry, he was too tired to try and do anything about it.

"You should get some rest," Kerry said. "Do you need anything?"

Jim grunted something close to a "no" and then shut his eyes. He thought he heard Kerry whisper something else as he drifted away from consciousness, but he couldn't hear the words. The job was over, and now he needed to rest.

30

SIX WEEKS LATER

*K*erry was parked outside Jim's house, the car idling and chatter coming in over the radio. They still had an hour before their shift started, more than enough time to make it in to the precinct, but their lieutenant wanted to speak to them before they got back to work.

Jim had finally received the all-clear from his doctor to return to active duty the week prior, and since then, he had passed both his physical and psychological tests to be reinstated with the department.

Kerry glanced around the neighborhood. It was still early morning, but there were a few families up and about, getting ready for day trips somewhere around the city or its outskirts. Seeing the kids and parents together caused Kerry's mind to drift back to her own family.

The kids had still been sleeping when Kerry had left that morning, but Brian had plans to take them on a whale-watching tour up in the San Juan Islands. It was a great time of year to see whales, and their youngest had never gone. It was going to be a surprise.

After the case she and Jim had worked together, Kerry had held out the smallest glimmer of hope that she'd be taken off the weekend shift, but in regard to seniority, she was still on the bottom rung of the ladder.

But she didn't complain, because while she still might have had to work the shitty shift, the mood at the precinct had changed.

The brass might have been able to keep Kerry's and Jim's names out of the papers, but they hadn't been able to stop the rumor mill from spreading their heroics throughout the department. And while Kerry received a bit more goodwill than Jim, he had still managed to get a few claps on the back, at least through word of mouth.

But despite the shift in mood, Kerry had been dreading today, unsure of how Jim would be received. Because today not only marked his first day back, it also marked IA's completion of their investigation into whether Jim's partner had any credibility into his allegations against Jim.

Kerry checked the time and then honked the horn again. For a man who had been punctual throughout most of his career, Kerry thought it was strange that he was already late. "What the hell is he doing?"

She was about to honk, but the door opened, and Jim stepped out. He was thinner than normal, but he

JAMES HUNT

looked strong. He offered a wave and a boyish smile as he opened the passenger-side door and sat down.

"Sorry," Jim said, reaching for the seat belt. "I'm a little out of practice."

"I was about to charge in and check on you," Kerry said, shifting into reverse and backing down the driveway to start the commute into work.

The ride was quiet. The pair hadn't talked in a few weeks, since Kerry had been busy still working the job while Jim focused on recovering.

"How's the side?" Kerry asked, unable to think of anything else to say to help break the ice.

"Still a little sore," Jim answered, twisting at the waist. "But I'm off the pain meds, so my brain is back to normal."

"Oh, good." The sarcastic tone came out involuntarily, but it made Jim laugh, and Kerry smiled. Maybe things could get back to normal after all.

"How has it been being partnered with Tony?" Jim asked.

Or maybe not, Kerry thought. "Fine. We've caught a few more cases since you went in."

"Yeah, I've been keeping track of my emails," Jim said. "You found all three kids, though, right?"

Kerry nodded but shrugged off the compliment. "It was easy pickings. All of the kids were the product of custody battles. It was just parents taking off with their kids because they thought it was the best thing for them. Nothing like what we worked on."

"That's good," Jim said. "If the job was nothing but

296

that, I don't think anyone could do it more than a few months."

The rest of the drive in to work was quiet, both detectives reflecting on their next moves. Kerry knew that both of them had said and done things during their shared case in the heat of the moment, but she wasn't sure how their short past would affect their future.

Lieutenant Mullocks had partnered Kerry up with another detective, and over the past six weeks, things had run smoothly. She and Tony had worked well together. Granted, they hadn't had a high-pressure case like the one she and Jim had worked, but it was like Jim had said: not every case would have such high stakes.

And for the first time in her career, Kerry had found herself in good standing with her fellow officers. No one saw her as the corrupted kid whose father had punched a hole the size of Jupiter through the department's credibility.

Now everyone saw her as the cop who could solve the hard cases even when her back was against the wall. It was a good feeling. And while people had stopped talking so much shit about Jim while he had been gone, she wasn't sure if that was going to stay the same once he returned. She also didn't know how the results of the IA investigation would affect him.

But Kerry had already made her decision. Now all she had to do was wait to see what Jim wanted to do.

* * *

JIM DID his best not to fidget. He knew Kerry could tell he was nervous, but he didn't want to let his emotions get the better of him the first day back on the job. It was out of his hands at this point. All he could do was bear the results when they were given to him.

When they finally arrived at the precinct, Jim followed Kerry inside, keeping a few steps behind. Despite Kerry's assurances that people had changed their minds about him, Jim wasn't convinced. A cop didn't just go from being a rat and back in everyone's good graces at the drop of a hat. But he would find out soon enough.

Jim stepped through the doors, removed his sunglasses, and took a breath. He caught a few stares his way in his peripheral vision, and he did his best not to let his cheeks get too red, but he wasn't sure how well he succeeded.

Thankfully, Jim wasn't out in the open for very long, and he ducked into Lieutenant Mullocks's office, finding their small but fiery leader sitting behind her desk.

"Lieutenant," Kerry said.

"LT," Jim said.

Mullocks was reading a file on her desk, but the angle didn't allow Jim to see the contents. She was quiet for a moment, lost in thought, but snapped the file shut and focused her attention on her guests. "Okay. Right. Kerry, will you go and grab Sergeant Ken for me?"

"Yes, ma'am," Kerry answered.

Jim flinched, unsure of why the sergeant was joining them. "Is everything all right, Lieutenant?"

"Yeah, Jim," Mullocks answered.

Ken was finally brought in, and Jim noted how Kerry remained behind the sergeant after he entered the office. "LT." He then looked to Jim and grimaced.

"Sergeant, I need your gun and your badge," Mullocks said.

Surprise flashed over Ken's face. "What?"

"You heard me," Mullocks answered.

Still stunned, Ken slowly crossed the office, placing his shield and his firearm on the desk. "What the hell is this about—Hey!"

Kerry moved up behind Ken quickly, cuffing his hands behind his back. "You're under arrest for breaking and entering and assault."

Ken squirmed, but once the steel was clamped around his wrists, he was helpless. "What the hell are you talking about? Let me go!"

"We're talking about the beatdown you and four other officers gave to Jim six weeks ago," Mullocks said. "Wyatt and the others already ratted you out."

Ken's cheeks reddened, his head looking like it was going to pop. "You can't do this! He's the rat! He's the bad cop!"

"No, the only bad cop here is you, Sergeant," Mullocks said. "Go ahead and process him, Kerry."

"Yes, ma'am," Kerry said. "Let's go."

Once Ken was out of the office, Jim remained in

stunned silence. He turned back to the lieutenant, shaking his head. "How did you know it was them?"

"Kerry figured it out," Mullocks answered. "Why don't you take a seat, Jim."

Jim did as he was told, and the moment he sat down, his heart kick-started in his chest. But while Jim might have been nervous, Mullocks was relaxed. She sat back in her chair, slouched with her hands over her lap.

"How are you feeling?" Mullocks asked.

"Good," Jim answered. "Ready for work."

Mullocks nodded and then sat up in her chair a little bit. "I read the analysis of your exams. According to those in charge of passing you, it seems that you're up to par. But you're not, are you?"

Jim remained quiet, taken aback by the question. "Um, ma'am, I don't—"

"Don't 'ma'am' me, Jim," Mullocks said. "I know what it's like to almost die on the job. It changes you."

Jim wasn't sure what Mullocks was trying to do, but he sensed she was sincere, and he hoped his time off hadn't caused his instincts to falter. "It's been hard to sleep," he admitted.

Mullocks nodded. "Probably hard to concentrate. Hard to keep your heart rate down anytime you're surprised. Not hungry. Tired, but your mind is wired at the same time." She leaned forward, hands clasped. "It's normal."

Jim shifted in his seat, maintaining his rigid

posture. "I'm not sure what you're trying to tell me, Lieutenant. Am I back on the job?"

Mullocks fiddled with her thumbs, rubbing them against one another for a moment, before she spoke. "You're back on the job. The only question is, what job do you want?" She leaned back. "Because you're going to have the pick of the litter."

Jim raised his eyebrows, confused. "I don't—"

"IA finished their investigation into your former partner," Mullocks said. "He was dirty, Jim. Dirty as they come. He had his fingers in several drug rings around the city, and nearly all of his informants turned on him the moment they learned he'd been taken into custody. He's going to jail, and for a long time." She leaned back in her chair. "IA also cleared you of the counter charges he filed against you."

Almost all at once, Jim's body relaxed. The weight of the world had rested on his shoulders, and he'd been at the mercy of people he couldn't control. It had been like being back in the foster system all over again. But hearing that it was over, that he was right, and that it was done, Jim had to fight the tears.

Mullocks gave Jim a few moments to collect himself, and then she spoke with a calmer, wiser voice than her age suggested.

"You're a good detective, Jim," Mullocks said. "And it might make me sound arrogant, but I know exactly what a good one looks like. I worked with one for many years at the beginning of my detective career."

She lowered her gaze, making it hard to see her emotion.

Jim knew about the lieutenant's old partner. The man was a legend in the city, but depending on who you asked, you'd get a difference of opinion on which side of good that legend landed. Jim had always landed on the right side with Chase Grant. Because that's where the evidence led him.

Mullocks straightened up again, returning to her normal self. "So, now that you've been cleared, I've got nearly every captain in the state wanting to recruit you, and that includes Major Crimes downtown." She raised her eyebrows. "The best of the best, if you believe the press hype."

Jim was well aware of the Major Crimes task force, and he knew the waiting list for cops wanting to join could be wrapped around the city limits a dozen times. It had been a dream of his to work for that unit, a place where he believed he could effect real change. But that had been early in his career.

"Talk to me, Jim," Mullocks said. "What do you have going in that mind of yours?"

Jim took a breath and took his time to find the right answer. "I've always been a bit of an outcast. Even when I was little. I never really played well with others, and I always believed that I was probably better off if I just stayed on my own."

Jim glanced down at his palms, where the scars lingered on his skin, and gently ran his fingers down the marks he had accumulated so long ago. "I've experienced things in my life that have shaped me. Experiences that are clearly marked in my mind where I was someone before it happened, and then someone else after it happened. Some of those events have been horrible." He smiled. "But there have been a few good ones." Jim lifted his gaze and stared the lieutenant in the eye. "I think I found something good here, Lieutenant. And I'd like to stay on with the Five and keep Kerry as my partner. If both would be willing to have me."

The lieutenant remained stoic for a minute. Jim was unable to read what she was thinking, which was unusual. Then she said, "Why don't you go and grab Kerry."

Jim remained in his chair, unsure if he'd heard the boss right, but then finally stood and opened the door. He found Kerry in the hallway, talking to Tony, who had been her partner while Jim had been in the hospital.

The pair were in deep conversation, Kerry doing most of the talking and Tony listening dutifully. It was too loud for Jim to hear what they were talking about, but he suspected it was about a case.

"Kerry!" Jim yelled, catching her attention, and then motioned for her to come into the office.

Jim returned to his chair, his stomach suddenly alive with so many butterflies that he couldn't sit down even if he'd wanted too.

Kerry entered, closing the door behind her without

needing to be told, and then took the empty chair next to Jim.

The three remained in the room, silence lingering, Jim eagerly waiting to learn why the lieutenant had called Kerry into the office.

Finally, Mullocks broke the tension. "Kerry, why don't you tell Jim what you told me last week."

Jim had the unsettling sensation that this was a trap, that he was being set up to fail for some reason, though he couldn't be certain why.

Kerry nodded, her expression and posture equally awkward, and shifted in her chair so she could face Jim as she spoke. "I told her that if you came back to the Five, I wanted to keep you on as a partner. I told her we worked well together, and I thought we could do a lot of good here."

Jim heard the words, but it took a few more moments before they registered.

"Jim?" Mullocks asked. "You still with us?"

The lieutenant's tone had a hint of playfulness in it, and when Jim finally broke out of his stupor, it was all he could do to laugh and nod.

"Yeah," Jim said. "I'm still here."

Kerry smiled. "So what do you say, Jim? Are we still partners?"

Jim had been looking for a place to belong his entire life, a place he could call his own, a family he could trust, people whom he cherished spending time with. It had taken him sixteen years as a kid before he'd finally landed in a good home with the people he called his parents, and it had taken him more than six years before he'd found those same kinds of individuals at work.

It was a rare thing to find a group of people like that, and Jim wasn't going to take that for granted.

"Yes. I'm in."

Made in the USA
Las Vegas, NV
21 November 2020

11261634R00174